# UNCHAINED FURY

## AXEL BLAZE THRILLER
## (BOOK FIVE)

## BILL RUNNER

RUNNER HOUSE BOOKS, LONDON
www.bill-runner.com

First eBook edition July 2023

978-1-7393196-2-5

www.bill-runner.com

## From Soldier to Vigilante: Blaze's Path

Dear Readers,

First off, thank you for joining Axel Blaze on his journey. Whether you've been with him since *Blaze Returns* or are just diving in now, I'm thrilled to have you along for the ride.

When I first created Axel Blaze, I envisioned a man who couldn't stand by when innocent lives were at stake—a man who acts decisively, even when it means crossing dangerous lines. In his first adventure in *Blaze Returns*, he was still tethered to a semi-official role, stepping in to help his old boss at the U.S. Marshals track down a missing Deputy.

But as the series unfolded, Blaze began carving his own path, driven by his unwavering sense of justice and a deep disdain for the wrongs he saw around him. In the first seven books—*Blaze Returns, Lethal Force, Hard Target, Mean Streets, Unchained Fury, No Escape*, and *Fear City*—all set across different American cities, Blaze operates as a lone ranger. He steps into situations where innocent lives hang in the balance, doing what others can't—or won't.

Starting with *Dead Calm* (Book 8), the series takes a deeper dive into Blaze's past. In *Dead Calm*, we see him as a Captain in the U.S. Army Rangers, followed by his Delta Force missions in *No Mercy*, and the upcoming *Warpath* (April 2025) and *Crossfire* (July 2025). These stories explore the intense operations and personal losses that forged Blaze into the man he is today.

The upcoming Book 12, *Nemesis* (November 2025), will be the final book exploring Blaze's military career. It's a deeply personal story where Blaze seeks justice for his brother Ryan—a U.S. Marine. This pivotal story will mark the turning point in Blaze's life, as he ultimately decides to leave the army. Disillusioned by the failures of the system, he becomes a man willing to cross lines to ensure justice prevails. Beginning in 2026, Blaze will be stepping fully into a world where the lines between right and wrong blur, and he's left to rely on his own moral compass to guide him.

In his words: You have to pay your dues. Period.

Your feedback and support have been instrumental in shaping this series. Blaze's journey has been as much yours as it has been mine, and I can't thank you enough for coming along for the ride.

Thank you for being part of Blaze's story.

Sincerely,

*Bill Runner*

# CHAPTER 1

A fog had begun to roll in from the San Francisco Bay, creeping silently through the city's streets—a giant eraser obliterating every landmark it slithered over. Silent and unsettling, the amorphous grayness was taking over the streets, swallowing up everything in its path, hiding unseen dangers under its thick gray cloak.

The woman moving about inside the house on a desolate street was unaware of the watchful eyes fixed upon her. She was too busy multitasking in the well-lit open plan kitchen—oblivious to any threats lurking outside. It was too dark and foggy for the woman to have noticed the three men sitting in the dark sedan parked on the street outside. They could easily have been standing outside her window, peeping in, and would still have been invisible to her.

The sun had set a while ago. Well before the fog had begun swallowing up whatever visibility remained in the streets. As the fog rolled in from the Bay toward the Golden Gate Bridge, the foghorns had begun emitting their familiar moan. The first thing that began to vanish from sight was the bridge itself. The grayness had spread toward both ends of the 1.7 miles long bridge until only the tops of the 746 feet high towers remained visible. From there, like the stupor taking over the consciousness of a junkie, the fog had oozed over the rest of the city.

The men in the car weren't some random group of perverts. They had been parked on the street for a couple of hours, waiting for the woman to arrive. A second team following the woman's car had been informing them about her exact movements. They knew her husband wasn't around. They knew that because a third team was keeping tabs on the husband, who was cooped up with some woman in a motel on the outskirts of Sausalito, up north beyond the Marin Headlands overlooking the Golden Gate Bridge.

At the center of the Marin Headlands lies Hawk Hill, which gets its name from being the lookout point for the flight of raptors—the predatory birds. With their keen eyes, sharp talons, and curved beaks, they are among nature's deadliest hunters. The three men in the car, packing handguns and automatic firepower, were no less dangerous.

The woman had arrived half an hour ago, pulling into her driveway in a sky-blue hatchback. As she got out of the car, it was clear she was a woman who could make heads turn. About five foot six and 135 pounds, with a toned, athletic body, she had long blonde curls that flowed out from under the baseball cap on her head. She was wearing designer sunglasses and a white cotton shirt tucked into close-fitting jeans. All three men craned their necks as she opened the back of the car and leaned inside to grab a gym bag and yoga mat, which she slung across her shoulders before picking up a bunch of grocery bags. She finally straightened up to shut the car door before heading toward the house.

From the looks of it, she was just a good-looking suburban housewife coming back from an afternoon of shopping, mixed with some yoga or Pilates. The well-proportioned body suggested she took her fitness regime seriously. Had she bothered to look, there had been enough daylight around at that time for her to make out the car parked on the opposite side of the street. But she seemed to have too much on her hands.

The men didn't make any move when she unlocked the front door and left it open while she headed inside to dump all her stuff in the living room. She returned less than a minute later to shut the door. Half an hour later, she was moving around in the kitchen, sipping wine from a glass, swaying lightly to the beat of the music playing on Bluetooth speakers, and laying out dishes on the table while she waited for the microwave to get her dinner ready.

The men still waited, watching her like hawks, but not making any move. The fog was getting thicker, reducing visibility by the minute. The eyes of all three men soon got fixated on another car as it turned the corner and cruised down the street very slowly. It came to a stop about twenty yards from the house, diagonally opposite the men's car. Its driver had switched off the headlights before it came to a complete stop.

A minute later, as if on cue, two men got out of each car, leaving one man behind in the driver's seat. The leader of the group signaled two of the men to start moving toward the back of the house.

Once they were out of sight, the other pair walked up to the front door. The boss man stood a little to the side, out of the range of the security camera that had its eye on the space immediately outside the front door. The other man posed as a delivery guy, holding a large packet in his hands. He pulled out a baseball cap from his back pocket, put it on, and rang the bell.

The men didn't seem too worried. They knew taking the woman would be an easy job. The fog was thick enough to eliminate any chance of someone from the neighboring houses spotting them.

"Who's it?" the woman asked as she walked toward the door, looking at the camera feed on the monitor beside the door.

"Express delivery for Frank Mitchell," the man said, lifting the packet in his hand toward the security camera.

The man's body tensed a little when he heard the woman turning the lock. She opened the door and looked at him enquiringly. She still had her baseball cap on, bill pulled low. The man handed her the packet.

"You need to sign for it," he said as he moved his right hand to the back of his pants.

In a quick move, the man drew a gun and pressed it into the woman's waist. Her mouth opened in shock, but not a word came out.

"Don't do anything stupid. You make a sound and I'll put a bullet in you," the man said in a menacing voice.

"What... What do you want? I... I don't have any cash in the house... I can get some from an ATM. Please..." she pleaded in a desperate voice.

"Shut up and get inside," he replied as he dug the gun harder into her, pushing her inside the house.

The woman had no option but to obey him. She stepped back with a terrified look on her face. The gunman signaled to his partner before following the woman inside. The second man gave a thumbs up to the drivers waiting in the two cars before following his partner.

The gunman had pushed the woman a couple of yards into the living room when the other man entered and turned to lock the door. The gunman glanced back for a second to look at his boss, his gun still pointed at the woman.

Never in his wildest dreams could the gunman have guessed that taking his eyes off the woman could be a deadly mistake. His lack of imagination proved costly for him.

Before the man had fully turned his head, the woman had taken a step forward and sideways, taking herself away from the line of fire, and grabbed the barrel of the gun with her left hand while jabbing him hard on the neck with her right hand. While the man moved his hand to his neck as he choked and sputtered, the woman followed the jab with a hard upward strike to his nose with the heel of her hand. The strike ruptured the man's nasal septum, smashing his nose into a bloody pulp.

The woman didn't stop moving as she swung up her right knee and smashed it into his groin. As the man began doubling over from the excruciating pain, the woman placed her left forearm behind his elbow and twisted it with a jerk, breaking it while kicking out his legs from under him. As she hurled the man onto the floor, she twisted the gun, breaking his index finger as she snatched it from his grip, and pointed it at the other man. The gunman had lost consciousness before his body hit the ground.

The entire sequence of moves had taken no more than three seconds. It took the other man, who had turned to lock the door, a couple of seconds to turn back and realize what was happening. He lost the third second staring unbelievingly at the action unfolding in front of him. The man had been too confident when he entered the house. He hadn't bothered to draw his gun. By the time he grabbed the gun tucked into the back of his pants, the woman already had a Glock pointed at him.

"Don't even think about it," she said in a commanding voice.

The man froze, shock written in large letters on his face.

"Hold the gun by the barrel and show it to me," she spoke in a voice that demanded compliance.

The man did as he was told.

"Place it on the floor. Very slowly. You make any sudden move and I'll put a bullet in you."

The man obeyed her, looking at her with a mix of surprise and anger in his eyes.

"Kick the gun to the far corner. Don't give me a reason to shoot you. I'm dying to do it but don't want to mess up the living room," she warned him.

The man looked at her with murder in his eyes, but complied with her command.

"Now flat on the ground."

"You're one dead bitch…" the man muttered in a menacing tone.

His words were cut short in mid-sentence as the woman suddenly took a step forward and struck him on the side of his face and neck with an open-handed strike. It wasn't a simple slap—the strike was much more painful and powerful. The woman smashed the heel of her palm into the side of the man's neck while the rest of her palm and fingers landed full force onto his ear in a resounding slap.

"You were saying…" she asked him in a calm voice as she took a quick step back.

The man could barely hear her over the ringing in his ear from the hard slap. He was also disoriented from the strike to his neck. He had been hit on the spot between the ear and chin where the vagus nerve lies between the carotid and the jugular. A solid strike on that spot knocks out the biggest of men. The woman seemed to have restrained herself, as if she wanted him to stay awake. The man's ears burned from pain and embarrassment at being slapped so hard by a woman half a foot shorter than him.

"You got lucky, bitch. You won't always have the gun with you."

"Oh, yeah? There," she said, starting to sound a little less calm as she tucked the gun into the back of her jeans. "Let's see what you've got."

She rushed toward him as she spoke the words. Everything the woman had done ever since the man had entered the house had been completely unexpected for him. She caught the man off guard once again when she rushed him. He kind of froze. All he could think of doing was try to push her back. The man outweighed the woman by at least half her body weight. Had it been any other woman, he could easily have shoved her so hard she would have landed flat on her back at the other end of the room.

But it was like the woman anticipated the move. She stepped sideways, grabbed his wrist, pulled him a little forward and downward, and placed her forearm behind his elbow, locking it. She had him perfectly positioned for an arm bar takedown—a standard tactic for any law enforcement officer. All she needed to do after that was apply a little pressure to the back of his elbow. The man would have no option but to go down on the floor—any resistance would break his elbow.

But the man was a slow learner. He didn't think the woman would go that far. He tried to resist and free his arm from her grip. This time, she wasn't holding back. She pushed his elbow beyond its range of motion and broke it. The man screamed as he gave up all resistance and fell to the ground. The woman cut off his scream with a sharp jab on the side of his neck, knocking him out.

"Whoa! Easy, tiger," a voice said from behind her.

The woman spun around to face the speaker, but the expression on her face had changed from anger to something close to a smile when she saw it was me. I had just come in after knocking out the two men trying to sneak in from the back.

When those men moved in for the kill, what they didn't realize was they never had a chance. They weren't the hunters about to make an easy kill. They were the prey. They would have been less cocky if they were aware of three bits of information.

One, the blonde woman in the kitchen wasn't the helpless prey she was pretending to be. She was Ex-Deputy Marshal Brittany Dixon. Until a couple of years ago, she was a Deputy in the Marshals' tactical unit, the Special Operations Group (SOG). Apart from their job description of responding to extreme threat and emergency situations, Deputies from SOG also provide specialized training to other law enforcement officers in hostage negotiations, tactical operations, and self-defense techniques. Deputy Dixon, or Britt, as we called her, was one of the best trainers in unarmed combat.

Two, not that Britt needed it, but she also had me watching her six. I had been keeping tabs on the men all the while they were parked outside the house. While they were cooling their asses in the car, I was stationed in the dark attic of the house, keeping an eye on the street, and monitoring the feed coming in from the security camera installed in a tree facing the backyard. Folks call me Blaze. I used to head SOG. I was Supervisory Deputy United States Marshal Axel Blaze until a few months ago, when I left the service.

Three, the men never had surprise on their side. The house belonged to Frank Mitchell, another former Deputy who had been part of my SOG team. He left the Marshals when he got married and began working in private security. The men had begun stalking Mitchell the previous day. What those guys didn't realize was shadowing unsavory characters is what Marshals do for a living. Mitchell was especially good at it. It didn't take him long to catch on to them. He had immediately begun countersurveillance to find out what they were up to. But what he discovered was something he found almost impossible to believe. Something that made him call me immediately. Information so shocking that it got me on the first flight to San Francisco.

Threats we believed we had dealt with two years ago were possibly alive and kicking. We had no option but to get to the bottom of it. If Mitchell was right, all of us involved in the operation two years ago were in grave danger.

We would have to strike first. And hard. End the threat once and for all.

## CHAPTER 2

I was at my ranch when Mitchell called me. I was out on the range with my crew, checking fences, mending breaches, and looking out for strays. It was almost the end of the day. We were getting ready to ride back to the ranch house.

After leaving the Marshals, I had been mostly hanging around my ranch, reacquainting myself with a cowboy's life. It was a medium-sized spread in Colorado, around 2,000 acres located in the shadow of the San Juan Mountains. Dad died while I was in high school. Mom loved the ranch and took over the reins. Up until the time cancer got to her. That's when I left the army after eleven years of active duty.

I had enlisted when I was twenty. A few months after 9/11. My big brother, Ryan, signed up first, joining the Marines. I enlisted six months later— that's how long it took me to convince mom. I joined the army. Eventually made it to the 75th Ranger Regiment.

In 2007, Ryan died under mysterious circumstances. It took me a while to get at the truth, but I did dig it out. And made sure his killers didn't go unpunished. After that, it became a kind of an obsession—getting justice done when it looked like the bad guys were getting away with any shit. I took early retirement to be with mom in her last days. I retired as Major Axel Blaze in the

1st Special Forces Operational Detachment—Delta (Sabre Squadron D). Most civilians know it as Delta Force.

When mom passed, I kind of lost direction. I had already lost Ryan. The bond I shared with my army buddies was what had kept me going after that. But after having lost that, I became a bit of a drifter. That was until I happened to bump into my old commanding officer during my last posting—Lt Colonel Seamus Flynn. He persuaded me to go meet his brother—Assistant Director Mark Flynn, Head of the Tactical Operations Division of the US Marshal service.

Flynn and I hit it off. Before I knew it, he had convinced me to join the Marshals. I stuck around for five years before deciding to leave. When I finally returned to the ranch at the age of thirty-six, it was after having been away for sixteen years.

Mitchell had left the Marshals a year before I did. When my phone buzzed in my pocket and I took it out to check the caller ID, I was surprised to see his name come up on the screen.

"Hey, Mitchell! Long time, pal."

"You said it, Cowboy. Long time. How you doing?"

In all my days in the army as well as in the Marshals, my nickname had been Cowboy. Not just because I grew up on a ranch... not only because I couldn't be separated from my cowboy boots any time I was in civilian attire... A large part of it had to do with my tendency to break the rules that didn't make sense.

"Just being a cowboy... herding cattle, mending fences... you know how it goes, pal. Nothing glamorous like what you city boys are used to," I replied.

Mitchell was born and brought up in San Francisco, but he didn't fit the stereotypical profile of West Coast city boys. Mitchell wasn't a surfer, didn't sport long hair, didn't smoke weed, drank black coffee without going nuts about the kind of milk or milk-substitute that went into it, had encyclopedic knowledge of every handgun developed ever since Samuel Colt patented the Colt Paterson in 1836, and was as good at using his fists as he was with his handguns. Long story short, Mitchell was the kind of guy you would want to watch your six on any risky mission.

"Yeah, sure," he chuckled. "But that's not what I've heard. Word is, you don't quite get the idea of retiring to a peaceful country life. I've been hearing stories about how you and trouble manage to find each other regularly."

"Who've you been talking to, pal?"

We shot the breeze for a while, but I was getting the feeling it wasn't just a random friendly call. I could sense something was bothering him.

"Something on your mind, Mitchell? Everything alright?" I asked.

"Uh... still the mind reader, huh? Well, the thing is... I saw some guys yesterday. And, two of them... well, even I'm not sure if I saw what I think I saw."

"What's it? I know you're not into dope... and you sure can handle your liquor. Whatever you think you saw, I'm sure we can trust your senses. Take me through it."

"Uh, right, that's why I called. You free right now? It's a long story. Well, not long, but I need your attention."

"Sure. Go on," I replied while signaling to my foreman to carry on with the boys toward the ranch house while I guided my horse to move off to one side.

"Yeah, right. Well, there are these guys who've been tailing me all day. Tough looking bunch, but not really pros ... didn't take me much to spot them on my tail."

"Where did this happen? Was it work related?"

"I don't know. There were two teams. Two cars. One of them was staking out my home."

"Home? Is Em fine?" I asked, concerned about his wife, Emily.

"Yeah. The good thing is she's not home at the moment. Flew to LA yesterday for a bachelorette party."

"Well, that's good. Go on."

"There was this car parked on the street outside my place this morning. Not directly outside but a little distance away... near the intersection. But the men sitting inside... they weren't the kind of guys you expect hanging around a residential street. But I wasn't sure. And I didn't want to give them a clue I was on to them. I ignored them and kept driving toward the intersection. That's when I knew for sure. As soon as I turned the corner, another car pulled out and began tailing me. I led them downtown. Made it easy to place a tracker."

"You placed a tracker on their car?"

"Yup. And while I was at it, I asked one of my boys to head to my place and check if the other car was still there. It was, and my guy put a tracker on it."

"Not bad. Sounds like you've got a good crew."

"You bet. I had to find out what they were up to. I parked my car in a parking garage, let the guys trail me on foot for a while before disappearing to place the tracker on their car, and then let them find me again and follow me around. An hour later, I headed back to my car and drove to work. The guys hung around for some time. But then headed off, with me on their tail. I have this hippie get up I sometimes use for surveillance—a wig with long, flowing hair, a droopy mustache, big sunglasses, loose silky shirt with weird symbols on it... even Em didn't recognize me the first time I wore it and came home."

"That doesn't surprise me," I remarked, recalling how he used to be a regular chameleon.

"I guess. Well, I followed them into the parking garage next to this mall in Union Square. Two guys stayed in the car while one got out and walked toward the elevator. I was feeling a little cocky about my disguise. So, I walked up and stood next to him while we waited together for the elevator. And then got in along with him."

"No kidding!"

"Yeah, really. The guy didn't have a clue. He was too busy in his phone and barely looked at me. Once we got out, I stayed at a distance and watched him walk inside a restaurant. Japanese place called Tokyo Dreams. Very upmarket. Prices through the roof kind of joint. The way I was dressed, they wouldn't have let me in. But good thing I was wearing new-ish jeans and boat shoes, and not the flip-flop sandals that usually go with that get up. They let me in, but I got a seat in a lousy corner. I didn't mind as I would have preferred it anyway."

Mitchell seemed to be stalling, as if hesitant to get to the point. But I didn't interrupt, letting him tell his story at his own pace.

"Well, the man went in and joined two guys already in there. They had one of those semi-private booths, with a slightly enclosed entrance. The guys seemed to be waiting for someone. And then, uh, two men walked in," Mitchell said, before going quiet for a few seconds.

"Who were these guys? Someone you know?" I asked.

"I think so. And... well, the thing is... I think they were guys both of us know."

"Who?"

"Uh, yeah, I'm coming to that. You remember the Cady brothers?"

"Cady brothers?"

It was my turn to sound a little hesitant, not sure where this was leading.

# CHAPTER 3

Before I could come up with a proper reply, my mind had wandered back to events from two years ago. To the Cady brothers—Carson and Dexter. Unscrupulous arms traffickers. Courted by warlords, dictators, terrorists and drug cartels from around the world. But for a long time, they were able to keep up the charade of being successful international businessmen who wined and dined in elite circles.

The brothers began their illegal arms network by fueling the civil wars that always seemed to be on in some part of west Africa. The Cadys changed the game by supplying increasingly sophisticated weapons, sometimes to both sides. The bloody conflicts soon got elevated—moving from machetes and small arms to AK-47s and rocket launchers. UNO-mandated arms embargoes in countries like Angola, Congo, Liberia and Sierra Leone couldn't put a dent in the Cadys operations.

Carson was the brains of the duo. Fluent in seven languages, he was a shrewd operator who helped the brothers carry on the charade of being legitimate international businessmen. Carson was a financial whiz kid who interwove their arms trafficking empire with a string of seemingly innocuous logistics and transport businesses. He built an operation so complex, hidden behind such a thick curtain of seemingly endless number of front companies, that even the US government unwittingly contracted their services a few times.

Dexter was the muscle behind the operation. Literally. About 260 pounds of beef on a six foot three frame. Dexter was a cold-blooded killer, devoid of a conscience. A methodical and vicious man, he took down rivals with brutal efficiency. In contrast to the smooth-talking Carson, Dexter liked to project a cigar-chomping old-world tough guy kind of image. I had seen photos of him standing shirtless, chewing a cigar while wielding an M60 machine gun with ammunition belts strapped across his tattooed chest. I had run across many wannabe Rambos like him. I had never gotten along with any of them.

The brothers learnt the ropes of moving cargo across continents from their old man. He was a pilot who flew chartered transport planes, often to Central America. But it was when the old man did a two-year stint at a transport airline in Eastern Europe that the brothers made the contacts they needed to set up their business. In the early 1990s, when the Soviet Union was crumbling, all types of arms from guns to missiles as well as the planes that could be used to transport them were up for grabs by anyone with the right connections.

That gave the Cadys an edge over other small-time arms traffickers. Not only could they get their hands on anything from guns to missiles to explosives, but they could also deliver them to any location on the planet. It was even rumored the CIA had dealt with them for some covert operations in central America.

From the late 1990s, the Cady brothers were on a roll for well over two decades. But investigative reporting by a persistent journalist brought the spotlight on how they were operating as equal-opportunity suppliers, selling arms to whoever could come up with the money. Arms supplied by them had been used by the Taliban, Al Qaeda and ISIS against American soldiers. That made federal law enforcement agencies look at them more carefully.

The final straw came when their involvement in supplying equipment and technology for Iran's nuclear development program was uncovered. That really brought them into the crosshairs. As soon as the brothers got wind of it, they fled the country. It took a year-long sting operation involving the DEA and ATF before they were finally apprehended in Dubai and brought back to the US.

It was when their trial began that the Marshals, specifically SOG, came into the picture. We handled security arrangements while transporting them from prison to court and back. It was a high-profile case. Flynn, my boss, had asked me to manage it personally. I didn't mind. In fact, I was looking forward to seeing the brothers locked up for good. I had seen too many good men lose life and limb because of weapons supplied by dirtbags like them.

At SOG, we were used to moving dangerous criminals. The Cadys weren't a big deal for us that way. But we knew they had dangerous connections—shadowy groups who would want the brothers out and about to maintain a steady supply of arms. We went for a five-strong security detail with a two-vehicle convoy. Three Deputies in the main van—two in the front and one in the back with the prisoners—and two in the lead vehicle. A five-man security detail for two prisoners sounded like a bit of an overkill, but we didn't want to leave anything to chance. We had mapped out many alternate routes to avoid any possible choke points and kept varying our routes during approach and departure.

But we had no control over what happened once they were at the court. There were two things about security within the court that worried me. The first was the security detail inside the courtroom. It was being managed by a team involving local PD, DEA and ATF. Getting too many players involved brought too many variables into the picture. But it was a high-profile case. Every agency wanted the limelight.

The second worrying thing was both brothers sat unshackled during the trial. The liberal judge didn't want to have defendants in cuffs and chains in his court unless the prosecution made a compelling case for it. The DA's office didn't try hard enough. They didn't understand the threat posed by the brothers.

The first time I set eyes on Dexter, I had no doubt about how much of a physical threat the man posed. He was a big guy, an inch more than my own height of six foot two and 60 pounds heavier than my weight of 200 pounds. Despite the suit he wore to impress the judge, the layers of muscle bulking up his shoulders and arms were easily discernible. The thick wrist and massive fist made it clear the guy could seriously hurt any man he could get his hands on.

What made him appear even more menacing were his eyes. They had a blank, empty look. Eyes of a killer. Zero emotion. Just cold, dead eyes.

The only physical thing Carson shared with his brother was his height. He was a lanky guy, easily over six foot two but weighing under 140 pounds. But the thing about him that made him stand out was his tendency to keep stretching some part of his body almost all the time. He would hardly be still for a minute before he would start rotating or stretching his neck, then moving to his shoulders, then the wrists, then knuckles... The guy just couldn't sit still.

On the first trip to the court, I got in the back of the prisoner vehicle. I wanted to size up the guys. Carson tried to strike up a conversation. All he got from me was silence. He couldn't stay quiet for long and again tried to sweet talk me with promises of an easy life.

"None of you will have to work another day in your life. All you need to do is get a flat tire. As simple as that. Once in a lifetime chance. Seriously, the peanuts you guys get paid aren't worth it," he said pompously.

I had heard that shit hundreds of times. We had an unwritten rule not to engage with prisoners. All Carson got from me was a mocking smile. Dexter had been silent all this time, not even attempting to establish eye contact. He suddenly began speaking.

"*Plata o plomo*. That's what cartels offer guys like you in Mexico. Silver or lead. You can willingly take the silver... or we make sure you get a bullet," he spoke in a deep voice filled with menace.

I simply stared at him. No reaction. The carrot hadn't worked, so he was going for the stick. A variation of the "good cop, bad cop" routine we knew too well. I had been there, done that... many times.

"Have you seen how cops take Cartel bosses to court in Mexico? They wear masks. Shit-scared of the bosses. And for good reason," Dexter continued speaking slowly, enunciating each word carefully.

I kept my stone face on. Dexter wasn't the first criminal who had tried to threaten me. They all shut up after letting off some steam. None of them was worth the bother of getting your blood up.

"You guys made a mistake. You should have worn masks. I've seen your faces. All five of you. I don't forget," he said, his voice thick with menace.

That was a line he shouldn't have crossed. I could overlook some of the shit we got from scum we dealt with, but threatening to go after my guys... Dexter succeeded in getting me to respond, but not in the way he wanted.

"Don't know about Mexico, but I do know things about America. You ever been to West Virginia?" I asked him in the same slow measured tone he had been using himself.

"I might have passed through," he replied, sounding curious.

"There's a city there. Not big. Place called Wheeling."

"What about it?"

"You know pit bulls?" I asked.

"The dogs?"

"Yeah."

"I own many. They can tear a man to pieces," he boasted.

"Yeah, right. They can be scary. Bit like you, right?"

"Yeah."

"The thing is, tough guy, in Wheeling, West Virginia, pit bulls like you are classified as vicious dogs. If you take them to a public place, the way we're taking you to the courthouse... they must be neutered and kept muzzled. You catch my drift?"

Dexter's face grew dark as my words bit him deeply.

"You've no idea who you're dealing with," he said.

"Works both ways, tough guy."

"You just signed your death warrant. You and those other guys."

"One more word out of you and I put a muzzle on you. Try me," I challenged him, my voice gone cold, my hand on my seat buckle, ready to unlock it and get up.

Dexter glared at me with murder in his eyes but didn't speak further. In fact, he didn't try speaking again with me or any other Deputy on any of the trips to the court. But we decided not to get complacent and kept our guards up.

The trial had become a big media circus. That was a pain in the ass, having to keep overenthusiastic reporters at a distance while we escorted the prisoners to the court and back. But we had planned it well. So far as prisoner transport was concerned, everything went without a hitch.

All it took was four court appearances for the jury to convict them. On the final day when the two were to be sentenced, the brothers appeared outwardly calm. Unfortunately, it was a different situation at the courthouse. We encountered larger crowds outside as well as inside the court. The district attorney was in a mood for grandstanding. Elections were around the corner. He was milking the trial as much as he could.

It wasn't anything like break time for us once we handed over the prisoners to the bailiffs in the holding cells of the court. We were aware most escape attempts during court appearances take place at the court itself. We also knew this was the only chance for the Cadys to make any escape attempt before their asses got dumped in a maximum-security prison.

We split up in teams and set up call signs for radio contact. The first team (call sign SOG-1) of two Deputies, Mitchell and Garcia, was stationed in the court's parking garage, which was located in the basement floor with the entrance and exit from a side road. They would be ready to get the vehicles in position to drive away once the business of the court was over. Deputy Mahone was SOG-2, seated inside the court room, ready to give us the signal as soon as it was time to leave. Britt and I were SOG-

3, positioned near the front entrance of the court. The back entrance was accessed through a corridor, which was blocked off on both sides by cops. Even though security within the court was in the hands of the cops, we were vigilant for any surprises.

The court entrance was like a scene from a madhouse. Television crews and vans were parked on the road, with eager reporters ready to grab sound bites. Adding to the confusion were many groups of protestors with placards railing against God-knows-what grievances. The cops had formed a cordon to keep the protestors away from the steps of the courthouse.

I was scanning the TV crews while Britt was keeping tabs on the protestors.

"That group in the middle is anti-guns. Next to them are the diehards for the second amendment," she pointed out two groups trying to outshout each other.

"No wonder they've got such a ruckus going on," I replied.

"That bunch on the left is anti-war. Four guys next to them are pro-democracy."

"Pro-democracy? A bit pointless, isn't it? This is America, last time I checked."

"Maybe that's the only placard they could get their hands on. But the groups yelling at each other on the right over there have even less of a point."

"Why's that?"

"They are for and against death penalty. That's not even on the table. Cadys are being tried for illegal trafficking and money laundering."

"Someone better go tell..."

My reply was cut short by a loud crack followed by an explosion in a parking garage across the road. As we instinctively ducked, we saw the force of the explosion lifting a car clear off the ground. Glass and shrapnel from the exploding car flew toward the protesters and news crews. There were a few seconds of almost dead silence before cries of pain and horror filled the air.

A couple of seconds later, another car parked fifty yards toward the right blew up, the force of the blast lifting it in the air, increasing the circumference of its blast impact, before it crashed back on the ground. Five seconds later, the explosion was mirrored near an intersection on the left.

The entire cordon of cops up front was frozen in place. Even though they were mentally prepared for the possibility of an escape attempt, nothing could have prepared them for the scale of the attacks on multiple fronts. Three well-coordinated explosions occurring at five-second intervals. Planned and executed with military precision. Meant to shock and awe. And cause confusion around and inside the court building.

But the course of action was clear to me. I didn't have the slightest doubt the explosions weren't random terrorist acts. I was sure they were meant to be diversions for the Cadys to make a run for it. Their only purpose was to create confusion. Put the security arrangements in disarray. But the explosions hadn't achieved much in terms of making a huge dent in the security detail. I was sure there was more to come.

"SOG-3 to all teams, explosions near the front entrance. Give me a Sitrep. Over," I spoke into the radio.

I had barely finished speaking when I heard the sound of automatic gunfire from the direction of the court's parking garage entrance on the side.

"This is SOG-1. Gunmen in a van have shot the parking garage guards. They're blocking the exit. We're exchanging fire as we speak. Over," Mitchell's voice came through my earpiece.

"SOG-1. Hold position. Don't let them control the entrance. And watch your six—there could be an attack from behind you. Over," I replied.

"Roger that."

It was possible the attack in the parking garage was meant to clear the way for the Cadys to escape from there. But I doubted that. There were too many obstacles between the courtroom where they were being tried and the parking garage. I had a feeling that like the other explosions, the attack was another diversion to keep us occupied.

My thoughts were interrupted by the sound of shots from the direction of the courtroom where the Cadys were being tried. I hadn't heard back from Mahone.

"SOG-3 to SOG-2. Do you copy?" I spoke into the radio again.

But all I got was radio silence. That worried me. If the Cadys could pull off the four external attacks, a fifth one inside the courtroom wouldn't be difficult for them. That would give them multiple options to get out of the building—front, back, parking garage…

"Hold position. I'm heading in. You see either of the brothers rushing out, shoot to maim or kill," I yelled at Britt as I sprinted inside.

"Copy that," she shouted back.

As I arrived at the courtroom, I saw cops with guns drawn, positioned outside its heavy wooden doors. It was locked from inside. There had been multiple shots fired inside. The cops had no idea what was going on. I was beginning to get a bad feeling about Mahone.

"SOG-3 to SOG-2. Mahone, you copy?" I spoke into the radio once again.

There was silence for a few seconds before I heard a crackle as someone pressed the radio mic to speak. I could hear a faint whirring sound in the background.

"You should have listened, Marshal. *Plata o plomo*. I gave you a choice. You chose bullets. Your man is dead," Dexter's cold voice came over the radio.

All sounds around me suddenly got muted. All I could hear was the throbbing in my ears as my blood rushed to my head, anger curling like a beast inside me, threatening to burn my insides. But experience had taught me not to be consumed by that passion. Not let it cloud my senses.

I realized I had stopped breathing and took a breath. That's when my mind focused on the other sound. A whirring sound, which was getting louder. A helicopter. A sound I wouldn't have heard in the commotion around me inside the courthouse. It flashed upon me—Dexter was on the roof of the three-story building. That was his escape plan.

My body had been bursting with pent up violent energy, which suddenly got an outlet. I sprinted toward the stairwell at the other side of the building.

"Lost your tongue, Marshal?" Dexter's taunting voice came through my earpiece as I ran.

I resisted the urge to press the mic and reply. I had enough presence of mind not to commit the same mistake as Dexter. He could have escaped in the helicopter by the time I realized what was going on. But he was too vain not to give in to the impulse of boasting about what he had done.

I was bounding up the stairs four steps at a time when he spoke. The only thing that mattered to me was the chance of breaking him with my hands. Turning on the mic could make him realize I was rushing up the stairs toward the roof.

When I reached the stairwell at the top of the third floor, I realized the heavy iron door to the roof was bolted from outside. Dexter had blocked access to the roof. I resisted the impulse of slamming my body into the door to force it open. The only thing it would do would be warn Dexter I was on the other side of the door. I knew that thing couldn't be broken open without a battering ram.

I could hear the approaching chopper through the door. It was close. I figured I had about twenty seconds before it got into hovering mode above the roof and let down a rope ladder. Without wasting a second, I leapt down the steps to get down to the third floor and barged into the first room I found with an unlocked door. There were three people inside, one man and two women, crowded near the windows, trying to figure out what was happening outside.

"Away from the windows. Now!" I shouted as I picked up a chair and rushed toward the window.

The three almost fell backwards in their rush to get out of my way. I slammed the chair against the windowpane, smashing it. I kicked off a couple of big shards of glass still sticking out from the frame before stepping onto the ledge outside the window.

I held on to the frame, leaned back a little, and looked up. I saw a ledge five feet above the top of the window frame, at least a couple of feet out of my reach. Above the ledge was the three-foot high border wall of the roof.

Adrenaline was pumping through my veins. I didn't think twice about letting go of the window frame and leaping up. My fingers landed on the ledge. I kept the motion going as I again hauled my body upwards with all my strength, let go of the ledge, and caught the edge of the roof's border wall.

As I pulled myself up and swung my leg over the roof wall, I saw the chopper with a rope ladder dangling from it. It was at the other end of the roof, about fifty yards away. Carson was already up the ladder and was being pulled into the chopper by a man inside it. Dexter had been waiting his turn and had just grabbed the ladder when I landed on the roof.

I drew my service weapon, a .40-caliber Glock-22, and ran toward him, firing off shots at the chopper. I clipped Carson in the back of his thigh and the other guy in the abdomen. Both men scrambled inside rapidly, away from my line of fire. Dexter had no option but to let go of the ladder as the chopper lifted suddenly and flew away. I fired a few more shots at it, but it was soon out of the Glock's range.

By that time, I had crossed over to the other end of the roof and was ten yards away from Dexter. It took a lot of self-control not to just shoot him in the head. I kept reminding myself shooting him would let him off too easy. He had murdered Mahone in cold blood. I wanted to make him suffer.

Dexter looked at me with murder in his eyes as I walked toward him. He had planned an almost perfect escape. Had I been a few seconds late, he would have been in the chopper.

I spoke into the radio as I walked. I gave Mitchell the direction the chopper flew in and asked him to immediately get air support. Then I turned off the radio.

"On your knees," I barked out an order.

I kicked Dexter on the back of his left knee. He cursed as he went down on the knee and held out his left arm to stop himself from falling flat on his face. I swept the arm out with another kick while pushing him forward, making him fall flat on the ground.

"You can play tough all you want. I know you don't have the balls to shoot me," Dexter shouted in a voice quivering with anger.

I didn't reply, but pushed my gun so hard into the back of his neck that he cried out in pain. Then I frisked him.

I found two guns. One was a SIG Sauer P226, which he had grabbed from a bailiff before shooting him and Mahone. The other was a Glock identical to mine, which he had grabbed from Mahone after shooting him. Dexter saw me examining the guns and gave me an evil smile.

"Is this the gun you used to shoot them?" I asked him, keeping my voice under control.

"What do you think?" he replied cockily.

"You shoot with your right hand?"

"Mostly. I'm good with both," he replied, still trying to sound cocky but starting to look a bit unsure.

I could sense my calm manner was unnerving him. I turned my back to him and walked toward the roof entrance, which Dexter had bolted from outside. I kept the guns beside the entrance and turned. He was still on the ground, looking at me unsurely.

"Cops will be breaking down that door any minute. You get through me, those guns are yours," I said as I walked toward him.

I could see hope return to Dexter's face as he saw a chance to escape. All he needed to do was get me on the ground once and there wouldn't be any stopping him. That's what I wanted to do to him. Raise his hopes and then crush his spirit.

Dexter gave me an evil smile as he got up and flexed his massive shoulders. He was clearly bigger than me. But the mood I was in, I barely noticed that. Guys like Dexter can be deadly so long as they have a weapon. They like to play dirty. They'll shoot, stab, slash you when you don't see it coming. But take the weapons away and they're suddenly clueless. You don't learn unarmed combat by shooting guys with an automatic. I would make him realize that the hard way. I was about to play dirty in a way he wouldn't forget until his dying breath.

Dexter made a sudden rush at me and swung out his right arm in a massive punch. Had it landed, I would have been flat on the ground. But I saw it coming a mile away. I ducked and threw in a couple of combination strikes. I punched him hard in the neck with my right hand, my knuckles making contact with his Adam's apple.

Before he began coughing and sputtering, my left hand was already moving toward his right eye. I held my three middle fingers straight out, making a deadly spear. I jabbed Dexter full force in the right eye. Combined with his own forward momentum, the impact was severe. The strike ruptured his cornea. Blood and slime oozed out of the eye. Dexter cried out in pain.

Those two strikes landing on target had already finished the fight before it had barely begun. Dexter couldn't see with his right eye and was gasping for breath, reeling from the impact of my punch on his throat. All he could do was instinctively try to step away from me. But I wasn't about to let him do that.

As I moved toward him, he covered his eye with his left hand while trying to push me away with his right. I caught the fingers of his outstretched hand, grabbing two of his fingers in each hand and ripped them apart with a jerk. All four fingers snapped, with his palm almost splitting in two with the force I exerted. Dexter screamed in pain. He tried to step back to get his torn right hand loose from my grip.

But I moved with him and closer to him, suddenly ducking and turning so my back was toward him with his arm held high above me. I brought his elbow crashing down on my right shoulder. The elbow snapped with a loud crack. The jagged edges of the radius and ulna forearm bones broke through the skin. Dexter screamed in agony, incapacitating pain coursing through his arm. He again tried to get away from me.

I let him stagger back a few steps before moving toward him with deliberate steps. I saw fear written large on the man's face as I closed the distance. I didn't feel any pity—all I could see was the face of Mahone. A good man unnecessarily lost his life because of this egomaniac who was now desperately trying to get away from me.

I took a step toward him and kicked his legs out from under him. Dexter fell heavily on his back. His body trembled with the intense pain from his multiple broken bones and ruptured right eye. He was blinking rapidly with his left eye.

"I need you to focus, tough guy," I said, bending down and lightly tapping his face.

"Arrest me. I'm not trying to escape. You can't do this," he whispered, gasping, barely able to speak.

Someone had begun banging on the roof door by then. A glimmer of hope appeared on Dexter's face, thinking his ordeal was finally over. I was about to shatter it again.

"You said you can shoot with either hand, right?" I asked, ignoring the banging.

He looked terrified when he heard my words. I grabbed his left hand and broke his index finger with a jerk, flattening it against the back of his palm. Then I raised his arm and smashed my knee into the back of his elbow, just below the joint, breaking both his forearm bones.

"You're never going to shoot straight with either arm. Think about that as you rot away in supermax for the rest of your life."

Those were the last words Dexter heard before he passed out.

# CHAPTER 4

Witnesses from within the courtroom later told us how the escape had taken place. When the first explosion occurred, no one realized its magnitude as the courtroom was deep within the courthouse. One of the bailiffs as well as Deputy Mahone began walking out to find out what was up. Dexter was waiting for that moment. He jumped up, used a shiv to fatally stab a second bailiff in the neck, grabbed his gun, and shot the two men in the back.

Dexter was charged with multiple murders on top of the charges already against him. No one was surprised when the DA sought the death penalty. The jury were unanimous in granting it. Dexter was sent to death row in Dry Creek State Prison. Executions in California have been on hold for many years. It wasn't likely Dexter would get the needle any time soon. But that didn't matter. What was important was the certainty about three things. He would never shoot straight, or even punch hard, with either hand again. He would never forget what caused him to lose his abilities. And he was never going to get out.

Two days later, the helicopter that broke out Carson was found crashed in the Sierra Nevada mountain range in northern California. There were three bodies inside. All burnt beyond recognition. One of them matched Carson in physical dimensions.

They weren't good memories. I hadn't really thought about them for a while. When Mitchell on the other end of the phone asked me about the Cady brothers, I had fallen silent for a few seconds.

"You there?" Mitchell asked when he didn't get my reply.

"Uh, yeah. What about the Cady brothers?" I asked.

"Well... I need to confirm a few things. After what you did to Dexter's right hand, he should have a big scar running through the middle of his palm... multiple stitches on the palm and its back side, right?"

"I guess."

"And both his arms were broken at the elbow?"

"Yeah."

"Compound fractures in both arms, right?"

"Uh-huh."

"So, even after surgery, his arms will always be stiff?"

"I guess. Those kinds of breaks don't heal completely. That's why I gave them to him."

"I know. No one would have blamed you if you had killed him that day."

"I'm still not sure where you're going with this," I replied.

"Getting to it. Just trying to get all the facts right. Just humor me, will you?"

"Sure. Go on."

"Thanks. You remember the tattoos Dexter had?"

"I think so. It was all part of his macho posturing bullshit. Lots of ink on his back—guns, crossbows, crosses..."

"Yeah, but I was thinking of the ones on his forearms."

"Um... didn't he have some big cat on one arm... and a big ass gun on the other?"

"Exactly. He had a roaring lion on the left and a machine gun kind of tattoo on the right. I confirmed from his file."

"You went back to his file?" I asked, sounding a little surprised.

"I had to... to confirm all his identifying features."

"Identifying features? I still don't get the point."

"I'm getting there. I promise. You remember Carson's profile? He was big-time into Japanese stuff. Spoke it fluently, had kind of a fetish for Japanese women, and was into that Origami stuff, making things out of paper."

"Yeah. I'm not sure he made a lot of things. I just remember this dragon he used to make."

"Exactly. And another thing I clearly remember is he was really weird the way he kept stretching all the time. Sitting, standing, whatever... He would always be stretching something—his shoulder or arm or neck. The guy just wouldn't be still."

"Yeah, weird guy," I said, my voice conveying a little impatience.

"Alright, I know I'm being a pain. But I had to confirm all this stuff. Anyways, the thing is, these two guys that walked in... I think they were the Cady brothers."

Mitchell waited for my reaction. He again had me at a loss for words.

"Well?" he asked.

"You said brothers? With an 's'?" I confirmed.

"Yeah."

"So... just to be sure... you're not talking about bumping into Dexter in prison?"

"I wish I was... but no. I'm almost certain I saw Carson and Dexter in that restaurant."

I again fell silent for a few moments. My mind was in turmoil, trying to make sense of what Mitchell had just told me. Had it been any other guy, I would have straight off told him he was talking bullshit. But not Mitchell. He was as solid as they come. If he said he saw something, then he did.

"Now you know why I'm so unsure," Mitchell said.

"I know, pal. But I don't know what to make of it. Take me through it. Every detail. Did you look at the guys closely?"

"Close enough. Maybe fifteen feet. Twenty tops. The second I saw them walking in, my gut told me it was Dexter I was looking at. He looks different. He's no longer clean shaved. He's this shaggy man now. I don't think he's had a shave or haircut for months. As he walked in, he kind of surveyed everything in the room. He was wearing dark glasses even inside the restaurant. That was odd, but you do see some dudes do that. I too was wearing them in my hippie avatar. But the thing that struck me was... he had to turn his body to look at anything on his right."

"Like he was blind in the right eye?" I asked.

"Exactly."

"Did he look at you?"

"He did, but I don't think he recognized me. It's a good thing I had my sunglasses on, or he might have seen something like recognition in my eyes."

"I still don't get why you're so sure it was Dexter."

"I'm getting there. I looked carefully at the rest of him to confirm my gut feel. And I'm reading this out from a list in my hand. He had the same facial structure... the same powerful build and height... both his arms were very stiff in movement... it felt like he was blind in his right eye... and... he had this ugly scar running from the back of his palm, through the middle of his fingers, and onto the front."

"Hmm... that does sound intriguing. Can't argue with that. What about the tattoos?"

"That I couldn't see clearly. He was wearing a full-sleeved shirt. The tattoo on his left arm is above the wrist, so it wasn't visible. But the machine gun one on his right arm, that's all over his forearm, with the barrel flowing onto the scar at the back of his palm. I think I could make it out. It wasn't visible initially as he was wearing a glove on his right hand when he walked in."

"Just one glove?"

"Yes. There wasn't any reason for it. It was a warm day, temperature almost touching 70. No reason really to wear a glove."

"Except to hide his scars and tattoo," I said, finishing his thought.

"Yeah. I guess he must have been feeling hot as he took it off without really thinking about it. But put it back on a few seconds later."

"I gotta agree, pal. It's beginning to sound more and more like him."

"That's what I'm saying. I couldn't shake the feeling from the moment I laid eyes on him. To get some confirmation, I took a quick video of the guys."

"Good thinking."

"It wasn't too difficult. I kept my phone under the table with only the camera lens above the edge. I sent the video to my tech guys to match it with Dexter's face using facial recognition software."

"And?"

"It was a 97% match."

"Which isn't bad given the distance and camera angle. Almost a positive match," I said, thinking aloud.

"Exactly. I'll forward some photos to you. Have a look and tell me. Just hang on a second."

Mitchell put me on hold while he forwarded the photos. They landed on my phone ten seconds later. I opened the first one to see a close up of a man. Shaggy-haired guy with unruly beard. Despite the hair, the man looked surprisingly familiar. My blood began to rise simply by looking at the photo.

"What do you think?" Mitchell asked as he got back on the call.

"I can't believe I'm saying it, but yeah, it does look like Dexter. Have you checked with the prison? Any chance he could be out temporarily?"

"I checked. They laughed at the idea when I asked if he could be out for any reason. They confirmed the only way he's getting out is if he's dead."

"And what about the other guy? What makes you think it was Carson? You got facial recognition?"

"No. Uh... here's the thing—Carson doesn't look like himself."

"Huh? So... you think it's him because he was hanging around with this other guy?"

"No, it's more logical than that," Mitchell replied, laughing. "Hang on, I'll again read from this list in my hand. This guy was the same height and build... spoke to the maître d' in fluent Japanese..."

"What about the voice?"

"Sounded like him. He was in real show-off mode, speaking a little loudly to impress everyone."

"Did you catch his voice on the video?"

"Unfortunately, no. A voice match would have cleared everything. But it took me a while to get over my initial shock. He was done talking by the time I began recording. They didn't hang around there for long... maybe a minute or two before moving to a private room."

"Never mind. What else?"

"Yeah. Well, this guy wouldn't stop stretching. Stretched every part of his body like he was about to run a marathon. Never stood still for a second."

"That does sound like..."

"And one more thing," Mitchell said excitedly, cutting me off, "They were in there for about half an hour. I hung around. While I was waiting, a waitress came out from the room after serving them food. As she walked past me, she was smiling, looking at something in her hand. Take a guess what it was?"

"Origami dragon?"

"Bingo. He must have made if from a napkin and given it to her."

"Sounds like you're on to something. What happened next?"

"It was only the Cadys... uh, the guys who looked like the Cadys... who went into the private room. The other guys stayed out. I couldn't figure out why. I realized when they got out of the room. Two guys had gone in and four walked out. Two guys I hadn't seen before were already inside the room. Sharply dressed guys... expensive suits, alligator shoes, gold Rolexes... the works."

"Any idea who they were?"

"No. They looked Latino. I managed to click a quick photo but it wasn't very clear. They came out too suddenly and didn't waste a second hanging around. They walked straight to the elevator, got down, and jumped into two Hummers waiting for them near the mall entrance. The brothers in one and the other two guys in the other. Both drove off in opposite directions. My car was stuck in the parking garage. By the time I got in a cab, they were gone."

"You got the license plates?"

"Yeah. That's the curious thing. Both had diplomatic plates. Registered to the Venezuelan consulate."

"Venezuelan diplomatic plates? Really?"

"Yeah. So... what do you think? Am I nuts?"

"No, pal. You're the sanest guy I know. And you know what... I couldn't shake the feeling that Carson had somehow given us the slip. Something wasn't right about how conveniently we found his body a couple of days later. Burnt beyond recognition."

"That's exactly what I thought. What do you think I should do? I haven't made a move on those guys yet. I figured I would have a chat with you first."

"Good thing you did. Don't make a move. I'll take the first flight out to San Francisco in the morning. Let's figure out what the hell's going on."

"Sure thing."

"Touch base with Britt and Garcia. Tell them to be alert. If it's really the Cadys, they'll be after everyone who was on that security detail."

"Roger that. And Blaze... they're going to have special love for you. Watch your six."

"Roger that."

By the time I got off the call, I was beginning to believe Mitchell might not be off the mark. I had never been entirely convinced about Carson's death. It somehow seemed too easy. Too much of a coincidence. Having found out how resourceful the Cadys were, I didn't put it past him to arrange for a charred body to fool the authorities into believing he was dead. And there was something else as well.

Carson's body as well as of the other guy didn't have bullet wounds. I was positive I had shot them.

But the Feds and the DA wanted to tie up the case. From being a feather in their cap, the case had turned into a big embarrassment. Even before a DNA match, they were dying to announce to the world they had got Carson. But finally, the DNA match came out positive. That settled it. I had no option but to accept I might not have shot him after all. It was a distance of thirty yards. I couldn't be one hundred percent sure. I still didn't know what to believe.

Next morning, I took the first flight out from Denver at 0600 hours. When I landed in San Francisco, I had moved from Mountain Time to Pacific Time and saved an hour. I walked out of the airport at eight.

Mitchell was waiting to pick me up. He hadn't changed at all after two years of married life. Fit guy, 175 pounds on a six-foot frame, with not an ounce of fat that guys tend to put on when they settle down. Looking at his pleasant face and demeanor, it was hard to visualize the man could turn into a mean fighting machine in the boxing ring. Mitchell had made it to UC Berkeley on a boxing scholarship.

But what really surprised me was the person standing next to him. When I asked Mitchell to call Britt and ask her to watch her six, I had no idea she would turn up in San Francisco before I did.

"Welcome to California, Cowboy," Britt said with a big smile.

After leaving the Marshals, she had set herself up as a sought-after self-defense and fitness trainer in Los Angeles, teaching clients in hip studios in Malibu and Santa Monica.

"Brittany Dixon! I've heard the name's making big waves on Malibu beaches," I replied, as we hugged.

"Not a big deal. Half the time I'm just a glorified nanny for spoilt brats."

"Spoilt but loaded," Mitchell pointed out.

"Yeah, for the most part. That's the only thing that makes it worth it most days."

"I'm sure you're one hell of a badass nanny. Good you came," I said.

"I had to come. If Mahone's killers are on the loose..." she replied.

"I know. What do you think? Could it be them?"

"I don't know. Mitchell called. Said you think it's possible. That was good enough for me."

"That was good enough for Garcia as well. He's flying in from Miami this evening," Mitchell added.

"Miami? Is that where he's posted these days?"

"Yup. He was stuck someplace in the Everglades when I called. Chasing gator poachers."

Deputy Luis Garcia was the only one of us who was still with the Marshals. Garcia was a skilled investigator, and a tough as nails lawman. If he had gator poachers in his sights, their future was sealed.

"So, how are we playing it?" Britt asked.

There wasn't a lot to be discussed. It was time for action. We were all in agreement we needed to go on the offensive. Grab the men who had been tailing Mitchell. And make them talk. That was the only way to get to the bottom of it.

Mitchell had already done half the groundwork. He had identified two teams. They didn't have a clue they were moving around with trackers on their cars. After staking out Mitchell's home and following him the previous day, the cars had gone to a building in the industrial area of the city. As per records Mitchell accessed online, the place was supposed to be a warehouse.

It was time to lure the men in. The only problem was we didn't know exactly what they had in mind—if they were planning to make a move on Mitchell, or were playing a waiting game with some other motive. Mitchell's wife, Emily, wouldn't be back for another couple of days, so he wasn't too worried.

We decided to give the men some more bait by bringing a fake Emily into the picture. Give the men choices and keep them busy. We planned to set the trap in two places. Mitchell would lead one team north over the Golden Gate Bridge to a motel near Sausalito. Britt and I would set the trap in Mitchell's place.

The key to lure those men lay in a little bit of disguise and a lot of misdirection. Show them something very similar to what they expected to see. Make them believe in the truth we would create for them. That's what magicians do on stage all the time. The same principles apply in warfare.

All it took was make the men believe Britt was Emily. They didn't really look that much alike. Emily was blonde while Britt was a brunette. Britt was also three inches taller than the five foot three Emily. But the two women did have one similarity—both looked fit and athletic. All that was needed was for Britt to color her hair blonde, dress the way Emily dressed, and arrive at Mitchell's house with him, with both displaying the comfortable body language long-time couples exhibit with each other. The difference in height wouldn't figure in the consciousness of an onlooker.

Mitchell and Britt knew the men had fallen for it when they left his home around midday in two separate cars—Britt headed downtown for Emily's gym while Mitchell led the other team to his workplace. Each car had a tail.

All that was left was for Mitchell to make the guys believe he was screwing around behind Emily's back. All it needed was for Mitchell to pick up a woman and take her to the motel. And not get out for hours. That way, the men would know Emily was alone at home when she returned in the evening. A couple of hours before she returned, a third team had made its way to Mitchell's place and had parked outside. But by then, I was already inside the house and was watching the men.

The trap was set. All we needed was for them to make a move. When the four men finally walked out of the two cars, we were ready for them. I saw two men moving toward the front door and alerted Britt on the radio. A second pair made their move through the back entrance.

What the men didn't know was they weren't the only ones making use of the fog and the shadows of the approaching night to make a stealthy attack. I was taking advantage of the reduced visibility as well, crouched behind a tree in the backyard, waiting to take them down.

I was ready for quick takedowns. It had to be as noiseless as possible. Any sounds coming from the backyard might alert the two guys Britt was dealing with in the front of the house.

I left my gun in the holster at the back of my jeans. Instead, I had an expandable baton ready in my hand. While one man tried to jimmy the back door, the second man stood a couple of feet behind him. The loud crack when the baton expanded to about two feet was the only sound the man heard before the baton smashed into the side of his neck. He collapsed—knocked out cold.

The man jimmying the door turned toward me, his hand reaching for a gun at his side. I let him grab the gun. As he began to line it on me, I brought the baton down hard on the middle of his forearm. There was a loud crack as the steel baton slammed onto the radius bone of his forearm, shattering it. The moment the baton broke his arm, I had already begun moving it up in a reverse swing.

The baton slammed into the man's chin, cutting out the cry of pain he had opened his mouth to emit. The force of the blow lifted the man a few inches off the ground. He had lost consciousness before his feet touched the ground again. The cracking sound of his jaw breaking was followed by complete silence as the man collapsed soundlessly.

I moved back to the other man, raised his right arm, and smashed my knee into the back of his elbow. His arm got bent at a crazy angle. These men were killers and I wasn't about to leave any of them able enough for another attack until I had figured out what the hell was going on.

I pulled out flexicuffs from my back pocket and cuffed the two guys' left hands to each other. Even if they woke up, which was unlikely, they wouldn't be going anywhere.

Then I took out a key, opened the back door, and walked quietly toward the living room. When I reached the doorway, I saw Britt taking out the second man. She had his elbow locked in an arm bar takedown position. When the man tried resisting, she broke his elbow and knocked him out with a sharp jab on the side of his neck.

"Whoa! Easy, tiger," I said.

Britt turned her head and looked at me. The fierce expression on her face got replaced by a smile.

"Those were some badass takedowns," I said, as I walked over to look at the two broken men lying knocked out on the floor.

"I think I lost it a bit... thinking of what would have happened to Em if she was alone here," Britt replied.

"Yeah, I know."

The plan had worked perfectly. We had taken out all four guys. None of them was going anywhere for a while. It was time to grab the two men who were waiting in the two cars parked out front.

# CHAPTER 5

"Let's grab the guys in the cars outside before they begin to wonder what's up," I said to Britt.

"Sure. How are we playing it?"

"There are two cars out front... on both sides of the road. You take the near one. I'll take the other."

"Copy that."

"And Britt..."

"Yeah?"

"Try a gentler touch. We need to get these guys talking. Best to have them awake for that."

"Roger that, boss," she laughed, giving me a mock salute.

We knew the guys in the cars would be watching the front entrance. We went out the back door, walked to the end of the backyard, opened the small access gate in the fence, and walked into the back alley. We circled around the house and split up once we were on the main street. We crept up behind the cars using the cover of the fog and darkness. Once we were positioned behind the trunks of our respective target cars, we moved forward simultaneously.

The guy sitting in my car had already made it easy. He had the driver's side window open, trying to peer through the darkness at the house to make out what was taking his partners so long. I took out my gun and jammed it into his face. I was surprised to see he was a kid not more than twenty.

And not the punk kid I would have expected to be moving around with a crew of killers, but a skinny, baby-faced guy wearing a hoodie. The curious thing was the hoodie was inside out.

"You make a sudden move and I'll put a bullet in you. Got it?"

"Yes, sir," he replied very obediently.

He surprised me yet again with his words. He looked and sounded like he had just gotten out of high school. I was momentarily distracted by a cry from the direction of the other car. When I turned my head, I saw the driver of that car lying face down on the sidewalk. Britt was kneeling on him, one knee on his back, her gun digging into his ear, as she retrieved a gun from the back of his pants.

"Open the trunk," I ordered the kid.

He looked at me nervously, raised his right palm above the window to show me it was empty, before reaching for the car key with his left hand slowly to pop open the trunk.

"Get out," I said, opening the door and signaling with my gun.

He didn't have to be told twice. He was the most compliant prisoner ever. I frisked him. He wasn't carrying anything except a wallet and a phone. It was a facial recognition one. I pressed the home button, pointed it at his face, set it to permanent unlock, and slipped the phone and wallet into my pocket. The kid looked like he was about ready to cry.

"Where's your gun?" I asked, as I turned him around and pressed my gun into his gut.

"My gun?" he asked, a bit incredulously. "I'm not carrying any gun."

"I know that, genius. I just frisked you. But if I find any guns in the car, I'll..."

"No, no, sorry, hang on. I misunderstood. I thought you asked about my gun. There is a gun in the car. But that's not mine. I'm just the driver."

"Just a driver, huh? An innocent Uber driver caught up with these gangsters?"

"No, not Uber," he replied very earnestly. "But I swear..."

"Cut the crap. How many guns in the car?"

"Uh, just one. It's a... uh, Uzi... in the glove compartment."

"Uzi, huh? Still claim to be an innocent driver?"

"I swear."

"Shut up," I cut him off.

I walked him to the back of the car, opened the trunk, and threw him inside. When he tried to protest, I dug the gun into his neck.

"I'll be back for you in a few minutes. I'll need you to do a lot of talking then."

He didn't make another sound as I closed the trunk door. I checked inside the car to confirm if what the kid had told me was true. It was. There was a mini-Uzi in the glove compartment. It looked brand new. I hid it under the driver's seat.

I locked the car and crossed the road. Britt was hauling up the other guy to his feet, his hands cuffed behind him. The man's face had hit the sidewalk when Britt tackled him and threw him down. His nose was badly bruised, and his lips were bloody and beginning to swell up.

"Remember our little talk about gentle touch?" I asked Britt, trying to restrain a smile.

"He tried to jump me when I was frisking him. But I did keep him conscious," she replied defensively.

"You're right. That's all we need. Come here, tough guy," I said, my voice turning cold as I grabbed him roughly by the collar and frog-marched him toward the house.

It was time for Britt to take a step back and for me to take the lead. We had done such interrogation routines dozens of times. Part of our "bad cop, worse cop" routine. Britt's violent takedown of the guy had already primed him. I would drive him further toward the edge by scaring the shit out of him.

While I interrogated the man, Britt would get on with other tasks we had planned. The first was to let Mitchell know we had taken out both teams at his house. That would be a cue for him to take out the third team staking him out at the motel. That part was fairly easy. Garcia had landed in the city an hour ago, grabbed a pickup truck from the Marshals' District Office, and had driven straight out to the motel. He already had eyes on the stalkers. All he needed was Britt's signal to take them out.

As I began hauling the guy toward the front door, Britt had already moved inside, where she began frisking the two knocked-out men. While I interrogated the only man conscious and able to answer questions, Britt would work on getting information from the men's phones and IDs.

Before Britt walked off to the back of the house to frisk the two men back there, I handed her the phone and wallet of the kid I had left locked in the trunk of the car outside.

I finally pushed the man through the front door and stopped a few feet away from the two guys lying unconscious on the floor. Both men's right arms were twisted at a weird angle at the elbow. One guy's face was smashed up as well. I could see the sight was having the intended effect on the man.

"Look at them carefully and then look at me," I said in a sharp voice.

The man tried to put on a cocky expression as he turned his face to look at me. He looked quite ridiculous, trying to look tough with a swollen nose and lips. But I knew he didn't have a choice other than putting on a tough act. I also knew the next few seconds would decide how much he would reveal.

I pushed him while kicking his legs out from under him. The wind flew out of him as he landed hard on his back. Before he had a chance to catch his breath, I rolled him over. I grabbed his cuffed right hand and pushed his middle finger back to the point of breaking. That made sure I had the man's complete attention.

"Listen to every word I say very carefully if you want to avoid pain. Got it?" I asked, my voice cold as ice.

"Yes," he said, gasping from the pain.

"You guys broke into this home. All of you have guns. If I break your fingers and limbs, before putting a bullet in your skull, I'll have no problem passing it off as self-defense and getting away with it. Get it?"

I had taken the pressure off his finger while I spoke. That gave the man the false hope I might not be following through on my threats. He kept silent, just staring at the floor without replying.

"Maybe you're too thick to get it. Let me explain," I said.

Without warning, I gave a sudden jerk to his middle finger and broke it. The man yelped in pain. Any traces of cockiness in his face were replaced by shock and fear.

"I hope this demonstration helped. I don't mind repeating it if I get the feeling you're going to need it again."

The man couldn't reply, too busy dealing with the shock of his broken finger.

"So... as I was saying, I could easily put a bullet in you and carry on with my life. And it won't be the first time I'll take out guys who come after me and my family. Tell me you get that."

"Yes," he gasped, nodding vigorously to convey his understanding, not wanting to take the chance that I had somehow not heard his answer.

I hauled him up and sat him down on a chair. I pulled another chair, sat directly facing him, and tried explaining his hopeless situation to him.

"This isn't your lucky night by a long shot. But here's the deal. You're either going to prison or you're dying tonight. There isn't a third option on the table."

I paused to let my words sink in. He just stared at me, his face wracked with pain.

"Your best option is to answer all my questions. That will mean your play in this thing is over. I'll let you live, hand you to the cops, and go after whoever asked you to do this. If you don't talk, I'll kill you. Then wake up one of these other guys and carry on with them. But without getting answers, I won't even take the risk of handing you guys to the cops. I know you'll all lawyer up as soon as a cop comes into the picture. Now it's up to you what choice you make."

The man remained silent. Not trying to look tough or any such shit, but processing my words. I could almost hear his brain whirring. I took off a crossbody bag I had slung across my bag, unzipped it, and took out a suppressor.

"You have ten seconds to make up your mind. The first bullet will take out your finger. But, hey, it's broken already... so might not be as painful," I said as I pulled out my gun from the back of my jeans and began screwing the suppressor on.

"Hang on, man, listen... you gotta understand... I'm gonna be a dead man if I talk."

"I know that. But they won't get to know you talked. The thing is, whatever you tell me, I'm not just going to take your word for it. I'll wake up these other guys and crosscheck everything you tell me. Each one of you is going to talk. No one will pin the blame on you."

I knew if I had to get him to talk, I would have to convince him he had a sure shot chance of staying alive after that. What I had said seemed to finally make sense to the man.

"Uh... right."

"That's the only thing I'm going to offer you. Take it or you lose your finger. What will it be? Five seconds," I said, as I pulled him forward and pressed the gun on his badly bent and bruised finger, which had begun to swell.

"Alright, alright..." he winced. "What do you want to know? I don't know much but... just tell me what you want," he said in a defeated tone.

I pushed him back into a seated position again.

"Way to go. But let me warn you, I already know quite a bit about what you guys were up to. You lie once and... well, I won't let you lie again. Got it?"

The man nodded.

"Let's start with your name."

"Mike."

"Who's the boss man of your crew?"

"Sharky."

"What's his real name?"

"I don't know, man, I swear. No one knows it. Everyone just calls him Sharky. He's got a rap sheet a mile long. I'm sure you guys can find him out."

"What do you mean by 'you guys'? What do you know about us?"

"Nothing, man. I'm just reaching. You guys must be law enforcement. That's practically stamped on your forehead. But breaking fingers and shit... you're one of those 'shoot first, ask later' kind of cops. But you know what, I don't know shit. I thought we were going after regular people...

office boy and his old lady. Easy job. Grab blondie and get the fuck out of here. If we knew blondie would turn out to be fucking GI Jane on steroids, you think we would have taken this gig?"

"Why were you trying to grab her?" I asked.

"I don't know why. Sharky asks us to do shit. We keep our mouths shut and fucking do it."

I tended to believe him. Low level street thugs like him just followed orders from the boss.

"What did he ask you to do?"

"Case this place. See who's around. Then grab the guy and the wife. We've been tailing him since yesterday. He was alone. We were to grab him tonight, but then Ninja blondie showed up and there was a change of plan. Dutch said to grab her instead. And then... you know the rest."

"Who's Dutch?"

"Sleeping beauty over there," Mike said, pointing to the knocked-out guy, the one with an intact face.

"Is he making the decisions for this crew?"

"Yeah. Sharky's the boss man. But once he tells Dutch what to do, Dutch calls the shots on the job. Fuck, man, it really hurts. At least uncuff me so I can hold the damn finger," Mike said, trying to caress his broken finger with his other hand, the pain shooting into his arm clearly visible on his face.

"Keep talking and I might do it. What was the plan after grabbing her?"

"We had to take her back to the warehouse. There's this place near Hunters Point."

"The one in the alley behind Fitch Street?"

The shock on the man's face was genuine. He forgot his pain for a moment.

"You know the place?" he asked incredulously.

"I told you I know stuff. So, don't try to bullshit me."

"I'm not, man. I've laid out everything straight. Please, man, cut off the cuffs. I'm going to pass out. I'm not running off anywhere."

I could see he was on the verge of passing out from the pain. The beads of sweat on his brow were clear signals.

"OK. I'll fix the finger. It will hurt like hell for a second but then the pain will subside."

"Uh, you sure you know what you're doing?"

"You better start praying I do. But don't scream. If you do, I'll break it again. Got it?"

"Yes," he said as his body tensed up and he drew quick breaths in anticipation of the pain.

The man's finger was still bent backwards at a crazy angle. I kept my thumb between the bent finger and the back of his hand, placed my fingers on the other side of the finger on the edge of his palm, and with a jerk of my thumb, pushed the finger back into its joint. There was a distinct click as the finger popped back into place. The man tried to stifle his impulse to scream but couldn't suppress a long, painful groan.

"There. The pain will go down. You won't pass out."

"Thanks, man," he said, the relief from the pain visible on his face.

"Back to the questions. We're not done yet."

"Yeah. Alright."

"How many men were on this job? Is there another car cruising the streets?"

"No, man, just the two cars out front."

"Think carefully before you answer," I said, my voice conveying a warning to him.

"Uh, there's another car, another team, but that's not out here."

"Where's it?"

"Motel near Sausalito. This guy we had to grab... he's holed up there with another broad...," he stopped speaking for a second as he looked at me and realization dawned on his face. "You already know that, don't you? You've been fucking with those guys the way you did with us."

"Yeah, you got that right. And seeing as how you've been cooperative, I'm going to let you live. You know I wasn't bullshitting."

"I know, man. No bullshit. You and GI Jane in there... I ain't messing with you guys."

"Wise decision. What's the deal with the kid driving the other car? He doesn't look like he's part of your crew."

"Little G-Man. Part of our crew? No way. He's a regular little choirboy. Him and another punk-ass broad he hangs out with got caught up in a jam. Ended up owing Sharky. And you know how that's gonna end. Sharky gave him a way out. The kid's got a clean license. And he sure can drive. Dutch uses him sometimes for dope runs, and gigs like the one today."

I took out my phone and searched for a photo Mitchell had forwarded me the previous night. A couple of the photos he sent were of the two guys he thought were the Cadys. But there was one more with three men who waited outside while the other men had a meeting in a private room. The man on the left was Latino. Wiry guy, medium height. The man in the center looked Caucasian. He looked reasonably well built and had a neatly trimmed beard. The third man was black, shorter than the other two, and skinny. And he dressed funny. White silk suit, white tie, and a white fedora. When I had looked at the photo earlier, I had thought that it reminded me of someone. Then it hit me. The skinny guy was trying to pull off Michael Jackson's Smooth Criminal look.

"Who are these guys?" I asked Mike.

"That's Sharky in the middle," he said, pointing to the man. "The other two guys aren't part of our crew. This Mexican guy... he was with these two weird guys Sharky's been doing business with."

"What weird guys?" I asked interrupting him.

"I don't know, man. There are these two guys. I've just seen them once."

I flipped through the photos on my phone and showed him another photo.

"You talking about these two?"

"Yeah, man. You're on to them as well?" he asked in a surprised tone.

"What do you think? Who are these two?"

"I don't know, man. I've just seen them once. But Sharky has some deal going with them. That's how we've got our hands on a lot of new guns."

That seemed to fit with the Cadys profile. Even if they had been out of the game for two years, they would know how to get their hands on guns if that was what Sharky wanted in return for his services.

"And who's this third guy?" I asked going back to the previous photo.

"His name's Slick. Not part of our crew."

Slick was the wannabe Smooth Criminal.

"What's Slick's story?" I asked.

"I don't know, man. I'm too low down in the chain. Sharky's the only one who deals with him. But Slicks's some kind of a fixer. Calls himself shot caller. But shot caller my ass... all I've seen him do is pass on some jobs to Sharky at times."

"What jobs?"

"You know the shit we do, man. Moving stuff, grabbing people, breaking someone... shit like that."

"What stuff do you move?"

"Uh, I don't know, man," he replied a little evasively.

"Have you already forgotten the broken finger?"

"Uh, no. Stuff like coke, dope, sometimes guns... that kind of stuff."

Britt came into the room at that point and signaled me to join her at the back. I had got all I needed from the guy. I decided it was time to put him to sleep.

"Don't move. I'll be back," I said.

I stood up, moved behind him, and knocked him out with the butt of my Glock.

"Found something?" I asked Britt.

"Yeah. This was on one of the phones. Have a look," she replied, handing me a phone.

I saw my own face staring back at me. It wasn't a photo I had seen before. Someone must have taken it clandestinely. As I swiped the screen to look at the other photos, I found faces of Britt, Mitchell and Garcia.

I looked up at Britt. She looked in deep thought. But there wasn't any fear on her face. She just wasn't wired that way.

"Looks like we're on someone's hit list," I said.

"Yeah. We've got to get these bastards before they get their act together and come after us," Britt replied in a tone of steely determination.

# CHAPTER 6

"Do you recognize where your photo is from?" I asked Britt.

"I think so. It took me a while to figure it out. All these photos are from the security detail we did for the Cadys. They've been zoomed into the faces, but there's a bit of background visible."

I took a careful look at each photo.

"You're right. It looks almost certain Dexter is behind this. We'll have to figure out how he managed to get these guys to work for him. He can't have access to any money. All their assets were seized."

"Yeah, he's getting help from someone."

"Whose phone is it? This guy's?" I asked, pointing to Dutch, the knocked-out guy Mike had said was leading their crew.

Britt nodded. I brought her up to speed with all Mike had told me.

"I think his story checks out. I sent all the names and mugshots I got from these guys' IDs to Garcia. He ran them through the database. All of them have got rap sheets... except that kid out there. Garcia gave me a quick lowdown on these guys. They are all part of Sharky's crew," Britt said.

"Who's this Sharky?"

"Started out as a low-level drug pusher. Known to be violent and ruthless. Has been rising fast even though still not a big-time gangster. But very ambitious. His crew has been trying to muscle in on drug distribution in the Bay area, which is mostly under Latino and Asian gangs. But Sharky's crew are more like jack-of-all-trades. Grab whatever business comes their way. They got into gunrunning as well. That's put them on ATF's radar."

"Sounds like he's the one we need to grab. Any word from Garcia or Mitchell?"

"They are on their way over. Should be here in ten minutes. What do we do with these guys?"

"Let's wait until they're here. In the meantime, I'll have a chat with the kid."

"Yeah, do that. He seems to be in over his head."

"Looks that way. Let's see what he has to say. What's his name? This guy was calling him G-Man."

"G-Man, huh? Well, that's a cool street name for a guy whose real name is Eugene Weizmann," she replied. "Take a look at this before you talk to him," she said, handing me a student ID card.

The card had the kid's mug printed on it along with his name. It was a Cal 1 Card—a UC Berkeley student card. Eugene Weizmann was an undergraduate student at UC Berkeley College of Letters and Science. Studying Comparative Literature.

"You've got to be kidding me. Is this legit?" I asked.

"Yeah, I checked. The kid studies at Cal."

"Then what the hell's he doing hanging around with this crew?"

"That's the million-dollar question."

"Oh, boy, this is going to be interesting. What about his phone? Anything on it that might suggest he's part of the gang?"

"No. Just a regular college kid's phone. Some weird apps on it. But nothing incriminating," Britt said, handing me the phone.

I took the phone, walked out to the car, stood by the trunk, and drew my gun.

"I've got a gun in my hand pointing at the trunk. I'm going to open it now. If you make a sudden move, I'll shoot. Got it?" I spoke loudly so the kid inside could hear it.

"Yes, sir. I promise I won't move a muscle. Please let me out," his muffled voice came through the trunk.

I pressed the button on the key. The trunk popped open. I needn't have bothered with my warning. Eugene couldn't have been more compliant. He was lying huddled up in a ball, his arms wrapped around his knees, which were pressed close to his chest. I could see beads of sweat on his forehead. The hoodie he wore looked partially damp with sweat. The kid looked like he was having a panic attack. I didn't have the heart to scare him further.

"C'mon, let's get you out," I said, holding out my hand.

"I'm sorry, I don't do well in closed spaces," he said apologetically as he hesitantly took my hand to step out.

He looked a little wobbly as he set his feet on the ground.

"Sorry," he apologized again as he leaned back against the trunk to get a hold of himself.

I nodded but kept quiet. I still wanted to keep up the pressure on the kid... not let him get too comfortable with me.

"Would it be alright if I grabbed a water bottle from the car?" he asked.

I nodded and kept a wary eye on him as he opened the driver's door. I had more or less come to the conclusion he was a harmless kid who happened to be in a tough spot. This was my final test for him. If he made a move for the glove compartment, he would lose my sympathy. But he didn't do any such thing. He grabbed a bottle propped in a cavity in the central console and got out, closing the door behind him. He glugged the water like he had just come back from a desert trek. I gave him a few seconds to get a hold of himself.

"What's your name?"

"Euge... uh, G-Man," he replied.

"You think G-Man is a cool name?"

"Uh... no, sir. I used to... Not anymore."

"So why did you give me that name?"

"Uh... these guys I was with... I don't feel good using my real name."

"What else do you think is cool? Hanging out with gangsters?"

"No, sir," he said, with an expression suggesting he was appalled I had such a low opinion of him. "Hanging out with them is the last thing I'd want to do."

"And yet, that's exactly what I found you doing. Now what should I make of that."

"I know. I'm very sorry. I'm not trying to justify myself. But I didn't have a choice."

"Why? Give me straight answers or you're going to end up in prison. And I'm not talking about a vague possibility sometime in the future. It will happen tonight. You were part of a criminal group that's going to be booked for kidnap, home invasion, and whatever else I can get the cops to throw at them."

The kid's face told me he was fully aware of the mess he was in. He looked like he was about to burst into tears. I really didn't want a crying kid on my hands. I decided to make him focus on specific questions to get him talking.

"How did you end up with these guys?"

"Uh, it's a long story, but... well, the thing is, I and my, uh, friend, Nova... Nova is, like, this entrepreneurial girl... we've been planning to start some kind of a venture together and... uh... she thinks running a cannabis dispensary would be cool. She's got the experience... worked as a budtender for four months. She's even got a name for the place. Hazy Days. And then, Nova thought it would be a good idea to do a kind of trial run... sell weed to guys in the dorm..."

"What dorm?"

"Where I live... residence halls at Berkeley... That's where I, uh, study."

I already knew that. But I didn't want to let him get the feeling I would cut him any slack because of that.

71

"Studying what?"

"Comparative literature."

"Well done. And after gaining deep insights into literary traditions from around the world, Eugene Weizmann arrived at the logical conclusion that selling illegal weed in dorms was the sure shot route to success. Does that more or less sum it up?"

"I know now it was a stupid idea."

"You got that right. Go on."

"Nova knows this dealer. She told him we'd sell weed for him in the dorms for a cut... and he agreed. We also discussed him coming in as a silent partner in our venture... put in some seed capital. I know it sounds stupid even as I speak the words. Anyway, the guy left a stock in my room and... uh..."

"Let me guess. It got stolen."

"Uh, yeah," Eugene answered sheepishly.

"That's how these guys scam dumb kids."

"Yes, sir, I realize that now. But once it went missing, it turned out we owed big-time to this guy called Sharky we'd never even heard of."

"And that's why people shouldn't mess around with illegal shit. What was the deal with Sharky?"

"The only deal is he won't break our bones so long as I come and drive their car any time they snap their fingers. Nova's still moving around with her hand in a cast."

"What's the deal with driving a car? Why did they ask you to do that?"

"Because I'm good at it. Uh, I don't want to sound boastful but... well, I can't run for shit... I can barely ride a bike... but put me behind a wheel and... you can't catch me," he said with a touch of pride.

But then thought better of it and quickly added: "But I've never broken the law... and have a clean license. I think that's why..."

"So, what you're telling me is you're this hotshot driver but you've never been in a Bay Area sideshow earning your chops?"

"No, I didn't say that. I'm being completely truthful with you. I have been in some sideshows."

"And you think all the swingers burning donuts out there are doing it by the book?"

"Uh... I kind of figured... uh, it's kind of borderline legal."

"Exactly the kind of thinking that's landed you in this mess," I replied.

"Yeah. I know."

"Is that why they call you G-Man?"

"Yeah, you know G-force... and how those hot rods look like they're ready to take off."

"Yeah, right. Now back to the shit you're in tonight. How long have you been driving for them? And what kind of runs do you do? And before you answer... I'm trying to figure out if there's a way to get you out of your mess. But I'll be nice only as long as you don't try any bullshit with me. The moment I feel otherwise, this conversation's over and your ass gets back in the trunk before we haul you off to lockup with these guys. Get it?"

"Yes. Absolutely. I haven't lied to you once. I won't do it, I swear. And... uh, thank you, sir, for giving me the benefit of the doubt. Uh... and just so you know... and I'm not being a smartass... but lying is one thing I really suck at."

"We'll see about that."

"Sure. About what you asked... I've been doing it about a month. Twelve times including tonight. They give me a call every second or third day... and I have to drop everything and run to them."

"What is it? Drug runs?" I asked.

"I don't know. I don't want to know. They give me the keys and I drive the car someplace and walk off."

"Who calls you? Is it Sharky?"

"No. Sharky is their boss. I only met him once and never ever want to meet him again. He's a psycho. He broke Nova's arm just to scare me to work for him. He told me he wasn't hurting me as I'd need both hands to drive. And he laughed while Nova cried in pain. Real psycho."

"Is Nova a classmate at Cal?"

"No. Just a friend. I met her at, uh, a sideshow."

"Right. It figures."

That explained a lot. Nerdy kid with a crush on a rebellious girl with an attitude. Willing to go to any length of stupid to impress her.

"Anyway, back to my question. Who calls you?"

"It's usually a guy called Dutch. You know him? He, uh, went into the house."

"Yeah, we just got acquainted. He's sleeping it off."

"Sleeping? Uh... right," he replied when the import of my words dawned on him.

"What was the plan for tonight?"

"Plan? Uh, I'm not really part of the gang. They don't talk to me. Just give me the keys and location. And I do it. Tonight, we went to a motel near Sausalito. They mostly don't discuss stuff in front of me. There was another group of guys at the motel. They talked for a while and then gave me this location. From here, I was to drive them to a warehouse near Hunters Point."

"What's inside the warehouse?"

"I don't know… Gang stuff? Drugs, weapons… I think. I haven't seen anything. They don't really let me move around much, but I hear things sometimes. But I'm too scared to look around. These guys are psychos. I don't know what would piss them off. I don't want to take a chance. So, I just keep my mouth shut, look at the floor mostly, and drive the car to wherever they ask me to."

"Alright, here's the deal. If you really want to get out of this mess, you'll have to stop bullshitting yourself. Take responsibility. Just closing your eyes to what you're doing doesn't help. Keep fooling yourself you're just an innocent guy stuck in all this, and you'll be doing this for the rest of your life. And now that you've fallen in with this crowd, the rest of your life isn't going to be too long or too bright. You get that?"

"Yes, sir. I swear I'm not trying to justify myself. I know what I've been doing is illegal. I'm not proud to be working as a mule."

"Not just a mule. It's worse. Let me tell you the plan they had for tonight. It was a hit on the guy who lives here. They would have kidnapped his wife and you would have driven the woman to the warehouse to be murdered. I don't want you to be under any illusions. That was your role tonight—help kidnap and murder an innocent woman."

Eugene was rendered speechless. That was my intention. I wanted him to have a clear idea about the shit he was in. It wasn't some cool college prank he could have a laugh about with his pals. I continued giving him some more reality bites.

"You lucked out tonight I saw your face before I grabbed you. Had it been one of their crew in the driver's seat tonight instead of you, the guy would have been lying with half his bones broken."

I let him take it all in during the silence that followed. I was interrupted by Britt's voice coming over my earpiece.

"Garcia and Mitchell are less than a minute away."

"Roger that," I replied.

It was time to head inside to plan an assault on the gang's warehouse. But I had to figure out what to do with the kid.

"How long have you been claustrophobic?" I asked Eugene.

He looked a bit surprised at the question.

"Since I was a kid," he replied.

"You should have told me before I dumped you into the trunk."

"I was too scared. I thought you were going to kill me. Uh, the mood you were in, I'm not sure it would have mattered."

"Probably not. But I'm not going to lock you in there again. Stay in the car. Had it been any of those guys, I would've broken an arm or leg and cuffed them so they don't run away. But I'm trusting you. Think hard about all the times you have spent with these guys. Any names, places, clues... anything that can help us take them all out. That's your only ticket to freedom—getting these guys off the streets. But you need to earn it. Got it?"

"Yes, sir. Uh, if you don't mind my asking, are you a cop?"

"Kind of. I was in law enforcement," I replied, keeping it vague. "And one more thing..." I said as something suddenly struck me.

I took out my phone and showed him the photo with Sharky, the mystery guy called Slick, and a third unnamed man.

"You know these guys?"

"I just know Sharky. And I've seen the African American man. I don't know the third man."

"This Michael Jackson lookalike... his name's Slick. Did you ever catch the name in any conversation?"

"I've heard the name. He's some kind of... I don't know the word for it... but they called him a guy who makes things happen. Um... I'm not sure I remember much else."

"Well, rack your brains and see if you can dig out anything. I'll be back in a few minutes. And stay miles away from this stuff," I said as I opened the car door and got the Uzi from under the driver's seat.

"I wouldn't know what to do with it. I've never used a gun in my life."

"If cops find you with it, it won't matter if you've used one or not. And here, hold on to your phone in case any of those guys call you. Remember, don't think of making any calls. You're messing with very dangerous men. It's a miracle you're not dead or in prison. Count your blessings. You follow my advice and I'll do my best to get you out of this mess. Got it?"

"Yes, sir. Absolutely. I promise I won't move a muscle unless you tell me to. And, uh, thank you, sir."

"Keep that for later. We're still nowhere near getting out of the woods yet. Keep the doors locked and windows up. And one more thing... you're wearing your hoodie inside out."

"Uh, I know. It's a Cal hoodie. I felt embarrassed wearing it while I was with these guys."

"Good you feel embarrassed. Gives me hope for you."

I turned around and saw a pair of headlights turning into the street.

# CHAPTER 7

When the vehicle came closer, I saw it was a van. Britt's voice in my ear confirmed it had Garcia and Mitchell inside. It was too dark and foggy to be able to see their faces.

I heard a loud whoop from the driver's window. I didn't have to see the face to know it was Garcia. The van screeched to a halt inches from me. I had to work hard to resist the automatic impulse to jump out of the way. It was a dumb game of nerves guys love to play. And never grow out of.

"I can see age hasn't rusted those nerves of steel, Cowboy," Garcia called out as he opened the door, jumped out, and walked toward me.

"But chasing gator poachers has surely improved your driving skills, Garcia," I replied, as we hugged big time.

"Oh, man... don't get me started."

"And here I was thinking you were having the time of your life in Miami."

"This guy... he jumped bail and escaped into the Everglades. Knows the fucking swamps like the back of his hand. Took us a week to finally nail his ass. This surely wasn't what I had in mind when I was posted to the Miami office," Garcia replied, laughing.

Garcia had been a Marine for six years before he left the army to eventually join the Marshals. We had been deployed in Afghanistan at the same time on two tours, but had never bumped into each other. But when I met him for the first time as part of my SOG team, the knowledge that we had faced the enemy at the same time gave us a close bond.

Garcia still had the don't-mess-with-me look he carried back in the days. And it wasn't because of his size. He was a wiry guy of about five foot ten, not weighing more than 165 pounds. But the sinewy muscles on his lean frame were like coiled cables of steel. Prominent veins running across his biceps and muscular forearms, the bulldog tattooed on the right one and USMC on the left, gave some indication the guy wasn't one you'd want on your wrong side.

There was also something about his eyes and the way he slightly squinted them when someone was acting like an asshole—it made guys stop and think twice about whether they really wanted to mess with him. Garcia's thick, droopy moustache further added to his badass look. That, coupled with the toothpick that he always seemed to be chewing on. He had picked up that habit when he gave up smoking years ago, and the toothpick kind of became part of him. Any time he began rolling it around in his mouth, it was a sure shot indication the guy in front of him was about to have a hard time.

"I take it you've got passengers in the back?" I asked Mitchell as he jumped out and joined us.

"Yeah, two of them. Still sleeping. Britt told me you've got a bigger cargo here."

"Five in there. I guess some of them might be coming around," I replied.

"That the Berkeley kid?" Garcia asked, looking at Eugene.

The kid was dutifully sitting inside the car with doors locked and windows up. But the second Garcia fixed his gaze on Eugene, the kid nervously broke eye contact and began looking straight up at the road.

"Yeah," I replied.

"What the fuck's he doing with these guys? I thought you needed brains to make it to Cal?" Garcia asked, still looking hard at the kid.

I could see Eugene getting visibly nervous under Garcia's intense scrutiny. Those eyes could make toughened criminals squirm—the kid really didn't have a chance.

"He got caught in a scam. And now these guys have their claws in him. Let's head inside. I'll fill you in."

"Sure thing. I'll get the van in the driveway," Garcia replied, jumping back into the van.

I could almost feel the kid starting to breathe again as Mitchell and I turned and walked toward his house.

"Whoa, who did all this?" Garcia asked as we walked in and saw the three men lying knocked out in the living room.

"Let me guess. Was that Britt Dixon in a rough mood?" Mitchell asked.

"Bingo," I replied.

"Guys, I need you back here," Britt called out from the other room.

When we went inside, Britt told us there had been two missed calls on Dutch's phone. Both were from Sharky. The boss must have been waiting for an update from his guys.

"What do we do? He's going to get suspicious if he doesn't hear back," Britt said.

"Yeah, we'll lose our advantage. If he moves from the warehouse, it'll be back to square one," Mitchell agreed.

"What are we waiting for? Let's get going and raid the place. What do you say?" Garcia said, looking at me.

"Let's do it. We'll have to decide what to do with all these men," I said.

"I'm sure you've already figured that out," Garcia replied.

Britt and Mitchell looked at me expectantly.

"These guys have drugs and weapons at the warehouse. The best thing would be to dump them there after we make the bust. Then call the cops. They'll take care of the rest. Best to avoid the drama of calling cops to Mitchell's place. What do you say, Mitchell?"

"I'm with you, Blaze. I can really do without having to explain to the neighbors why I had gangsters paying me a house visit."

"I was wondering why you had asked me to get the van," Garcia said.

"Yeah, that was the idea. Let's start dumping these guys in the back of the van. Garcia, get someone to start tracking Sharky's phone. Britt, give him the number and throw some water on Dutch. We'll need him awake if another call comes in."

We were interrupted by someone calling out from the front door. It was Eugene.

"Excuse me... uh, excuse me. Sir, I'm sorry to intrude, but it's important," his voice kept rising with each word he uttered.

"You've got to be kidding me. Is that how gangsters from Berkeley talk?" Garcia asked.

We couldn't help laughing.

"Leave it to me. I'll have a word with him. You start dumping the men in the van. There are two more lying by the back entrance," I said, before walking out to see what Eugene had to say that was so important it couldn't wait.

I saw him standing just inside the front door, staring wide-eyed at the three broken men lying unconscious, his jaw almost touching the floor.

"Are they..." he whispered, not quite sure how to finish the sentence.

"No, they're alive," I answered his implied question. "What is it? Let's go outside."

I led him back to the street outside.

"Sorry, I know you asked me not to move. But it's important. I think you'll agree with me."

"What is it, Eugene?" I asked, trying to hide my impatience.

"Sharky called on my phone."

"Oh. What did he say?"

"He sounded mad. He's been calling Dutch but he's not taking the call. He asked me 'what the fuck's going on'... uh, those were his exact words."

"What did you say?"

"I froze for a few seconds. Didn't know what to say. But then he got madder. I told him Dutch and

83

the other men are inside the house and they asked me to stay in the car. He told me to get in and tell Dutch to, uh, 'get off his fucking ass and call Sharky the fuck back'. Uh, those were his exact words. He made me repeat the words back to him so I'd relay his exact message."

"Good work. I'll take it from here," I said, but saw he was staring wide-eyed at something behind me.

I turned and saw Garcia and Mitchell carrying one of the men and dump him in the back of the van. I snapped my fingers in front of Eugene's face to get his attention.

"They're not dead. Just knocked out. Now, back to the car. Doors locked. And switch off your phone until I tell you to turn it on."

"Yes, sir."

I turned and signaled Garcia and Mitchell to meet me in the backyard before rushing inside. Britt had dumped enough water on Dutch to get him back into the land of the living. He was half lying on the floor in an awkward position, trying to prop himself up on his intact arm. His unbroken arm was still cuffed to the other guy, who hadn't woken up yet. Dutch couldn't use his other arm as it was broken at the elbow.

I signaled Britt to follow me to the back, where we found Garcia and Mitchell waiting.

"Slight change of plan. Sharky's getting hopping mad Dutch isn't taking his calls. Garcia, we'll have to scare the shit out of the guy so he makes the call. We don't have much time. Ready?" I asked.

"Sure. We improvise? Bad cop, worse cop from hell routine?"

"Yes. Let's go."

Both of us walked menacingly into the room. Dutch tried to give us a defiant stare, but his expression soon changed. I took out the knife from the sheath inside my cowboy boot, cut the flexicuffs binding him to the other man, grabbed him roughly by the collar, pulled him up into a seated position, and threw him hard against the wall. He cried out in pain as the jarring impact sent shockwaves through his broken arm.

"Save your energy, tough guy. You've got a lot of pain coming your way," I said.

"I've heard you've got us on a hitlist, gangster boy. Do you have any fucking idea who you're fucking around with?" Garcia's voice sounded more like a growl, as he leaned in close, his eyes almost burning holes into the man, the toothpick rolling around from one side of his mouth to the other.

"What hitlist? What the f..."

I cut him off midway as I placed the tip of the razor-sharp blade below his eyeball and pressed lightly, drawing blood.

"You're not bullshitting your way out of this. Got it?"

"Yes," he whispered, barely breathing to avoid the knife nicking him again.

"We know Sharky's waiting at the warehouse."

"You know that?"

"Who the fuck do you think we are? We know you've been staking out this place and the motel in

Sausalito, dumbass. We know every move you guys have been making. That's what we do... see this star? And you thought you'd fuck with us?" Garcia said, taking out the Marshal's badge from his pocket.

"And before you think you're safe and we'll just arrest your ass... think again. There's only one way you're seeing the sun tomorrow. You talk to Sharky and lead us to him," I said.

"Or I put a bullet in you from my government-issued gun. You've broken into a Marshal's house. No one's going to ask questions. And this badge makes it even more legal. Might even get me a medal," Garcia said.

"So, what will it be—make a call or..." I left my sentence unfinished for Garcia to finish it.

"A bullet to the brain. No point letting you live if you're no use for us. We kill you, wake up these other guys, and take our chances with them. I'm sure one of them will be ready to talk."

"You have five seconds to say yes. Tick tock, tick tock," I said, pressing the knife slightly.

Garcia racked the slide of his Glock to add to the pressure.

Dutch was shaken to the core. Being a gangster is one thing. But an attack on a federal lawman's house... that's something the man wouldn't have done had he known better. We kept up the pressure, without giving him a chance to even breathe properly. The man had no choice but to cave in.

"Alright, alright, I'll do it."

"Wise choice. Tell him you've got the woman. But your men staking out the motel called you to say the husband is driving here from the motel. You're waiting to grab him and will bring them both."

"But he'll know I lied to him. I'm a dead man," Dutch said, doubt creeping into his voice.

"He won't. When I grab Sharky, I'll slip it to him Mitchell picked us up on the way home from the motel. And we beat the shit out of you guys. You can say all that happened after you made the call. That lets you off the hook," I said, giving him a clear way out.

"Uh, alright," he said, finally giving in.

"Wise choice. Before you make the call, how many guys are holed up at the warehouse?" I asked.

"Uh, I don't know."

"Lying won't help you. You'll be in the front seat when we raid the warehouse. If we're prepared, we'll avoid gunfire and make sure no one dies. If not, bullets will fly. And you'll be in the middle of it with your hands cuffed. Think about it."

Dutch's face told me he didn't need to think about it. The scenario I described was real and would result in him catching a bullet.

"There should be six men," he said.

"Including Sharky?"

"Yeah."

"Is Slick going to be around?"

I hadn't yet told Garcia about Slick. He gave me a questioning look but didn't say a word.

"At the warehouse? No. He's not part of the crew," Dutch replied.

"Where does he hang out? How do you guys contact him?"

"I don't know, man. He deals with Sharky. They meet at this club downtown. Called Wild Spirits. I think Slick mostly hangs out there."

"Alright. How many entrances does the warehouse have?"

"Um... there's the main one at the front... and two others, one at the back and another at the side."

"Any chance the other two would be open?"

"I don't think so. They keep everything bolted from inside."

I had all the information I needed. It was time to call Sharky.

"Right. Let's call Sharky. Stick to the script. Ready?"

Dutch nodded. I pressed Sharky's number on the phone and put it on speaker mode.

"Where the fuck have you been?" Sharky's voice thundered out of the speaker as he took the call.

"We've got the woman. But the guy made a move from the motel he was shacked up at. He's on his way here. We're waiting to grab him."

"Oh... OK. But why the fuck weren't you picking up the phone?"

"It was on silent, boss. And then the guy called the broad, uh... woman," he corrected himself, looking nervously at us, before continuing, "We had to make sure she didn't say anything to him."

"Alright. Let me know when you've grabbed the guy. And tell Murky to call me the fuck back. I can't get a hold of him either. Am I the fucking boss or what?"

"You're the boss man. Murky must be following the guy. I'll tell him to call as soon as he's here."

I disconnected the call.

"Who's Murky?" I asked.

"He was staking out the motel," Dutch answered.

"Alright. You did your part. You get to live. Stay on the floor. Don't move an inch," I ordered him.

Garcia and I went back to the other room. Britt and Mitchell were waiting for us.

"Who's Slick? What was all that about?" Garcia asked me.

"I'm not sure but I think he's the guy who floated the hit on us. Some kind of a fixer. He's the next target once we put Sharky out of business," I replied.

"Right. Sharky might start getting suspicious when he doesn't hear back from Murky."

"Who's Murky?" Mitchell asked.

"One of the two guys staking out the motel," Garcia replied.

"So... he's lying knocked out in the back of the van, right?" Britt asked.

"Yeah," Mitchell replied.

"We'll have to move now, or we'll lose the advantage of surprise," Garcia said.

"Yeah, we better move," I agreed.

"What's our play?"

"We'll try to make it as painless as possible. Hopefully, without any bullets fired, like we managed here. But if bullets do fly, we're not using our own guns. We don't want the cops tying anything that goes down there to us. We'll have to remain in the shadows until we get to the bottom of this."

"Roger that. These guys were carrying more than enough hardware. I'll sort it out," Garcia replied.

"Good. Let's hit the road in five minutes."

"Roger that," all three said in unison before each one of us went about our specific tasks.

There had been eight men involved in the stake out at the motel and Mitchell's home. Six of them, except Dutch and Eugene, were cuffed and dumped in the back of the van.

Garcia soon set us up with weapons.

"Three Glocks and a SIG... and four AR-15s," he said, pointing to the guns laid out neatly on the table.

Mitchell went for the SIG. We picked a handgun each and slung the AR-15 rifles across our backs. We decided to travel in three vehicles—the two cars the men had come in and the van with all the cuffed men in the back. Garcia drove one car, with Dutch seated next to him—uncuffed but hardly a threat with his right arm broken. Eugene drove the other car, with me riding shotgun. Britt and Mitchell followed in the van.

"What do you want me to do when we get there? Try to drive the car through the doors?" Eugene asked in a nervous voice as I got into the passenger seat.

"You've been to the warehouse before, right?" I asked.

"Yes."

"Are the doors made of cardboard?"

"No. They were metal."

"Then don't overthink or ask dumb questions. This isn't a movie set. Simply follow Dutch's car. He'll get them to open the doors. They expect to see you and Dutch driving. That's what they'll see. Once we're inside, just duck below the steering column and stay there until I ask you to come out."

"Uh, right. Got it," he replied, trying to sound a little more confident.

"We'll try to get it done without a bullet being fired, but you can't be sure. Just stay low and you'll be fine."

"Uh, OK."

"Once we grab Sharky, he'll be going to prison for a long time. That's your only ticket to freedom. He won't let you be if he's out and about."

"Uh, right. Thank you, sir. I really appreciate your help, and the fact you believe me."

"Don't worry about it. When you get out of this mess, don't act like a dumbass again. And you can quit calling me sir. My name's Axel."

"Uh, right... thanks... Axel. Uh, and one more thing..."

"Yes?"

"It's about Slick. You asked about him and I couldn't remember the word for what those guys called him. Well, it's shot caller. I'm not exactly sure what it means... Does that make sense to you?"

"Yeah, it does. It's beginning to make perfect sense."

I was convinced by this time the hit had come from Dexter. If those guys were calling Slick shot caller, he must have been in prison at some time and would still have connections in there. If the hit had come to Sharky's crew through Slick, it was logical the hit originated from someone in prison.

"One more thing. What I heard the men saying was he's always in a white suit and hat."

I had already seen that in the photo. But didn't know he wore that get up all the time. That would make it easier to grab him.

We were finally on our way to the warehouse in Hunters Point. We needed answers soon. Grabbing Sharky was the first step in getting to the men behind all this.

# CHAPTER 8

Hunters Point is called the forgotten neighborhood of San Francisco. Plagued by decades of industrial decay and a history of toxic spills, it tends to be in the news for all the wrong reasons, most of them having to do with crime and gang wars.

Less than a fifteen-minute drive from downtown, Hunters Point doesn't bear much resemblance to the city's shiny center. It lies on the south-eastern corner of San Francisco, east of US 101. The highway starts way up north in Olympic National Park in Washington and makes its way south through Oregon and California to finally end in Los Angeles. But Hunters Point is a place far removed from the tinsel dreams of La-La Land. With its graffiti-scarred housing projects and storefronts with faded billboards, large parts of the neighborhood have the nightmarish appearance of an urban wasteland.

Hunters Point did have its good days once. Candlestick Park was the first major league baseball park in the city. It was home to the San Francisco Giants for four decades until the year 2000. But the stadium had the reputation of being the windiest, coldest and dampest park in Major League Baseball, with winds blowing directly off the Pacific Ocean.

As with other good things that forsook the area, the Giants left Hunters Point to move to Oracle Park in San Francisco's trendier SoMa neighborhood. The new design reduced wind levels, but cold fog in summer months still remains a feature at Giants games. The Giants took their foghorn with them, which blows any time a player hits a home run.

We drove east down Golden Gate Avenue, continuing onto 10th Street before taking the on-ramp onto US 101. We took Exit 432 a couple of miles later to get onto Palou Avenue. In all, it took us twenty minutes to arrive in Hunters Point. As we left the projects behind us and moved toward the Bay, the residential area disappeared and all we could see were warehouses. It was growing late in the night and there wasn't much traffic or people around.

We stopped all three vehicles a couple of hundred yards from the warehouse. Britt and Mitchell parked the van in an empty parking lot next to another building.

Garcia got out of the car he was driving. He got Dutch out of the passenger side and into the driving seat. Mitchell had joined them by that time. He and Garcia jumped into the back seat and sat low.

"All you need to do is get them to open the doors and let you in. Once we are in, get as low as you can, and then stay there. Don't try to be a hero. You're getting the first bullet if the guy opening the door gets any hint that things aren't right. Those guys in there aren't worth losing your life over," Garcia warned Dutch.

I had already briefed Eugene on the way over. He was to stay close behind Dutch's car. Once Dutch got the men inside the warehouse to open the doors, Eugene would let Dutch go in but would stall the car just outside the doors. I didn't want the kid to get in the line of fire.

Eugene remained in the driving seat while Britt and I got into the back of the car. Guns drawn, we were good to go.

Dutch brought his car to a stop outside the warehouse. Facing the car were two heavy iron doors bolted from inside. Before our car came to a stop behind the lead vehicle, Britt and I opened the rear doors, jumped out, and took up positions on either side of the warehouse doors.

Dutch honked loudly. Nothing happened for a few seconds. He pressed on the horn for longer. We heard steps coming toward the door. One of the doors had a peeping hatch. It slid open and a face peered out. Dutch turned on the cabin lights inside his car. Eugene did the same.

"Open the fucking thing," Dutch called out.

That got an immediate reaction. The hatch closed, followed by the sound of a bolt being opened. A man with an Uzi slung by a nylon strap across his body opened one door and stepped out. Behind him stood a second man, similarly armed with an Uzi. The car couldn't head inside until both doors were opened.

But the men were being extra cautious. One of them came forward and stood by the driver's window, looking at Dutch. Garcia and Mitchell slunk further down behind the front seats. Garcia kept his gun pressed into Dutch's back, in case he got any bright ideas.

"Where's the woman?" the man asked Dutch.

"In the fucking trunk. You think I'd have her on my lap?" Dutch barked back at him.

The man must have been used to Dutch's cheery disposition.

"What about the others?" the guard asked.

"They'll be here in a few minutes."

"What happened to your arm?" he asked as his gaze fell on Dutch's broken arm.

"What do you think—we weren't out on a fucking picnic."

The man found the comment funny. He laughed. That brought the other gunman out of the door as well.

"You telling me the woman broke your arm?" the man asked, sniggering, as the other man walked over to the passenger side and bent a little to look inside.

That was what I had been waiting for. I signaled Britt. We moved forward simultaneously, smashing the butts of our Glocks into the heads of the two men with military precision. Both men collapsed without a sound. We caught them before they hit the ground, dragged them away from the doors, and dumped them in the shadows.

I crept toward the open gate to look inside the warehouse. The situation there was slightly different to what we expected. A couple of pickup trucks were lined up at the other end of the large hall, about thirty-five yards away. Four men were busy loading boxes inside one of them.

Behind the trucks was a cabin. I could see two men inside. I recognized one of them from the photos. Sharky. Dutch's information had been correct. I could see a small access door on one side and a larger one at the back. Both looked shut, most likely bolted from inside.

The only option was a frontal assault. We were four against six. We had the advantage of surprise. But there was a big distance separating us. And we had no idea about how well armed those guys were. I signaled Britt to grab the Uzi from the guy she had knocked out while I did the same. We slung the Uzis on top of our rifles.

I partially opened the second door to make space for the car. Dutch drove inside very slowly. Britt and I hunched behind the car and moved in step with it. The plan was to keep on moving behind the car until it reached the trucks and then catch the men by surprise. But Dutch made a sudden play that messed up our plans. He stopped the car barely ten yards inside the front doors, opened the driver door, fell onto the floor, and slid under the car.

We were stuck too far away to make a surprise attack. I tried pushing the car but had no luck—it was in parking mode. I signaled Britt to stay behind the car while I jumped into the driver's seat. I whispered to Mitchell and Garcia to get out and join Britt while I started the car.

But it was too late. The men at the other end had noticed something was wrong. The guys loading the truck turned and began drawing the Uzis hanging at their sides. But they didn't get a chance. Britt, Garcia and Mitchell were armed, ready and aimed. They took out three men with three shots.

That was when all hell broke loose. What I hadn't been able to see when I observed Sharky and the other man in the cabin was they had M-16 automatic rifles handy within the cabin. M-16s aren't something gangsters usually have access to. But I didn't have time to wonder about how they had managed to get their hands on those guns. We were suddenly pinned under heavy automatic fire as Sharky and the other man let loose at us, bullets thudding into the car like we were in a heavy hailstorm. As they fired, they dashed out of the cabin and took cover behind the pickups.

During the brief lull of a few seconds when they changed magazines, we let loose with all we had, Mitchell and Garcia letting off rapid shots from their AR-15s while Britt emptied her Uzi. But none of the shots hit home—Sharky and the other two men were hiding behind the trucks.

We had to take cover again while they let off another round of lethal automatic fire at us. We had no option but to lie low and let out a few wild shots, waiting for them to empty their magazines. This time when we got the chance to fire during the brief lull, we changed strategy and began disabling the trucks. We shot out the tires of the truck closer to us by the time they reloaded. Garcia was on the ground and was firing level on the floor. He managed to shoot off the ankles of one guy. Loud screams coming from the man confirmed the hit.

It was becoming clear this was going to be a standoff. That must have become apparent to those guys as well. The third time they pinned us with automatic fire, they stopped firing mid-way and threw a couple of smoke bombs in the empty space between us. Thick, red smoke covered the space, cutting off visibility. Then the men began firing again—short bursts at two-second intervals.

We had lost our visual on the target. But the sound of a door being unbolted told me what I needed to know. The men were making an exit from the rear door. My suspicion was confirmed when the truck at the back came to life and shot forward.

"Britt, Garcia, maintain position. Mitchell, follow me. The back alley opens on the front street. We'll cut them off," I said as I ran toward the exit, with Mitchell on my heels.

As I exited, I saw Eugene had displayed presence of mind. He had turned the car around, facing the street, and ready to shoot off. He was turned all the way in his seat, watching out for us. The second he saw us rush out the door, he leaned and opened the passenger door.

I was about to rush toward it when I saw the truck shoot out of the side street and come to a halt about forty yards from where we were. Sharky was in the open back, kneeling on his right knee with his left foot planted in front of him, the M-16 rifle in his hands. But it wasn't the rifle that worried me. The M-16 had an extra attachment under the barrel—an M203 grenade launcher. He had just inserted a 40×46 mm grenade cartridge into the launcher and was raising the rifle to his shoulder to aim it at the car.

Before Mitchell or I could shoot Sharky, his partner let loose another burst of automatic fire from the driver's window. It was wild shooting—the bullets flew all over the place, but both of us had to dive to the ground to avoid being hit. I rolled over a few times, before getting up and diving into the open passenger door.

"Get out of the car," I shouted at the kid as I reached in, grabbed his hoodie, and pulled him out forcefully.

The kid barely weighed 110 pounds. He literally flew out of his seat as I pulled him while falling backwards and out of the car. I wrapped the kid in my arms and rolled over a few times, trying to get as far away from the car as I could.

I was about ten feet away from the car when I heard the unmistakable thumping sound of the grenade being fired. The car made a huge target. Sharky didn't need to be a crack shot to hit it. The car burst into flames as the grenade hit it and exploded. We had managed to get out just in time.

But Sharky didn't hang around. Mitchell had begun shooting at him. The pickup's tires squealed as Sharky's guy stepped on the gas. The truck leapt forward and soon vanished from sight.

I got up and got the visibly shaken Eugene to his feet. I had a quick look at him. He would be fine.

"Hold position. Watch out for the kid. I'll clear the back exit," I shouted to Mitchell as I ran toward the back.

There was no one around at the back. All three men had managed to escape.

"Hold your fire. It's Blaze," I shouted as I entered the warehouse from the back.

Britt and Garcia looked at me questioningly as I walked toward them.

"They got away," I said, my voice heavy with disappointment.

"Not for long. We'll get them," Britt replied.

"We've still got a chance. I gave Sharky's number to my guy to track. He'll get back to me anytime now," Garcia said.

"Copy that. Better get the van now. Let's get out of here in two minutes," I replied.

"Roger that," Garcia said as he rushed out.

But he stopped for a second when he noticed Dutch trying to surreptitiously slide out from under the car.

"You're not going anywhere, asshole," he said as he bent down, grabbed Dutch's collar to pull him up, and punched him hard, knocking him out.

Then he rushed out to get the van. I signaled Britt to join me in the cabin.

"We have sixty seconds. Grab anything that could give us a clue later," I said.

"On it," she replied.

I walked toward a board on the wall opposite the entrance. Pinned to it were printouts of the same photos of the four of us, which Britt had shown me on Dutch's phone. Each photo had a name written below it. Mitchell's was the only one that also had his address written below his name. It was clear someone had made a hit list and given the job to Sharky's crew to locate each one of us. Mitchell happened to be in San Francisco. So, he was the easiest one to spot.

I already knew about the four photos and wasn't surprised to see them on the board. But it was the fifth printout that grabbed me by the throat and left me frozen for a few seconds. It wasn't a photo. It was just the empty outline of a face. The name below it was Kelly Mahone. Deputy Liam Mahone's widow.

This was the final confirmation I needed. Mitchell had been right all along. It was Dexter behind all this. He was making it as personal as it could get. He was going after everyone associated with me. Nothing off limits. No holds barred. It was a game I excelled at.

Some people, by committing egregious acts, lose their right to live. Dexter had just lost his.

# CHAPTER 9

I grabbed all the printouts pinned onto the board, took off my crossbody bag, and put them inside it. When I turned to leave, I found Britt watching me. Her face told me she knew. She had seen Kelly's name. But she didn't say a word. She would wait until I had broken it to the rest of our crew.

"Let's leave. We've got work to do," I said.

"Roger that," she replied in a firm voice as she turned, ready to leave.

I put my hand around her shoulder, and we walked out.

Garcia and Mitchell had removed the cuffs of the men in the back of the van. A couple of them who had woken up were put back to sleep again before they were dumped near the pickup truck outside the cabin. Inside the truck were neatly stacked boxes filled with automatics and handguns. We could already hear the sirens of cop cars on their way. We wouldn't have to worry about those men anymore. The cops and ATF would take care of them. It was time for us to leave.

We wiped our prints off the guns and dumped them next to the trucks. Then we jumped into the van and drove off. In a couple of minutes, we were back once again on Highway 101. No one talked. I could sense why. We had Eugene with us. The things we had to do in the next few hours, we couldn't talk freely about them in the kid's presence.

"You will have to go dark for a while. Stay completely off the radar. No cell phones. No social media. Nothing. No contact with the world at all. Zero digital footprint. Can you understand the concept?" I asked Eugene.

"Uh, yes. You think they're going to come after me?"

"I don't think you'll be top of their list of priorities. Sharky will be too busy saving his own ass to come after you. But these guys are killers. Until we take them down, the only way you're safe is if you're untraceable. Is there a place you can hang out until the heat gets over? Not your regular circle in Berkeley... some place those guys won't be able to figure out."

"Yes. I've got an aunt. Lives in Pacific Heights. I don't think anyone at Cal knows about her."

"Good. Call your aunt. Tell her you're coming over."

"Alright," he said, taking out his phone from his pocket.

"Hang on. What did I just tell you about using your phone?"

"Oh... sorry. Yes, no cell phones. So... uh, how do I call her?"

I took out a burner from my bag and handed it to him.

"This is your phone until all this ends. Only I know the number. The only number fed into it is mine. You won't call anyone else. Got it?"

"Yes."

"Good. Call your aunt now. Keep it short. We don't have time. And give me your phone."

Eugene looked up his aunt's number in his phone and then handed it to me before making the call from the burner. He kept it short and got off the phone within a minute.

"All done," he said.

"Good. Are you carrying coins?"

"Coins?" he asked, looking a little surprised, as he patted his jeans pocket to make sure. "No. I use Apple Pay or my card mostly."

I took out some coins from my pocket and handed them to him.

"We'll drop you at a bus stop on Van Ness and Jackson. Grab a bus. Use these coins to pay the fare."

"Uh, OK. But I do have a Muni card."

"Remember what I said about zero digital footprint?"

"Oh, yes. Sorry."

"Never mind. Get a bus. Get off and walk to your aunt's place. No taxis. Once you're there, send me a text. And then, sleep, watch TV, whatever... but no internet."

"Right. Got it."

"Be ready to get off in a minute."

"Yes. Uh... can I warn Nova?"

"If you call her from the burner... you might get burnt. I can call her and ask her to lay low. And explain what I just told you. Does that work for you?"

"Yes. Thanks," he said, giving me the number.

"That was good thinking, kid. Getting the car reversed and ready to leave," Mitchell complimented him.

That was typical Mitchell. High emotional quotient. Sensed the kid was nervous and tried to make him feel good.

"Uh, thanks. It didn't do much help."

"Not your fault those guys had a grenade launcher. Caught us by surprise as well," Mitchell replied.

"Just stay out of trouble, kid. You'll be fine," Garcia pitched in as well.

We dropped Eugene off near the bus stop and kept driving on US 101 to make our way to the motel in Sausalito.

"What's our next move?" Garcia asked the second the door shut behind Eugene.

"This thing is more dangerous than we thought," I replied, looking at Britt.

I told Garcia and Mahone about what I had found in the cabin.

"Kelly? What does she have to do with all this?" Mitchell asked.

"Nothing. Except that she's Mahone's widow. If they're going after her, it means there are no limits to what they are prepared to do," Britt replied.

"I should have ended it on the court roof," I said, almost talking to myself as a wave of anger mixed with a sense of guilt swept over me once again.

"Don't go there... this 'could've, should've' kind of thinking is nothing but a dark tunnel... The guy started it. You literally tore him apart. If he's fool enough to start again, we all know how this ends," Garcia said.

"You're right. This only ends one way," I agreed, getting a hold of myself.

"Yeah."

"Anyone still in touch with Kelly?" I asked.

Everyone shook their heads.

"Any ideas, Garcia? You're the only one still a Deputy. Can you get hold of someone?"

"Um... I'll have to make some calls. Not sure who'll have access to that info. I'll have to pull some strings," he replied.

"On second thoughts, leave it to me. Flynn can get it done. Not just locate her but get a security detail out to her," I said.

Flynn was way up in the Marshal's hierarchy—Head of the Tactical Operations Division. He didn't just have the rank to pull strings, he was the kind of guy who'd move heaven and earth to make sure Kelly remained safe.

"Of course, your boss and buddy. He'll do it way faster than I can," Garcia agreed.

"What about Emily?" Britt asked.

"Yeah, I was thinking that. We can't give them any easy targets. Mitchell, you and Emily are squarely in their sights. Where exactly is she in LA?"

"There are six of them on this bachelorette party. Renting this house in Manhattan Beach. Driving back tomorrow," Mitchell said, beginning to sound a little concerned.

"Dude, you better haul ass and get there pronto," Garcia said.

"But…" Mitchell began speaking.

"Garcia's right. We've got this covered. What time's the last flight?"

"Too late for that. That was at 2230 hours. The next one's at six in the morning."

It was too late. The time was 2245 hours.

"Give me Em's location and hit the road. I'll ask Flynn to send a couple of Deputies over. They'll hang around until you arrive."

"Right. I'll head out and get back tomorrow," Mitchell said.

"What about you, Garcia? Anyone back home you think could be in danger?"

"No, I'm good, bro. Nothing to worry about," he replied.

I didn't dig further. All the time I had known him, Garcia hadn't come across as the settling down kind of guy. Anyways, he was a capable guy. If he said things were fine… they were.

"Britt?"

"No, I'm good, bro. Nothing to worry about," she replied, mimicking Garcia.

"Smartass," Garcia mumbled.

Britt had already told me earlier her partner was in England on a business trip. She didn't have to worry about him.

"Alright, then. I need to make a quick call to this girl, Nova. She might be in danger," I replied.

"Kid's girlfriend?" Garcia asked.

"I think more of a crush than a girlfriend."

"So… nerdy kid decided to play gangster to impress her?" Britt asked.

"Not really. He agreed to a dumb idea she thought was cool. And got stuck owing these guys. You know how it goes?"

I called Nova. Gave her the same advice I had given Eugene—disappear for a couple of days with zero digital footprint. Told her how the kid had barely managed to scrape through. I couldn't be sure how religiously she would follow the advice of a stranger over the phone. But that was her choice to make. I had many other things on my to-do list.

As soon as I got off the call, I got disappointing news from Garcia. His guy told him Sharky had dumped his phone. We had lost that lead. We arrived at the motel as Garcia pulled into the parking lot.

"Never mind. We've still got some leads. You guys sort out the vehicles. I'll call Flynn in the meantime," I said.

"Right. What's our play now? Grab Slick?" Garcia asked.

"Yeah, that's our best shot for now."

"About this Slick character, I've got a buddy in SFPD. I messaged him earlier to send me the lowdown on him. He should be getting back any minute now," Mitchell said.

"That'll come in handy," I replied.

I got out of the van and called Flynn. Assistant Director Mark Flynn was based near the East Coast at Arlington, Virginia. That was on Eastern Time Zone. A three-hour time difference. The time was 0200 hours at his end. It took seven rings before Flynn took the call.

109

"This better be important," Flynn growled into the phone, sounding as cheerful as any man woken up in the middle of the night would be.

Despite his irritated tone, it felt good to hear his voice. Flynn and I had become good friends during my time in the Marshals, and even more so after I left.

"Blaze here. Did I wake you?"

"Blaze, you son of a gun! Why would you think that? It's only two in the middle of the freaking night. Don't you cowboys sleep?"

"I thought the tac team's supposed to be on call 24 hours."

"Yeah, right, smartass... what's up?"

I gave Flynn a quick recap of all that had happened, from Mitchell's call the previous day to finding the name of Kelly Mahone on the hit list.

"Jesus H Christ! Mahone's wife? These guys are going too far."

"Yeah. They're going to regret it," I replied, my voice cold.

"I know. But first things first, we've got to make sure she's safe. Do you know where she's living these days? Mahone was from Boston, right?" he asked.

"Yes, but I haven't really kept track. None of us know for sure. I'm guessing neither do these guys, but we can't take a chance."

"You bet we can't. Leave it with me. I'll get on to this immediately. It will be in the central database. We'll post deputies outside wherever she's living."

"Thanks. And the same for Mitchell's wife. She's in LA. We didn't realize the threat level until I saw their actual hitlist. Mitchell's going to hit the road now, but it'll take him about six hours."

"Sure thing. Send me the location. I'll get a couple of Deputies to park themselves there until Mitchell arrives."

"Thanks. Now we can focus on getting to the bottom of this," I said, feeling a bit relieved.

"It does sound like Dexter is behind this."

"Yeah, I don't have any doubt about that anymore."

"The question is how. He's on death row. He'll be isolated, if not in solitary confinement. No contact with other inmates. No phone calls. No visitations except from his lawyer."

What Flynn said made sense. It was highly unlikely a prisoner on death row and without any influence on the outside could pull it off.

"Mitchell says he saw him in the city," I replied, trying to sound convincing.

"But he's on death row, for Christ's sake... it doesn't make sense."

"I know. But I trust Mitchell's instinct. Everything he's said has been spot-on."

"You do have a point. The way he caught on to those guys... it does the Marshals proud. But you said he checked with the prison."

"Yeah, he called. But I want to physically confirm it. Something big is up. I can't put my finger on it. But I think the hit list is only part of it. They are up to something else as well. If nothing else, I want to look into his eyes and decide for myself."

"You mean eye."

"What?"

"You left him with only one eye, remember?"

"Yeah, I should have taken both out."

"We'd both have been out of jobs," Flynn pointed out.

"I know," I replied.

Dexter was almost half dead when I arrested him. I got a lot of heat for using excessive violence during the arrest. The least it would have gotten me was suspension for a few weeks. Not that I cared. But Flynn stood behind me like a rock. The only thing that happened was Dexter got a death sentence.

"The thing is, you won't be able to get near him. Any visit will have to be pre-approved."

"You're right. Garcia will have to do it, in that case. He's the only one with the badge."

"They might even refuse Garcia. The warden has a lot of sway in this. It'll have to come from the top. I'll pull some strings. But it will be done. How far is Dry Creek Prison from where you are?"

"A couple of hours drive."

"The earliest you can visit is 9:00 a.m. That will be noon my time. I'll send you the paperwork on your phone by 7:00 a.m. your time."

"Roger that."

"We better deputize the three of you temporarily. If there's this unfinished business, you better do it as Deputies. And badges will help. It will give you access to safe houses as well, if you need it."

"Whatever you feel best, boss. I'm good with it."

"Good. You, Mitchell and Britt are deputized as of now. I'll send an official notice to your phones in a few minutes."

"Copy that."

"And Blaze..."

"Yes?"

"I can't believe I'm saying it but, going after our people... and families... these guys have taken it too far. This time, we end it for good."

"We will. It's a promise."

By the time I got off the call, Garcia had parked the van in a dark corner of the parking lot. Mitchell was standing beside his car, ready to leave, but looking unsure and a bit guilty.

"I've got news. We've all been deputized. It's back to the old times until we nail these guys," I said.

All three whooped. It felt like old times at SOG again.

"Mitchell, if you feel there's a threat, take Em to the safe house."

"Yeah, I'm sure it will be fine," he replied.

"You better hit the road then."

"Yeah. Before that... I've just received the lowdown on Slick. Real name Leroy James. He used to be a low-level pimp and dealer until he got busted by Vice and got sent to prison. His stature kind of grew there. He latched on to the Crips and became one of their procurers for drugs inside the prison. Got out six months ago and is still on parole. He still has connections inside."

"So that's how he's involved in this. The hit must have come from inside the prison. Dexter must have gotten in touch with his crew somehow," Britt said.

We got Mitchell on his way and got inside Garcia's truck. He had brought an official vehicle specially designed for witness transport. It was a modified Ford F-150 Raptor. A beast of a machine with a 5.2-liter V8 heart producing a mighty 700-horsepower, it was also ideal for all-terrain pursuit of fugitives. This one looked especially suited for ramming into vehicles, with a giant rammer fitted in the front.

"What does this Slick look like?" Garcia asked.

"Remember the song Smooth Criminal?"

"Michael Jackson?" he asked.

"Yeah."

"Well, amazing moves. But what about it?" Britt asked.

"That's the way Slick dresses. Skinny guy of about five foot eight wearing a white suit, tie and fedora. Shouldn't be too difficult to spot," I said, showing them the photo on my phone.

"Seriously? This should be interesting. Let's go."

Slick was our only lead to figure out what was up. We headed downtown to his hangout—the night club called Wild Spirits.

# CHAPTER 10

Garcia cruised slowly in front of the night club before making a U-turn and parking across the street. As we walked toward the club, we could see the words "Wild Spirits" flashing in dazzling red and blue neon lights. The words glowed brilliantly every few seconds as electricity pulsated through each letter on the billboard. Neon tubes shaped like martini glasses and a crazy dancing figure around the two words didn't leave anyone guessing what the joint was all about.

When we walked in through the large doors the bouncer stationed outside opened for us, we were met with the loud, thumping bass beats of techno music on full blast. The deep, throbbing rhythm reverberated off the walls, hitting us, making even the floor shake. It was like walking into a wall of sound.

The place was huge. But very dark and hazy. Strategically placed smoke machines were pouring out liquid carbon dioxide. As soon as the liquefied gas hit the room air, it got transformed into an artificial fog almost as thick as the one around the Bay. The alternating mix of red and blue lights oozing through the haze mimicked the colors of the neon signs on the billboard outside. Every few seconds, crazily angled strobe lights streaked through the haze, like flashes of lightning from a distant thunderstorm.

The seating area was set up in a large circle around the dance floor in the middle. About forty tables were spread out around the dance floor that was meant to accommodate maybe fifty people. It looked like there were almost double the number on the floor, sweaty bodies barely getting space to move. The place was packed.

Beyond the dance floor was the bar, with a large counter spread out over at least fifty feet. On each side of the bar, and slightly hidden from the dance floor, were private booths for loaded guys who were willing to shell out big dough for an even bigger hangover the next day.

It took a few seconds for our eyes to get fully adjusted to the weirdness of the lights. We had decided to split up and communicate over radio. That would help us cover more area. We immediately fanned out, eyes alert for any sign of Slick.

Britt and Garcia covered the seating area, spreading out on both sides before heading toward the restrooms. I scanned the dance floor. It didn't take long to make out there wasn't anyone wearing a white fedora on the floor. I began the longer process of moving through the crowd, looking at each face.

Five minutes later, I had come up with nothing. I stood in a space in the seating area, slightly above the dance floor, casting a final look before trying to peek into the private booths. Garcia's voice suddenly crackled in my earpiece, barely audible over the loud music.

"I've got confirmation Slick's on the premises. I haven't got eyes on him yet. He's not in his white outfit today. It's a pinkish... purplish kind of suit. And black fedora," he said.

"Copy that. I've gathered the same intel. Mauve suit. Look for a pinkish, purplish color," Britt confirmed.

Both of them had drawn a blank in the seating area but lucked out in the restrooms. Both managed to grab someone snorting a line of coke. In both cases, the users were completely cooperative once they saw the badge.

"Hey there, handsome. Looking good tonight."

I turned my head and saw a woman standing next to me. I had seen her earlier, trying to make eye contact when I was moving through the dance floor looking for Slick. Good looking woman, dressed in a form-fitting dress and high heels. Dressed for clubbing. The kind of woman men would be lining up offering to buy a drink. I hadn't given her a second look on the dance floor. I was too busy searching for Slick.

"Thanks, you too," I said, smiling, not wanting to be rude.

"I noticed you were standing here all by yourself and thought I'd come over and keep you company."

"Thanks. Very nice of you," I replied, my eyes focused more on the area behind her.

She looked slightly confused. She had expected a different reaction.

"You need to loosen up, babe. And buy me a drink," she persisted.

I looked at her. She had slightly bloodshot eyes. Dilated pupils. There was a distinct possibility she had just snorted a line. She could be another one of Slick's clients.

"You know what, sweetheart? You're absolutely right. I do need to loosen up."

"Why didn't you say so? I would've given you a line but I'm all out. I have some at my place," she said, giggling.

"Sounds like a plan. But I need to grab some for a pal of mine. Seen the candyman anywhere? Dude in pink suit, black hat. I need to hook up with him before I party."

"Yeah. He's over there in a private booth. C'mon, I'll show you," she said, taking my hand.

I followed her to the area where there were four private booths lined up one after the other. Each booth had a curtain all around it for privacy. I stopped the woman from going further. I didn't want her to get any heat later for leading me to Slick.

"Which one is it? Just point it out to me. I'll have a word with him and join you at the bar. How about that?"

"Uh, OK. That one," she said, sounding less cheerful than she did a second ago.

"Thanks. I'll be seeing you soon," I replied.

She looked unsure, but turned and swayed back toward the bar area.

"I have the location. It's the last private booth on the left of the bar," I said into my mic.

"Roger that. I'm on my way," Britt replied.

"Who was that, dude? She seemed to be all over you," Garcia spoke almost into my ear.

I hadn't realized Garcia had been following me.

"Just a lost soul," I replied.

We saw Britt walking toward us a few seconds later. A guy in a tight-fitting shiny shirt looked like he was about to make a move on her. He put on a cocky smile and started to kind of glide toward her. But something in her face made him rethink.

"Not in the mood, dude. Clear off," Britt said, kind of swiping him aside with her arm, without breaking stride.

Two seconds later, she was standing next to us.

"How are we playing this?" she asked.

"I'm sure Slick won't be hanging out alone in there. We don't want to start a firefight. How about Britt and I get into the booth... act like clubbers looking to party... take out whoever's in there with him? You act as lookout," I said to Garcia.

"Sounds like a plan. No guns, right?" he asked.

"Yeah. No guns."

"Roger that," he replied.

"Ready?" I asked Britt.

"Yeah. Let's go," she replied, wrapping her arm around my waist.

I placed my arm around her shoulder, and we were off, swaying and staggering toward the booth.

"I'm looking for my main man Slick," I said, grinning stupidly as I pulled the curtain aside to reveal the booth inside.

We found three men sitting on a U-shaped sofa inside the booth. Two tough-looking guys sat on opposite sides of the table, and a third man was sitting farthest from us with his back to the wall. It didn't need much figuring out to know that the third guy was Slick. And it wasn't just because he was wearing the mauve-colored suit and fedora. The guy had gone to some pains to pull off the Smooth Criminal look. He had done his hair the same way, with thin strands of hair falling across his face and forehead.

"The curtain's there for a reason, dude. It's a private booth. We call you in. You don't just barge in," Slick said in a sharp voice.

"Oh, sorry, dude. I thought after last week... you and I were, like, homies," I replied.

"Last week? I don't remember your face, bro."

Britt and I had separated while I talked, moving slightly closer to Slick's two bodyguards.

"Yo, listen up. You heard what the boss said. Wait your ass outside or... you catch my drift?" one of them interjected, pulling back his jacket to reveal a gun.

"C'mon, man... we're just looking for a little nose candy," Britt chimed in.

She looked at me as the man relaxed a little. That was the cue.

Maybe it was years of working together taking down criminals. Or it was simply the most logical move from our angle. But the moves we made were identical. Both of us hit the guy in front of us on the throat, using the arc formed by the thumb and index finger. When you hit a man just below the Adam's Apple by using the lowest joint bone of the index finger, the metacarpal phalangeal joint, it will in the very least render a man speechless and struggling to breathe. The strike was followed by a quick grab behind the man's head and banging it hard on the wooden table. In less than two seconds, we had two instant knockouts on our hands.

Everything had happened too suddenly for Slick to comprehend. He sat frozen for a couple of seconds. But then he tried to bullshit his way out of the spot he suddenly found himself in.

"Don't come near me. I'm warning you. I'm like a damn ninja. I got some deadly moves. I ain't gonna warn you twice," he said, his voice crackling a bit as his eyes darted around, searching for an escape route.

While we were pushing the two unconscious men inside to get closer to him, Slick suddenly sprang into action. He ducked under the table and scrambled like a rat, coming out the other side.

The guy was fast. But not too lucky. The moment he got out from under the table and began to make a dash toward the bar area, he ran straight into Garcia's outstretched arms. Garcia's boot knife pressed firm against his throat made sure Slick didn't make a sound when he was forced back into the private booth again. Britt drew the curtains once they were inside.

Garcia pushed Slick onto the couch and forced him back in the same position he was earlier. By that time, I had pushed one of the knocked-out men under the table. Britt had pushed the other man into a corner of the couch against the wall. She grabbed Slick's hat and placed it over the man's smashed face.

Garcia slipped in and sat next to Slick, his arm around his shoulder, like they were best buddies.

"Hey, shot caller. I've heard you've got a hit out on us?" he asked Slick in a voice cold as ice, his knife still pressing into Slick's throat.

Slick lost his voice for a few seconds. Britt and I had sat down by then, forming a snug circle around the guy we were about to scare shitless.

"Wha... What? Shot caller? Hold up, dude. Ain't no need for the blade, bro. I'm just a businessman," Slick replied, finally managing to find his voice.

"Just a businessman, huh? Well, word on the street is different. We heard you're the man if someone needs a hit done."

"What? Me... set up hits," he chuckled nervously. "Nah, man. You got me all twisted. Must be mistaking me for somebody else."

"Is that right?"

"Yeah, man. We were talking business when you guys barged in and messed up my business partners."

"You mean the two guys carrying burners with the serial numbers scraped off? These ain't legit, bro," I said, flashing the gun.

"What? Scraped off numbers? Damn! That ain't legit for sure. Appreciate that, man. You just saved me from them. How about I buy y'all drinks to show my gratitude?"

"Cut out the crap, Leroy James. We know exactly who you are," Britt spoke up.

That shut him up again. At that moment, the curtains moved, and a pretty waitress popped in her head.

"Guys, you want me to get you anything?"

"Thanks, sweetie. We're fine for now," Britt replied.

The waitress smiled and then looked questioningly at Slick.

"What about you, MJ? We're fine for now, right, buddy?" Garcia asked, his arm still around the shoulders of his new best pal.

"Uh... yeah, we're fine," Slick confirmed.

The waitress smiled and walked away

"Looks like you've moved up in life, lover boy... from pimping on the streets to selling dope to high-end customers," I said.

"For real, man? This ain't how you handle a legit businessman. I ain't no pimp or pusher. I don't know what the hell you're talking about," he attempted one last time to weasel out of the tight spot he was in.

"See this, wise guy," Garcia said, flashing his badge. "US Marshal. Chasing guys like you is what we do for a living. We know you're on parole. Remember the conditions your parole officer told you? How many of them are you violating just by being here in this place?"

Slick's face lost some color.

"Uh... I'm clean, man. Test me if you want. And I ain't got no guns."

"What about these?" I asked, holding up the guns of the two knocked-out men.

"I told you these dudes had me fooled, man. I thought they were legit businessmen."

Garcia suddenly pushed Slick forward onto the table and frisked his back.

"Bingo!" he said, holding a bunch of small packets filled with white powder. "Whoa! How many eight balls have you got there, dude?"

"I've no idea where these came from."

I decided to dial up the pressure a few notches. I placed my hand behind his neck, pulled him forward, and pressed the side of his face hard into the tabletop. I did that slowly and deliberately, letting him resist all he could, making him realize he didn't have enough power in his body to resist my actions. With the other hand, I pulled out my boot knife, and placed the tip almost into his ear, deliberately nicking him, drawing a little blood. The man was too scared to even wince.

"I don't think you're listening to us. You want me to clear up your hearing... remove some ear wax?" I asked.

"Nah, man, I got perfect ears. Crystal clear, like a ten on ten or however the fuck they measure it. Ain't no need for no medical procedure, bro."

"Good. Now here's the deal. Your sorry ass is headed back to prison if you don't cut out the bullshit. One phone call and you're back in the slammer. Get that?"

"Yeah, man. I hear you loud and clear. I got it."

"I'm not done yet. Someone asked you to put out a hit on us. We know Sharky's crew took the contract. Try denying it and you're dead meat."

"Nah... I mean, yeah. I ain't denying shit."

"Good. If you give us the straight dope, we'll let you walk... eventually. Tell us exactly where the hit came from. Everything you know. But if I feel you're trying to pull a fast one, I'm going to break you in so many places you'll never walk straight again. And then I'll throw your ass in prison. You don't want to test me. Tell me you get it."

"Yeah. I get it, dude. Completely. No more bullshit," he replied, sounding defeated.

"Good. Now we're all going for a drive. You've got a lot of talking to do," I said, removing the knife from his ear and flicking it back into its sheath, before letting go of his neck.

"Uh... I'll come with you, man. I'm all about peace. But we got homies scattered around this joint. They ain't just letting us stroll outta here. Bullets are gonna fly."

"That's for you to figure out, MJ. Feed them any bullshit story. I know you're good at it. We can moonwalk out of here peacefully if you pull it off. Or we do it the hard way. But your ass will be the first one on the line if them bullets start flying," Garcia told him.

"Yeah... I feel you, man. Let's dip through the back exit. No way we're making it out the front in one piece."

A couple of minutes later, we walked out the club's back entrance without incident. Britt and I waited with Slick near an intersection while Garcia ran to get the truck. A minute later, we were on our way.

# CHAPTER 11

Before we began turning the screws on Slick, we gave him a chance to explain his role in the entire thing. He tried to convince us he was nothing more than an ill-informed middleman in the entire deal.

"I know homies have been calling me shot caller and all... but that's all for fun, dude. I mean, look at me... do I look like some badass shot caller? All I'm doing is a little bit of hustling... a man's got to earn his living somehow. But it's mostly honest work, I swear. Getting two interested parties to come together... that's all I do."

"You're killing me, man. Earning an honest day's living. Such noble thoughts. Was that why you gave up on being a pimp?" Garcia asked, his voice heavy with sarcasm.

"Not the word I'd use, dude... especially in this fine lady's presence," Slick said, trying to win over Britt.

"Slick," Britt said in a voice that didn't sound like the guy had succeeded in achieving his aim.

"Yes, ma'am."

"You saw how this fine lady busted the head of the fine gentleman back in the booth?"

"Yes, ma'am."

"You try being a smartass again... I'll make you shut the fuck up. You dig?"

"Yes, ma'am. I dig… completely. All I was saying was… pimp is a word with, uh, slightly negative connotations."

"No kidding."

"Well, yeah, I was more like the People Manager all these fancy ass companies have these days. These girls… they were kinda short of money and I was like… I know ways we could get some bread. The girls kinda struggled with making and managing money… you know how it is with women and money, man. So, I've always been like this CEO-minded person. I don't know enough technology and shit but … I was like Uber… managing a workforce of these self-employed working girls… creating jobs out of nothing… stimulating the economy… trying to live the American dream."

"Yeah, right. We'll nominate you for business visionary of the year. Now cut out the bull and start talking sense. How did the hit come to you?" I asked.

"Uh, right. You know when I was, you know, incarcerated… Well, I needed to figure out real quick how not to end up being someone's bitch… uh, pardon my French, ma'am. I'm a survivor and all but, prison is a different ball game, man. I managed to pull some drug runs for this dude, Chainz. Dude turned out to be the Crips' shot caller. That kept me safe until I got parole two years later. And now, uh, I, like, owe them. I do stuff they tell me to do. They asked me to spread the word about a hit. And…"

"And? You gave out the hit on us?"

"Uh, yes. But... that was my only play in this thing. You gotta understand, dude... I'm like, just the medium... like the internet has tons of weird shit going through it, you know... kiddie porn and what not... but it ain't the internet's fault... It's the weirdos you guys go and catch, you know what I mean..."

"Yeah, Einstein. What happened next."

"Uh, the rest you know... Sharky's crew took the hit."

"We already know all that. Who gave out the hit?" I asked.

"Sorry, I'm getting to that. This hit... it's like the weirdest thing. It came from a man on death row. That hasn't happened in, like, ever. Those guys are in isolation. And more importantly, they don't have access to the kind of dough you need to get a crew to make such a hit. But this guy, he's got connections."

"What's his name? I won't ask again nicely."

"See here, Marshal, I've been many things but a rat ain't one of them," he said, quickly adding when he saw me reach out to grab him: "But... hold on, man... there was a but coming... I'm doing this in the spirit of being a law-abiding citizen. Because you Marshals asked me to do my bit. I hope you all make a note of that."

"Yeah, noted. But the next words out of your mouth better be the name of the guy."

"Uh... Dexter Cady."

I exchanged glances with Britt and Garcia. It felt strange, but the confirmation of what we already suspected came as a bit of a relief. We finally knew the enemy. Sharky and his crew were simply pawns in the game. And Slick had been nothing more than the grapevine.

"How the hell did he get word to the Crips? He's on death row. Those guys are locked down... isolated from other inmates."

"Marshal, I swear, I don't know nothing about that. They just tell me to spread the word, and I do. No questions asked."

"How do the Crips contact you?" I asked.

"Well, uh, they hit me up on the phone."

"No way they're using the prison phone. Those calls are monitored. Give me a straight answer."

"They've got this sweet deal going with a guard. He hooks them up with a cell when they gotta make a call."

"And how much did you and your crew make off this deal?"

"Uh, I don't know. It was the Crips who got the dough. I'm just a measly messenger."

"You remember this, Slick?" I asked, taking out my boot knife and waving it in front of his face.

"Yeah, Marshal. It's not like I'm ever gonna forget that. I'm a sensitive soul. The memories gonna haunt me, man," he replied, gently touching his ear.

"You try stalling me again, and I won't just graze the other ear."

"Hundred grand. Fifty for spreading the word and another fifty when the deal was done."

"And your cut?"

"Uh, five grand. That's it. I told you I'm at the bottom of the damn chain."

"Why didn't the Crips handle the hit themselves? They're deep in the game and bigger than Sharky's crew," I questioned.

"Nobody wanted to mess with the Marshals. Any other hit, they'd be all over it... but not this one. No one wanted to fuck around with law enforcement. Crips, Latinos, Chinatown... nobody touched it. Then I got word Sharky wanted in. All I did was connect them with the cats who were doing the negotiating. But here's the twist... Crips were the ones who put out the hit, and now they feel like they got played."

"Why's that?"

"Most of the payment came in the form of weapons, man. Not your regular street shit, but heavy artillery... grenade launchers... military-grade firepower. Turns out this cat Cady had some big-time arms connections. Sharky's crew got their hands on some serious hardware, way beyond what them other crews got. Word is, the streets of San Francisco are about to run red. Sharky's gunning to be a damn godfather. This shit's spiraling outta control."

"Who was doing the negotiating for Dexter?"

"I ain't sure about that. All I did was pass Sharky some weird names and video game logins. I think they made contact through that."

"What were the names? We need exact details."

"Uh, right... it's on my phone. You guys jacked it when you mugged me," he said, throwing an accusing look at Garcia.

"Here. You try erasing anything from it... your sorry ass is gonna be mugged in a way you can't even begin to fathom," Garcia growled, handing him the phone.

"Peace, brother. I said I'm doing all this shit as a law-abiding citizen. All citizens have a right to privacy on their phones and shit," he said, before quickly adding: "Just saying, Marshal... I mean, we're on the same side now."

"Yeah, cut the chatter. Just give us the details."

"Yeah. Here it is... The game's called DeadForce. Dudes looking like zombies trying to blow each other's heads off. Sharky's crew had to log in as '*Mayhem_Kings*' with the password '*GeTrevenge541*'. They were supposed to play with a dude called '*Havoc_KD*'. All the communication happened during the games. I don't know what they talked about."

I believed that was true. The games and chats are end-to-end encrypted. Only the participants would have a clue about what was going on in there. It was also quite apparent he wasn't fudging the details about the game. All the names in the log in details sounded like no one but the Cadys could have created them. The password '*GeTrevenge541*' said it all. And it wasn't a coincidence the letters KD in the name '*Havoc_KD*' sounded like Cady.

"How did you hook up with Sharky's crew?" I asked.

"Uh, on the phone... and they swung by the club."

"Which club?"

"The one where you busted my ass. Wild Spirits."

"What about the other guys? You never crossed paths with them?"

"Um... lemme think."

"Need a reminder? Does the name Tokyo Dreams jog your memory?" I asked.

"Tokyo Dreams? Oh, the Japanese joint. Damn, it slipped my mind. I swear, bro, I forgot. But for real, how long y'all been watching my every move?"

"Don't you worry about that. Who were those guys?"

"Honestly, I ain't got a damn clue. Sharky hit me up, said I needed to be there because some deal was going down. But I didn't do jack shit. Don't even know why the hell they dragged me there. I was just hanging around like some damn busboy, with Sharky and some other dude I never met before."

"Break it down for me. What exactly happened?"

"We hung around for, like an hour, drinking fucking green tea. Then these two straight-up freaks showed up. They had a quick chat with Sharky and dipped into some private room."

"Freaks, you say... in what way?"

"One of them was scarier than the devil himself, man. Big-ass dude, rocking long hair and a beard, moving all weird... like some damn Robocop, stiff as hell. And get this—he had the nerve to rock shades inside that dim joint, like it wasn't dark enough with them damn lanterns. And here's the kicker—the dude had a gnarly-ass scar on his right hand, looking like it got torn to shreds in the middle. Just looking at it gave me the creeps, man."

I exchanged glances with Garcia and Britt. Everything Slick was saying seemed to be further confirmation Dexter was the man Mitchell had seen in the restaurant. But it was still impossible to believe a man on death row in a prison two hundred miles away could be moving around in the city.

"And what about the other guy?"

"He was a whole different kind of weird, man. Not scary. More like Rain Man kind of weird. Dude had some serious stretching game going on, like them dancers priming up before they bust out a routine. Trust me, I know what I'm talking about. I'm a dancer myself, so I've seen it firsthand, you feel me? And the languages, man... it was like a damn symphony. He's the first white dude I ever heard speaking Japanese like he popped outta Tokyo itself... no stuttering or nothing, just opened his mouth and Japanese flowed out smooth like Southern whiskey. Then later, I caught him chatting away in Mexican with them other dudes."

"You mean Spanish, you dumbass," Garcia chimed in.

"Huh? Spanish? If you say so, boss. They looked Mexican to me."

"Forget it," Garcia sighed, shaking his head, "Who were these other dudes?"

"They were holed up in that private room, the same one them other two dudes went in. We had no clue they were in there until all four of them stepped out."

"But who the hell were they?"

"I dunno, man. All I can tell you is they looked damn loaded. Both sporting legit Rolexes. I've seen my fair share of fakes, but these were the real deal. And they were deep in some serious convo. Must've been in there for like an hour."

"We've got to get a grip on these guys. The only lead we've got is in that Japanese joint. Think it might still be open?" I asked Britt.

"Hard to say. Most joints around the Bay area shut down before midnight. Only a few remain open into the late hours."

"Well, considering I spilled my guts to you all... you folks go ahead. I'll send you all the luck you need and bid you farewell. My black ass and Japanese grub ain't a match made in heaven," Slick said, trying his luck.

"Nice try. You aren't going anywhere until we've got our hands on all those men. The hit list you floated has just got a notch bigger. If they come gunning for us... well, guess who we'll be using as a human shield," Garcia shot back.

Tokyo Dreams was just a couple of blocks away. It turned out it was one of the few joints in San Francisco that kept its doors open well into the night.

# CHAPTER 12

We parked the pickup in the building's underground parking garage and took the elevator to the eighth floor.

"How are we playing it? Do we flash the badge and chat with the manager? Or play it cool, slide into a table like regular Joes? Just so you know, my stomach's screaming for some grub," Britt chimed in as the elevator ascended.

"Let's do both. We get a table, put in an order for whatever they can rustle up quickly, and have a word with the waitress before we approach the manager. We better cover all bases," I replied.

"Works for me," Garcia agreed.

"Not that anyone cares for my opinion..." Slick began saying.

"Yeah, you're right. No one cares," Garcia replied.

"Britt, mind taking charge of the order? That way, we won't waste time trying to decipher the menu."

"You think I'm the sushi expert or something?"

"Well, I reckon being a trainer in LA, having some deep sushi wisdom would be a fundamental pre-requisite."

"You might be on to something there," Britt chuckled.

"Any chance they'll have a regular old burger in there, huh?" Garcia asked.

"Sure, the day they start serving sushi and ramen in diners."

When the elevator doors opened, the first thing we saw in front of us was a wall. Not just any plain old wall but a large fluorescent canvas painted in vivid pink, purple and green. A holographic image of Tokyo's skyscrapers made up the background of the wall while the words Tokyo Dreams were emblazoned across it in large, flowing neon letters. The entrance to the restaurant was at the right end of the wall, which looked like it was standing by itself in the middle of the large reception area.

As we walked toward the entrance, a pretty waitress came out. On second thoughts, pretty was an understatement—the woman in her mid-twenties was drop-dead gorgeous. A beautiful face framed by long, dark hair. Delicate features and perfect complexion with porcelain-like skin. With a healthy touch of rosiness to the cheeks. Her almond-shaped deep brown eyes, veiled by long, thick lashes, had a welcoming warmth to them. She wasn't tall—I doubted if she was more than an inch above five feet. And she was lightweight—she would barely touch hundred pounds on the scale. But she wasn't skinny. Just a nicely proportioned petite woman.

Her nametag said Naomi.

Naomi seemed to be the perfect choice for the job of welcoming customers into the restaurant. Once she smiled that brilliant smile of hers, any guy with doubts about his keenness for Japanese cuisine was likely to shut up, follow her inside, and take a table.

Naomi took a couple of steps toward us, bowed, and said the word, "*Konbanwa*".

We just nodded and smiled back. I had been to a Japanese joint some time back and knew the word meant "Good evening". That, along with maybe two other words, summed up my expertise in the language. But Naomi's one-word greeting was followed by what sounded like a very long sentence in Japanese, ending with the words "Tokyo Dreams".

"I think she's welcoming us to this joint," Slick whispered in my ear.

"Thanks. I managed to figure that out," I replied.

At that moment, Naomi switched to English. And we breathed a sigh of relief.

"Hi, I'm Naomi. Welcome to Tokyo Dreams. Sorry guys, I didn't mean to scare you off with too much Japanese in your face, but we are supposed to give a traditional welcome to all customers before we can switch to English."

"You know what... you caught us just in time. We were about ready to run away scared," I replied.

She found that funny and laughed.

"You know something funny... I've actually had people thinking it'll be too much effort to order food here and decide to turn back. And sometimes, when I switch to English, people start talking funny... speaking slowly and loudly... like I'm fresh off the boat from Tokyo. I was born here, for crying out loud."

"You don't need to worry about us. We're starving. No way are we turning back. And our friend here won't let us... he's a big connoisseur of Japanese cuisine. We're here on his recommendation. Right, MJ?" Garcia asked, putting his arm around Slick's shoulders, like they were the best of pals.

"Uh, yeah. I love it," Slick said, not sounding too convincing.

"Did you say MJ? I thought you looked familiar. Weren't you here yesterday? We were talking about how you had that Michael Jackson look. You were wearing a white suit, right? With those scary... uh, men," she said, faltering a little in trying to find the right adjective for Slick's companions.

"Were the men with him really scary?" I asked.

"Uh, not really," she replied, faltering a bit.

"We know MJ here is one hell of a smooth criminal. But don't you worry about it. We're working to convince him to change his ways," Garcia said.

"Uh, right," she said, suddenly looking a little less confident. "Uh, table for four?"

"That'll be great," Britt answered her in a reassuring voice.

"Great. Follow me," she said, perking up again, before turning and leading us inside.

The moment we stepped inside, we could see it was clearly an upmarket place. The interiors were very aesthetically done, combining traditional Japanese designs with a futuristic high-tech ambience. The walls were adorned with intricate wood carvings and paintings with Japanese calligraphy. The lighting was soft, with rows of small lamps made of rice paper casting a gentle glow.

Naomi got us a table and rushed off to grab menus. She was back barely a minute later, with menus in one hand and a tray with four small ceramic glasses in the other. She placed a menu as well as a glass in front of each one of us.

"Green tea to welcome you. It's on the house. You can have as many refills as you want."

"Great. Slick here was telling me how much he loved it yesterday." Garcia replied.

"Great. But, guys, I'm sorry but you'll have to order within ten minutes. The last order is at 1.30. We close at two."

"We're ready. What's the quickest thing you can get us?" Britt asked.

"Um... sushi... ramen..."

"Let's go for ramen."

While Britt sorted out the order, I looked around the restaurant, trying to figure out where Mitchell would have sat the previous day. He had mentioned a corner table close to the entrance, diagonally opposite the private rooms. The rooms were laid out behind a thin wall of faux rice paper. They weren't visible from the table area.

"That was a lot of talking for a simple order for ramen," Garcia commented when Naomi finally rushed off with the order.

"You've no idea. That was like the shortest conversation ever. You can go on forever, choosing the type of ramen, noodle firmness, broth strength, topping... I get the feeling you don't eat out much at Japanese joints," Britt replied with a twinkle in her eye.

"Twenty-four hours ago, I was in the swamps chasing gator poachers. Take a guess about the kind of cuisine that gets served out there."

"I get the idea."

Naomi was back with our orders within seven minutes, which wasn't bad at all for an upmarket joint like Tokyo Dreams. I had already asked Garcia to get Slick away from the table for a few minutes while Britt and I tried getting information from Naomi. I guessed she would be more forthcoming talking about the "scary guys" with Slick if she didn't have to talk in his presence.

"Hey, Naomi... those guys our wannabe MJ was with yesterday... are they regulars to this place?" I asked her as she laid the dishes on the table.

"Those two. No, I've never seen them before."

"You mentioned they looked scary."

"Oh boy, you can say that again. One guy was really scary—one of those perpetually angry types. He even had a gun. I caught a glimpse of it when his jacket got slightly pulled back. I don't think he said a word the whole time. All they did was try some green tea and make faces before ordering iced coffee. I don't think they even touched the sushi those other guys ordered for them."

"What other guys? The ones who were in the private room?"

I kicked myself a second later. My question had suddenly made her wary. She looked at me nervously, not sure how to answer. There was no option but to play the Marshals card. I showed her Garcia's badge.

"Let me tell you why we're asking. My name is Axel. This is Britt."

"Hi," Britt said.

"We are US Marshals chasing dangerous fugitives. I believe the men in that private room were part of the gang," I explained.

"Oh... you mean, your friend MJ ... is he...?" she left the question hanging in the air.

"He's mixed up in things way over his head. Even he doesn't know who the guys in there were. We need to establish their identity."

"Oh... I see. Yeah, they did look like gangsters. Hmm... let me think... I'll tell you what I remember about them. Well, the two guys who booked the room... I've seen them around before. But not the other two."

"Can you give us any idea about who they were? It's really important we catch them soon," Britt jumped in.

"Uh, alright. The two guys who booked the room... I've seen them before... I've no idea who they are... like, I don't know their names and all... but, there's one thing I found strange—they were dressed very flashily yesterday. Shiny suits, bright golden watches, gator shoes... I mean, they looked like regular guys before. But yesterday, they were like... I don't know, high-end pimps or something. Does that make sense?"

"It makes perfect sense. Anything else... about those two or the other two men?"

"Uh, I don't know... nothing about those two... but the other two men... they were weird. One was, like, scary weird... big man with beard and wild hair... a big, ugly scar in the middle of his hand. The other guy was weird as well, but more like, creepy weird."

"What do you mean?"

"His mannerisms... He couldn't be still. Always stretching parts of his body... if nothing else, then cracking his knuckles. Except when he focused on something. When I went inside the room with their order... he took a napkin and made a dragon out of it. Not some kid's stuff, but a proper dragon with a tail and claws and... really well done."

I exchanged glances with Britt. Naomi had just confirmed what Mitchell had told me earlier.

"Interesting. Anything else about him?" I asked.

"Yeah. He spoke Japanese very well. Actually, even better than I do. I don't remember any other customer in like, ever, who could speak fluent Japanese. Obviously, I mean people who aren't Japanese. And it's not like I don't run into wannabes everyday... dudes who pick up a few words, look up random stuff online, and then try to act like gurus about Japanese culture. It all stems from their subliminal desire to impress others with their language skills, you know... a need for validation... to somehow be viewed as intellectually superior..."

"Let me guess... Psych major?" I asked.

"Is it that obvious?" she asked, giggling.

"Not at all. Axel is kind of clairvoyant. You were talking about this guy..." Britt intervened, trying to keep Naomi on track.

"Yeah, right. But just in case you were wondering, this waitressing thing is a temporary gig. My true calling is in psychology, I just haven't figured out exactly what it is," Naomi said to me, a little bit defensively, before carrying on talking about Carson, "So, this guy, he had, like, native fluency. And... I'm not sure if it's relevant, but he kind of hit on me. At first, I thought he was just being sweet, when he made the origami dragon and gave it to me. But when I went in the room next time, he began talking to me in Japanese... kind of asking me out... dropping big hints about how he was planning to open this fancy restaurant in J-Town."

"J-Town? That's Japantown, right?"

"Yeah."

"Did he mention where exactly in Japantown?"

"At the Peace Plaza. Next to the Pagoda. He said I could come with him after my shift, take a look if I was looking to go places in life. Those were his literal words. Like that would make me throw myself at him."

"What time were they here? Did he know your shift ends at 2:00 a.m.?" I asked her.

"It was early evening. But he did ask when my shift ended when he was making polite conversation in the beginning."

"Then he was surely hitting on you," I agreed.

"He was, wasn't he? And he was, like, old... mid-fifties... and as I said, he was weird. I was like, eww..."

"Did the other men have any reaction while he was hitting on you?"

"I don't think they even got to know what was up. He was deliberately talking in Japanese. And his tone didn't indicate he was doing anything other than making polite conversation. But when I began replying in English and told him I had a busy schedule all evening, he shut up quickly. I think he was scared of the other guy... the scary one."

"That was good thinking."

"I guess. It happens sometimes. More often than I like it. Goes with the job, you know."

"It really shouldn't. Don't let them ever get away with it," Britt said, the words coming out of her mouth almost like a reflex action.

"I know. I usually don't."

"Good for you. Is that why you called him creepy kind of weird?" I asked.

"Yeah. He really gave me the creeps. It's nothing specific... it was, I don't know, the way he spoke and acted. And he came over again today. But that was before my shift started. I started late today. Another girl told me he hung around for a while, asked about me, and then a couple of guys came over and kind of took him away."

"Was he here today?"

"Yeah, and I know it sounds paranoid, but when I left work yesterday, I got this weird feeling I was being watched. Actually, forget it, I think I'm being silly."

"Where did this happen, when you felt you were being watched?"

"Uh, in the parking garage. There were these guys inside a big SUV. They weren't doing anything. They were just sitting there. Watching. It just gave me the creeps. But then I drove off. Nothing happened."

"Did you see their faces?"

"Not really. I just caught a glimpse of the guys in there and didn't look again."

"Hmm... do you remember the SUV? What make was it?"

"Um, I don't know. I don't know much about SUVs. It was large and black."

I opened an image of a black Hummer on my phone and showed it to her.

"Could it be this?"

"Uh, could be. But I'm not one hundred per cent sure. All I remember is it was a big tank-like thing and looked huge parked next to my little Chevy Spark. The thing is, I wasn't really looking directly at it. I could just sense there were guys inside. I was feeling nervous and didn't want to look that way. You know what I mean?"

"Yeah. Anything else you remember about this guy?" I asked.

I had noticed the maître d' had begun glancing toward our table. He was a stern-looking man of about forty-five. Looked like the kind of guy who would be a stickler for rules. A waitress hanging around one table for too long must have been flouting some weird rule in his book. I knew we couldn't hold Naomi for much longer.

"I think he had a face job done."

"Face job? Are you sure?"

"Pretty sure. I've got an aunt in showbiz... she's not like a star or anything, but she keeps getting bit parts on TV... Anyway, she had a face job done last year. And there were these scars around her hairline, behind the ears, and under the jawline. This guy had the same scars. They were light, so I'm guessing it must have been some time ago, but I'm pretty sure he did."

"Naomi," I said.

"Yes?"

"You'd make a great detective."

"Thanks," she replied, beaming. "You know what? One of the career paths I'm seriously considering is forensic psychology."

"I'm sure you'll excel in it."

"Thanks. But I better head back now, or I'll get pulled up for talking too much."

"I noticed that guy at the reception has been watching you."

"Shit. Oops, sorry. His name's Kata. He's like this stern old schoolteacher. He can be a real buzzkill," she said, avoiding looking in his direction.

"One last thing... do you think there would be a record of the guys who booked the private room yesterday?" I asked innocently.

Britt gave me a knowing look.

"Yeah, it'll be in the booking system. We're not supposed to give out the details. But, uh, those guys... were they really gangsters?"

"I'm not sure about the ones who booked the room. But the two weirdos... they are psychopaths. Responsible for multiple murders. It's them we're after. Those two are the only lead we have."

"Leave it to me. Kata's watching like a hawk right now. I'll try to get it for you once he moves away," she said and scooted off in a direction away from the reception counter from where Kata was monitoring the restaurant.

Kata tried to attract her attention to get her to come toward him, but she pretended not to have noticed and disappeared into the kitchen.

# CHAPTER 13

"That was smoothly done," Britt remarked when Naomi was gone.

"I figured it'll be easier for her to get the details. That guy Kata... the way she talked about him... he sounds like the type who'll insist on a search warrant."

"Looks that way. I'm more worried the man might end up alerting them. It sounds like those two guys are regulars here."

"Yeah, there's that too."

"Let's see how your magic works on Naomi."

Naomi's plan of avoiding Kata hadn't gone too well. He wasn't a guy who would be ignored.

Kata walked over to the kitchen door, signaled her to come out, asked her to follow him to the counter, and had a conversation with her there. He seemed to be doing most of the talking. Naomi walked back toward the kitchen a minute later, avoiding eye contact with us. But the moment she was out of his line of sight, she looked at us, rolled her eyes, smiled, and walked back into the kitchen. Kata seemed too absorbed in the computer to have noticed.

"Ouch, looks like we've got her in trouble. Doesn't look like she'll be able to get her hands on the details," Britt said.

"She's a smart girl. And she's got attitude. I'd be willing to place my bets on her."

By that time Garcia had joined us at the table, with Slick in tow.

"Dig in, guys. We've set the wheels in motion," Britt said as soon as they were seated.

"What about the manager? Are we leaning on him for intel?" Garcia asked.

"That's a negative," I replied.

"Blaze is relying on his charm for a change," Britt said, recapping the conversation with Naomi for Garcia when she saw the puzzled look on his face.

"We don't trust the manager. He might tip off the men we're after," I explained.

"Alright then, charm offensive it is," Garcia replied.

While we ate, we brought Garcia up to speed. We weren't too worried about Slick hearing things—we weren't planning to let him go free until this thing was over. Despite Slick's serious misgivings about the "sloppy shit" in the bowl in front of him, he wolfed down the ramen in record time, keeping pace with the rest of us.

I felt my phone buzz. It was a message from Flynn. He had located Kelly Mahone. A protective detail had been posted outside her house as well as the place where Emily Mitchell was staying in Los Angeles. I relayed the information to Britt and Garcia and slipped the phone back into my pocket.

Naomi had been busy with customers at other tables in the meantime. It was getting near to closing time. Most of the customers had begun to leave. Naomi was busy getting them their checks. A few minutes later, Kata moved away from the counter and disappeared into one of the private rooms.

As soon as he went, Naomi left everything and headed straight toward the computer terminal. She had a look of intense concentration on her face as she stood in front of the computer for a couple of minutes, punching keys, scrolling through the screen, while glancing toward the private rooms every now and then to make sure Kata was still inside. She finally walked off with a triumphant look.

Kata emerged from the room a minute later. But he didn't go back to the counter. He went around the tables, talking to the remaining customers, before making a courtesy stop at our table.

"Good evening. I hope everything is fine at your table?" Kata asked, speaking in a deep voice with a distinctive accent.

"All fine. Thanks," Britt replied.

"May I be so bold as to ask what brings you to our fine establishment tonight?"

"Our friend here's a fan of your fine establishment. And we thought, why the hell not give it a try," Garcia chimed in.

We waited to see what kind of a reaction the man would have to Slick. But there wasn't any. He didn't take the bait about Slick and sidestepped the issue.

"I hope you enjoyed it," Kata replied.

"Yup. Thanks."

"Good. Are you from around? I mean, I haven't seen you before."

"Yeah, we're from around. You can expect to see much more of us," I replied.

"Oh, good. I apologize if the waitress was taking too much of your time with her talking."

"Not at all. It was a pleasure."

"OK. Thank you. Please let me know if I can be of any service," he said, before bowing and moving to the next table.

"I don't like the guy," Britt gave her immediate assessment.

"I'm not exactly in love with him either. He'll surely rat us out the first chance he gets," Garcia agreed.

Once Kata moved a few tables away, Naomi was back with a paper in her hand.

"Would you want to join our loyalty program?" she asked, using the form as an excuse to hang around our table.

"Sure. I hope we didn't get you into trouble," I asked as I took the form from her.

Naomi turned her head to check on Kata before she spoke again.

"Kata's a crafty devil. I got played. When he asked me what I was chatting to you guys about, I said we were talking about the city. But he started talking about your friend MJ and then suddenly asked me if you all were connected to the other guys from yesterday. I let it slip you knew those guys. I shut up after that, but it was too late. When I checked the records in the computer, I found he had deleted them. There are no entries for yesterday afternoon."

"You think he deliberately deleted them?" I asked.

"I'm certain. We're very meticulous about the entries for the private rooms. Those are the high-end customers, and the records go into a database at the end of every week. You've no idea how mad it made me."

"That's a bummer," I said, almost to myself.

"No, it's not. Remember what you said?"

"Huh?" I replied, not sure what she meant.

"About how I could be a great detective? Well, Kata may be sly, but he's up against me. All he knows about that computer is keying in information... or deleting it. He doesn't have a clue all data is backed up in the cloud. And guess what I was doing at the terminal when I realized I'd been played?"

"You found the entries in the backup?" I took a guess.

"Yup. I got their names, phone numbers and an address. There you go," she said, sliding me a slip of paper, turning her head slightly to make sure Kata couldn't see her.

The paper had two names—Daniel Cruz and Hugo Ortiz. Apart from their phone numbers, there was an address, which was on a commercial street. It looked like an office address.

"That's a big help. Thanks."

"No problem. I got a big kick out of it. I was mad as hell when I found what Kata did. I couldn't let him get away with it."

"I think we might as well make her an official investigator on this case," Britt gushed with praise.

It made Naomi's cheeks rosier than they already were.

"Thanks. I better get the check before Kata begins wondering again. Not that he's got the brains to figure this one out," she said, before walking over to the counter for the check.

We were among the last customers remaining. Kata made it a point to hang around our table when Naomi came with the check.

"Garcia, the guy's watching us like a hawk. Keep him busy," I whispered.

"On it," he whispered back, immediately got up, and blocked Kata's view.

"Hey, big man, great place you've got here. How do I go about booking one of those private rooms?" Garcia asked him, as he put his arms around Kata's shoulder and almost dragged the reluctant man toward the rooms.

"I've got my details on the form. Didn't want to hand it to you in front of him," I said, handing the form to Naomi.

"Good thinking," she said, putting it in her pocket. "I'll let you know if those guys come back."

"Thanks. One more thing…"

"Sure."

"When this weird guy came over today, where were you?"

"I was close by, in a mall across the street."

"Where did you park your car?"

"In the parking garage below. We get free parking here."

But then the import of what I had said struck her.

"You think he knows my car? Saw it there and came up?" she asked, looking alarmed.

"No need to be alarmed. I'm just looking at all possibilities."

What I didn't tell Naomi was I thought the man might have put a tracker on her car. I knew if I mentioned it, she would freak out. I decided to check it out.

"If you're nervous about the SUV, do you want us to hang around in the parking garage until you get off?"

"Uh, I don't want to bother you," she replied, not exactly saying no.

"It's not a bother. We'll be around a few more minutes. Let us know if it'll make you feel safer."

"Uh, actually... it'll be great if you guys could hang around while I get my car," Naomi agreed without wasting a second. "But it'll take me twenty minutes before I head out. Is that fine?"

"No problem. Do you remember anything else about the SUV? Like the license plate?"

"No. Sorry. It didn't strike me at the time. All I remember is it was big and black. And looked like a monster parked next to my little Chevy."

"What color is your car?"

"Red," she replied, giving me her license plate number as well.

"Alright. Don't worry about it. When you come down to the parking garage, don't look for us. We will be there... hanging around in the background... Just get inside your car and go home. I'll let you know later if we see something suspicious. Sounds good?"

"Thank you so much. But..."

"Yes?"

"How will you tell me?"

"You've got my number on that form. Text me your number before you leave."

"Of course. Right. I'll do that. Thanks," she said and rushed off to finish her remaining chores for the night.

"Girl must've been really spooked out by the men," Britt remarked after Naomi walked away.

"Yeah. If that guy she's talking about turns out to be Carson, she could be in danger. Carson was a weird guy. He had a thing for Japanese women. I won't be surprised if he's stalking her."

"You think he's tracking her car?"

"We'll get to know soon enough."

Garcia was back with Kata after his quick tour of the private rooms. The grin on Garcia's face as he walked back was in stark contrast to the sour-faced look on Kata's mug.

By the time we settled the check, it was 0200 hours—time for Tokyo Dreams to close. We made our way to the elevator to get down to the parking garage.

# CHAPTER 14

We got into the elevator on the eighth floor and pressed the button for the underground parking garage. But as soon as the doors began closing, I reached out for the panel. Garcia beat me to it. He was closer to the panel. He pressed the button for the seventh floor.

"Is that what you had in mind?" he asked.

"Yeah. Any floor before the parking level," I replied.

"What's going on?" Britt asked.

"You go first," I said to Garcia.

"I think Kata has already informed his guests we've been asking about them," he said.

"Go on, Sherlock. How did you arrive at that conclusion?" Britt asked him.

"Remember how the guy disappeared into a private room for a few minutes while we were eating?"

"Yeah."

"I assumed he was attending to guests in there. But guess what?"

"There weren't any guests," I replied.

"Bingo. All private rooms were empty. Also, he was looking into his phone as he walked there, as if reading a message... or searching for a number. It was a busy time. There was no reason for him to leave the reception unless..."

"...he was making a call," I finished his sentence.

The elevator stopped on the seventh floor. As the doors opened, we saw the floor was deserted. We got out. The doors shut behind us and the elevator proceeded to the parking level.

"But he could have been calling anyone," Britt pointed out.

"Call it a hunch."

"You do have a point. And why did you want to stop the elevator here?" Britt asked me.

"I'm certain what Mitchell said was true. I don't know how, but Dexter was here yesterday. Which means he's out of prison. We take that as fact until we check him out at the prison. A prison guard confirming over the phone that he's still locked up inside doesn't cut it for me anymore."

"What about Carson. You think he's alive?" Garcia asked.

"I don't know what to think, pal? All we can do is try to track down these guys before they get a chance to take another hit at us. Or decide to simply disappear. We can't be looking over our shoulders for the rest of our lives."

"I hear you, bro," Garcia said.

"But what are we doing on this deserted floor?" Britt asked.

"We still have an active hit out on us. If Garcia is right, someone could be waiting for us down there. The main advantage we have is surprise. We can't lose that," I said.

"Yeah, that's what I thought. We'll have to split up," Garcia suggested.

"Dude, I'm a man of peace. Don't do well in violent situations. I'll just be getting in the way of all you Marshals. How about I say good night and see you later," Slick, who we had ordered to keep his mouth shut in the restaurant, finally spoke up.

"Get one thing straight in your head—you're as much of a target now as we are. Those guys know you were with us. They'll think you're a rat. How long do you think you'll last on your own?" I asked him.

The usually glib Slick was suddenly at a loss for words.

"We're in the same boat now, shot caller. The only difference is your ass is going to prison unless you help us put an end to all this. For now, your only hope is to stick close to us. Fending off attacks is what we're trained to do. *Comprende*, amigo?" Garcia asked.

"Uh, yes, boss. Completely *comprende*. I know I'm screwed."

"Not necessarily. There's still a chance things will turn out right for you. But it all depends on how much you're willing to put into it to make it happen," Britt said.

"I'm all in. I ain't planning on kicking the bucket anytime soon... and, uh, staying on the outside of them prison walls sounds mighty fine to me."

"Great. Now button it and let us handle the rest," Garcia told him.

"Yes, boss."

"What's our play now?" Britt asked.

"How about you and I head down the stairs while Garcia waits here with Slick? We'll do a recon of the place. Once we give the signal...

Garcia... you and Slick come down in the elevator. After that, we wait until Naomi drives out."

"Copy that. Watch your six, guys," Garcia said.

"Roger that," we replied and walked off toward the stairs at the other end of a corridor.

We rapidly descended the stairs to arrive at the landing at the parking level. We stopped to inspect the parking area through the peeping window in the exit door. The place looked deserted. The elevator was about forty yards from where we were.

We fanned out, moving in opposite directions, staying low and keeping an eye out for two vehicles—a black Hummer and a red Chevy hatchback.

I moved anti-clockwise, scanning the few vehicles still parked there. I came across two SUVs. Neither of them was black. And neither looked like a Hummer.

"Found the hatchback. It's parked in K12," Britt's voice came through my earpiece a minute later.

"Copy that. I'll do a full perimeter check and join you."

I stayed close to the boundary wall as I moved toward the elevator entrance. Something about a black van parked near the elevator didn't feel right. As I moved closer, I noticed it wasn't parked inside the demarcated parking spaces, which started ten feet further on from where the van was parked close to the elevator door. I grabbed a pair of binoculars from my bag and focused on the front cabin. I saw a man in the driver's seat. He was simply sitting there. Waiting.

"Garcia, maintain position," I spoke into the mic.

"Roger that," Garcia replied.

I made my way toward parking space 12 in row K. The tiny red car stood parked in the corner space. Britt was on her back, inspecting the car's undercarriage with a small flashlight.

"Found anything?" I asked, holding out my hand.

"Yup. There's a tracker in the tire well. But the undercarriage is clear. Naomi was right. The guy's a psycho," she replied, taking my hand as I pulled her to her feet.

"She's a smart girl. But we've got other problems. There's a black van parked near the elevator. Something about it doesn't feel right."

"You think there might be hitmen inside?"

"Yeah. It's parked strategically so the second you open its sliding door on the side, anyone coming out of the elevator would be a sitting duck."

"What do you say... shall we get into our truck and ram the hell out of the guys inside it?"

"Let's make sure we don't ram into some regular guy who just happens to have poor parking skills. That beast Garcia has brought along for the ride can do serious damage," I replied.

"So, what do we do?"

"I have an idea. You get into the truck and wait for my signal. I'll circle around and take up position so I can observe the driver. Once I'm there, I'll ask Garcia to send the empty elevator down. Then watch what happens when the elevator door opens."

"Sounds like a plan. I'll get in the truck."

I circled around to approach the van. I took up position behind a pillar located at a 45-degree angle from the front of the van. It gave me a view of the driver as well as the sliding door facing the elevator. I took out my binoculars to focus on the driver. He was looking toward the elevator. It was too dark inside the van to see anything behind him.

"Garcia, send the empty elevator down. Then wait for my signal."

"Roger that," he replied.

"Elevator's on its way," Garcia's voice came through my earpiece thirty seconds later.

I heard the elevator stop about thirty seconds later. The van driver heard the sound as well. I noticed him sitting up straighter and say something to someone in the back of the van. As soon as the elevator door opened five seconds later, the van's sliding side door opened as well. The M24 miniature binoculars in my hands had 7x optics—powerful enough to give me a clear view of the barrel of an M-16 rifle, with its distinctively designed handguard behind the front sight assembly and the flash suppressor at the end of the barrel.

I no longer had any doubts in my mind. I was looking at a team of hitmen. Judging by the rifle, they were part of Sharky's crew.

"Blaze to all teams, there's a kill team in a van parked outside the elevator. We're taking them out."

"Roger that," Britt and Garcia replied.

"Britt, be alert and wait for my signal."

"Copy that."

"Garcia, you and Slick are the bait. Take the elevator and make your way down. As soon as the elevator door opens, fall flat on the ground. Britt and I will do the rest."

"Copy that. I'm calling the elevator now," Garcia replied.

After a few seconds, his voice came over the radio again.

"We're inside the elevator. Will touch ground in thirty seconds."

"Copy that. Britt, turn on the ignition. Put vehicle in gear. When I give the word, start moving slowly for three seconds, then hit the gas and ram the hell out of them."

"Copy that," she replied.

As soon as I heard the sound of the elevator landing in the parking level, I drew my gun and gave the next command to Britt.

"Britt, start moving."

"Roger that."

As the elevator doors opened, the sliding door of the van moved almost in time with that. But by then, I was already running toward the van. The van driver was too focused on the elevator door to notice me approaching the van from an angle.

I began firing a second before a rifle barrel came into view. I let off rapid shots into the van, not really aiming at anyone but more with the intention of pinning them down before Britt rammed into them. One of the bullets hit the barrel of a rifle just as it was coming out to let loose automatic fire toward the elevator. The burst went high, and sideways, not even close to the elevator.

I saw the van driver pulling out a gun to line it on me. I needn't have worried about him. Because that's when Britt rammed into the van. The impact was violent. The beast of a truck weighing six thousand pounds slammed into the side of the van, making a huge crater in its side. The van was lifted clear off the ground. It kind of flew a few feet off the ground and landed with a resounding thud a couple of yards away before skidding to a stop. The smell of burnt rubber filled the air. Garcia's truck didn't show very visible signs of the impact. The rammer fitted on its front made sure that not even the headlight got smashed in the collision.

The van hadn't flipped over but the impact had sent every man inside it crashing onto the van's inner wall. The man firing from the open door flew out of the van and slammed headfirst into a wall. He was dead before his body dropped to the floor.

The driver's window had cracked from the driver's head banging hard into it. The man sat with a dazed look, the side of his head cut and bloody. I walked toward the side of the van, holding my gun straight out in front of me with both hands. I saw three men inside. All looking broken and bruised and in a state of semi-consciousness.

"Threat neutralized. But be watchful. And call 911. I'll have a chat with the driver."

"Roger that," I heard both voices confirm.

I opened the driver's door, grabbed the driver by the throat, roughly pulled him out, and dumped him on the ground. The man cried out in pain. His visible injuries included at least a dislocated left shoulder, a broken humerus bone just below the shoulder, and a few broken ribs. He was part of a kill team that would have drilled us all with gunfire without batting an eyelid. I wasn't about to show him mercy.

I also knew cops would be on the scene in a few minutes. Once they arrived, the man would clam up. I needed to get him to talk before that. There wasn't time for any bullshit psychological tactics. I needed to put the fear of death in him. Fast.

I grabbed the man's hair with my left hand and pulled up his head to make him observe my next action. As he watched, I pumped bullets into the right shoulders of all three men lying in the back of the van. The man flinched with each shot.

Then I dragged him toward the wall, close to where his partner's broken and lifeless body lay grotesquely twisted. The body gave the man a clear idea of what I had in mind for him. He tried to avert his eyes—getting too scared to look at the face of death.

"Look at him," I said, grabbing him by the back of his head and forcefully turning his face.

"That's how dead you'll look in a few seconds," I said, before turning his face toward me.

I bent over him to let him see the deadly intent in my eyes.

"We've taken out your entire team. You're next. You've got just one shot at staying alive," I said, my voice cold as ice.

"Anything. I'll do anything. Don't kill me," he pleaded, his voice coming out in a hoarse whisper.

"Just one chance. I'll ask questions. You answer. You lie once, I'll put a bullet in you. Get it?"

"Yes. I won't lie."

"Who sent you?"

"Sharky."

"How did you get our location?"

"Uh, I don't know for sure," he said.

I pressed my Glock into his still intact right shoulder.

"No, no, wait... listen to me, man. I don't know for sure but... Sharky's been working for these two guys."

"What guys?"

"Dexter and Ronin."

"Dexter and Ronin?" I asked.

I hadn't come across the name Ronin before.

"Yes. They've got the contacts. They and these two guys they've been dealing with... both Latinos. Those Latinos have connections to do stuff... like tracking phones. Maybe they tracked your phones, man. I'm only guessing. All I know is Sharky called me and told me he had solid intel you guys were here."

"What are the Latino guys' names?"

"Cruz and Ortiz."

Those were the two names Naomi gave me earlier. The ones who booked the private room. The ones Kata must have called to rat about us.

"What about Kata? Is he the one who called Sharky?" I asked.

"Huh? Kata? I've never heard the name."

I wasn't sure what to make of that. His answer suggested Kata wasn't involved with the gang. But it was possible this guy didn't know everybody Sharky and his contacts were involved with.

"What do Dexter and Ronin look like?"

"I've just seen them once from far. Dexter is a big guy. Well built. He's just got one eye. Ronin is tall and skinny."

"Anything else about him?"

"Who? Ronin?"

"Yeah."

"Well... he twitches a lot."

That confirmed my suspicion. The guy we were thinking was Carson was operating under the name, Ronin. It kind of fit his profile. I knew Ronin was a Japanese word. Some kind of a samurai warrior.

"How many people were you supposed to take out?" I asked him.

"Uh, four."

"Who?"

"Uh, we were just doing what we were ordered."

"Who? I won't ask again."

"Uh, you and... uh, the photos are in my phone."

"Where's your phone?"

"In my pants pocket."

I took it out, got him to unlock it with his thumbprint, and went through the messages. The latest one had four photos. Apart from the three of us, I saw Slick's face staring back at me. He too had come into Sharky's crosshairs.

At that moment, we began hearing the faint sirens of approaching cop cars. I could see a flicker of hope in the man's eyes.

"Don't even think about it? You're done talking only when I'm done asking. The cops are a long way off. It only takes me a second to put a bullet in your skull."

"Yeah, I know," he replied in a hopeless voice.

"When did you get the call for the hit?"

"About twenty minutes ago."

"Bullshit. How could you arrive so quickly, armed with all this hardware?"

"No man, I swear. You can check on the phone. We were told to be ready for such a call. We've been cruising downtown for a few hours."

I checked the call log. The last incoming call was from twenty-two minutes ago.

"Is that Sharky's number?" I asked him.

"Yeah. It's a burner."

"How many other crews are there?"

"Two more."

"Where are they?"

"Uh, one's north of Golden Gate. Covering Sausalito, Marin City... the other's around Japantown."

"Same vans as yours?"

"Uh, I guess so. More or less."

"Their license plate numbers?"

"I swear, man. I don't know. I don't even know the number of the one I was driving. I swear."

I believed him. I had no more use for him. I had gotten all the information he had.

"Get up," I ordered, slipping his phone into my pocket.

It took him a few seconds to maneuver his body into a position that made the process of getting up least painful. Once he was close to the van, I clipped him on the back of his head. The man fell down unconscious.

The sirens of the cop cars had grown louder. I saw Slick standing obediently by the elevator door, not moving an inch from where Garcia had ordered him to stand. Garcia and Britt stood by the truck, keeping a wary eye out for any other hidden threats.

I had one more task to finish before I was ready to talk to the cops. I walked over to them.

"You OK?" I asked Britt.

"Yeah. I was the one inside the tank, seatbelt on and braced for impact. Not a scratch."

"Good. How's it looking?" I asked Garcia.

"We've got one dead. The others are still breathing. But we're in the clear. This was a hit. We've got all the evidence confirming that. Got anything out of the guy?"

"Yeah, lots. I'll fill you in later. But before the cops arrive and we get detained for a while, I'll go up and question Kata. Jolt him with some reality bites and get answers. We might not get a chance later."

"Copy that. We've got this covered. When you do come down, the story is you went up to ensure there isn't any threat in the restaurant. And better keep Slick close to you. We don't want the cops getting their hands on him."

"Copy that."

As I turned, I saw the elevator had come down with some passengers. Standing just inside the elevator door, rooted to where they stood, were Naomi, Kata and another waitress from the restaurant. The shock of witnessing the busted-up van and broken bodies was written in bold letters on all three faces.

The intensity of the sound of the sirens had increased. The cops would be turning into the parking garage any second. I walked inside the elevator, gently herded them back, and signaled Slick to join me. Then I pressed the button for the eighth floor.

It was time to scare the living daylights out of Kata.

## CHAPTER 15

"What happened here?" Naomi finally found her voice just as the elevator doors shut out the scene of complete mayhem outside.

"Kata's gangster friends turned up," I replied, looking at Kata with a grim expression.

The usually stern man lost some of his composure as his face visibly paled. He opened his mouth, but nothing came out.

"There will be a slight delay for you girls tonight. Cops are going to be all over the place. There's nothing to worry about. The threat is over. But you better head back into the restaurant and wait a few minutes," I said in as soothing a voice I could manage under the circumstances, looking at Naomi and the other girl in turn.

They simply nodded. Their eyes were filled with questions, but they instinctively understood it wasn't the right time to ask them.

When the doors opened, I stood between Kata and the others, and gestured with a sweep of my arm to indicate they should walk out. Kata understood he wasn't going anywhere—he didn't make any attempt to get out.

"We'll go down and have a little chat. Back in ten minutes. Don't worry," I said to Naomi.

She nodded, her expressive eyes still looking unsure as hell. I pressed the button for the seventh floor. Ten seconds later, Kata and I stood alone on the deserted floor.

"You and I are going to have a chat. But before we do, I want you to understand something. The people I was with today, the ones who got attacked in the parking garage by hitmen armed with automatics, they are family to me," I said, lifting my finger to keep him quiet when I saw him opening his mouth.

"People who come after my family... I have a reputation for breaking them with my hands. Let me know if you think I'm bluffing."

Kata stood transfixed, not being able to do anything except shake his head.

"You're doubly screwed. It's not just me you have to deal with. There's a dead body downstairs and three men on the brink of dying. That attack on federal agents happened based on your phone call. That makes you complicit with those gangsters. That means prison time, not just a slap on the wrist. You've messed up big time. Get it?"

"Yes," he barely managed to whisper.

I could see beads of sweat forming on his brow.

"I'm the only one standing between you and prison. If you come clean, I might decide not to ask the cops to book you. Because if I do, no lawyer will be able to save you from prison time for a deadly assault on federal agents. Get it?"

"Yes. I will tell you everything. I had no idea. I'm very sorry," he said, bowing as he apologized.

I was a little surprised by Kata's apology. The look on his face told me he realized he had messed up big time. And he looked sincerely regretful. I had expected him to put up some resistance. But I kept up the pressure.

"Who did you call tonight after you came to know we had asked Naomi about the guys from yesterday?"

"Daniel Cruz," he replied immediately, without making any attempt to feign ignorance.

"Who's he?"

"Uh, I don't know for certain. He works for the government. Exactly what he does... I don't know. He never told me. And I never asked. It's impolite to ask customers what they do. They only tell if they want to. Mr. Cruz and his friend Mr. Ortiz are regular customers. They sometimes book private rooms for meetings."

"Why did you call him?"

"He asked me to tell him if anyone asked about him. He told me he does important government work, and he needs to know if something happens. I was just doing my duty to my customer. I did not know who you were."

"What exactly did you tell him?"

"That there were four people. One of them was the black man who was in the restaurant yesterday along with the other men."

"What was his response?"

"He just said thank you. And to tell him if I learn anything else about you. That's why I came to your table after making the call... to see if I could find anything. But I'm not good at small talk... as you must have noticed."

"Is that all that happened? Just an innocent conversation where you mentioned three anonymous people. Those men down there got the order to kill us five minutes after your call. Don't test my patience, Kata. I won't warn you again."

"Oh, sorry. There was one more thing I forgot to tell you. Mr. Cruz asked me to take a photo of you all and send it to him."

"And you did that?"

"Yes. I'm very sorry."

"That was a very big mistake. You put the lives of federal Marshals at risk," I said in a grave voice.

"I sincerely apologize. I did not realize what I was doing. Mr. Cruz and Mr. Ortiz betrayed my trust," he said, his voice trembling with emotion.

The man was killing me with his apologies. I had become convinced by then he wasn't really involved. He was a straightforward Japanese guy, very prim and proper in his manners, who got played by Cruz and Ortiz. But I did not let any of it reflect in my tone.

"Why did you delete their records from the computer?" I asked.

"Uh, I knew Naomi would give them to you. It's against our rules. She is not good with following rules."

"And yet you're the one looking at prison time."

He couldn't figure out a response to that.

"Was there anything different about Cruz and Ortiz yesterday?"

"Uh, the men they came with yesterday... I haven't seen them before. They were not the kind of men they used to bring for meetings before that."

"In what way?"

"Uh, they did not look like nice men. They looked dangerous. And Mr. Cruz and Mr. Ortiz were dressed very differently. I have always seen them in normal clothes. I mean, they wore suits like any government people. But yesterday, they wore very different clothes. Very shiny suits. Gold watch. Gold necklace."

"Did you ask why?"

"No. It would be impolite to ask."

"Too bad. What do you know about the other guys in the restaurant yesterday?"

"Mr. Cruz and Mr. Ortiz booked the room. They and two other men had a late afternoon meal there. Three men sat on a table outside. One of them was the man who was with you today. I do not know the others. They did not look like nice people."

"They didn't look like nice people... and yet you went squealing to Cruz when we asked about them," I said, my tone still far from being even borderline pleasant.

"Uh, I'm sorry. All those other men yesterday, they looked like bad men. I thought because you were with one of them, you were also bad men."

"No shit. What else do you remember about those bad men?"

"Uh, they all looked dangerous. Like gangsters. Except one. He was very charming. And spoke very good Japanese. But..."

"But what?"

"He was strange in many ways. Hard to explain."

"What was his name?"

"Ronin. In fact, his is the only name I know. He told it to me when we were talking."

"Ronin is a Japanese name, right?"

"Yes. It comes from feudal Japan. It means a wandering samurai who has no master."

"Wandering warrior, huh?" I said, almost to myself.

"Yes. But he didn't really look like a warrior."

All the clues about Carson seemed to be falling into place. He had somehow managed to fudge his death and escape. All the physical characteristics I had heard from multiple witnesses pointed to him. Naomi's observation about him having had a face job done provided an answer to why his face looked slightly different. His choosing the name Ronin seemed to fit with what had happened to him—he had been underground for two years.

It suddenly occurred to me the Cadys had spent a lot of time in California before they fled the country three years ago—a year before they were captured and brought back to face trial. Knowing Carson's obsession with Japanese stuff, it seemed logical he had been to the restaurant before.

"Are you sure he's never been to the restaurant before yesterday?"

"Uh, you know, I did get the feeling there was something very familiar about him. The way he stretched his body... the fluency with which he spoke Japanese... He speaks as good as I do, and without much accent. I grew up in Osaka and came to America only ten years ago. For an American to speak my language so fluently... that is very rare. I thought about it a lot yesterday. There was a man I remembered from maybe three or four years ago. I can almost swear he was this man's brother or close relative. But I'm very sure I haven't seen this man before."

"Did you ask him if he had been here before?"

"No. But he did say it was his first time to Tokyo Dreams. Even though..."

"What?"

"When I went back into the room later, he did say something to the other man he had come with. He said, 'Man, I missed this place. It's good to be back'. That puzzled me a little, but I thought maybe he meant San Francisco, the city."

I took out my phone, found a mugshot of Carson, and showed it to Kata.

"Do you know this man?"

"Yes. He was the man I was talking about. He was who the man from yesterday reminded me of. How did you know?" he asked.

"Never mind that. How do you know him?"

"He used to come here. I was just a waiter at that time. But then he disappeared. And many months later, I read in the newspaper he was a bad man. An arms dealer. And then he died."

"And that's how you know the man who came yesterday wasn't the same guy?"

"Yes."

"But if you ignore the fact that he died, can you say with reasonable surety the man you saw yesterday could be the same man?"

"Uh, I don't understand."

"Compare what you remember of the two men—the physical structure, voice, mannerisms... Think about it and answer."

"Right. Let me see. Well, as I said, I felt like this man could be the other man's brother. I thought that because he had the same height, same kind of thin body, same way of speaking, same mastery over Japanese, same strange way of stretching... The only difference was in the face. He looked different from what I remembered, from what I can see in this photo. And he looked younger."

"Different how? Take another look at the photo."

Kata studied it for a few seconds before replying.

"The man who was here had more hair. The man in the photo has a receding hairline."

"That's right. What else?"

"The nose. This man in the photo has a slightly large and hooked nose. But the other man had a smaller, straighter nose. And... he just looks younger. Like he was the younger brother of this man."

It suddenly hit me this guy would have security camera feed from the previous day. I could get a close-up view of all the men.

"You must have the security feed from yesterday."

"Yes. I can show that to you now. Also, I just remembered... I have the business cards of Mr. Cruz and Mr. Ortiz. They gave them to me last year, when they made a booking for the first time. I keep all the cards very carefully."

"That's good. Before we head upstairs, listen to me carefully. Your little honeymoon with Cruz and Ortiz is over. Those guys won't leave any loose ends. And you, pal, are a very loose end. You'll need to disappear for a couple of days while we sort this out. You get that?"

"Oh," was all he managed to say as the gravity of my words sunk into him.

I could see fresh beads of sweat forming on his brow. His eyes had grown larger. He was just a simple man stuck in really bad shit. I couldn't just leave him there to be killed.

"Don't worry. We are Marshals. We deal with this kind of thing all the time. Just do exactly as I say."

"Yes. Please tell me what to do. I will follow your every command."

"It's more like advice... but never mind. When you leave tonight, switch off your phone and leave it in the restaurant. If you carry it with you, it can get traced even if it's off. Got it?"

"Yes."

"Who else is in your family?"

"My wife and daughter. But they are not here. They are visiting family in Osaka."

"Right. That's less to worry about. Don't go home tonight. Go to any friend's place. Alright?"

"Yes. Uh, what about the restaurant? Should I take leave for tomorrow?"

"What did I just tell you about disappearing?"

"You asked to disappear for two days."

"Does that answer your question."

"Oh... yes."

"But tell the other staff to open it as usual tomorrow. The only other change is Naomi will be on leave as well."

"Uh, is she in danger as well? Is it my fault? I'm so sorry."

"Not your fault. That guy... the one we just talked about, he's a nutcase. He's been stalking her."

"Oh, no. Can I do anything to help?" he asked, looking genuinely concerned.

"No, leave it to me. Don't mention this to her or anyone else. She doesn't know it. I'll tell her... and arrange for a safe place."

"OK. I understand."

"Good. Let's head upstairs," I said, pressing the button to call the elevator.

"Uh, does that mean I will not be arrested?" he asked in a pleading voice.

"You've answered all questions honestly. I won't mention your involvement to the cops."

"Thank you. I am very grateful," he said, bowing deeply.

"Don't worry about it."

We got into the elevator, and I made my way once again to Tokyo Dreams.

## CHAPTER 16

When the elevator doors opened, the multi-colored fluorescent display announcing Tokyo Dreams looked somewhat less flashy—the neon lights had been dimmed after closing time. The dining area was empty. The free-standing tables and chairs had been pushed to one side. Naomi and three others stood with their backs against a wall. Slick was sprawled out on a couch in one of the booths. He sat up straight as soon as he saw me. All eyes looked at us inquisitively as we walked out.

"We'll be ready to leave in five minutes," I announced before following Kata into his back office.

It was a neat little room, organized and tidy. Invoices and reservation books were neatly arranged on the desk, in the center of which stood a large computer screen. There were some framed photos on the walls with some celebrities who had dined there. But I didn't really have the time for them.

Kata was in a corner of the room, standing in front of an open cabinet, flipping through what looked like a photo album. It had laminated slots for slipping stuff inside them. When I looked closely, it was a business card holder. I didn't even know those existed anymore. Kata had at least a dozen of them on a table beside him. He finally found what he was looking for.

"There. I knew I had them," he said triumphantly, handing me a couple of cards.

They were Cruz and Ortiz's cards. Both worked in a government-run trade office. Cruz was a Trade Analyst and Ortiz was an Export Manager. I felt sure it was a front. But it gave us a lead.

I was about to slip the cards in my pocket when I saw the look of pain on Kata's face knowing there would be a hole in his prized business card collection. I took out my phone, clicked a photo of the cards, and handed them back to him. The look of relief on his face said it all. He placed all his card holders back into the cabinet and turned to me.

"I will ask Naomi to look for the footage. She will do it faster," he said.

"Sure."

"I will talk to the others. You can use the room to, uh, tell Naomi about the man."

"Yeah. Makes sense."

Kata called in Naomi. He walked out as soon as she came in.

"Is everything cool?" Naomi asked.

"Yeah."

"With Kata, I mean. You looked mad as hell when you took him down in the elevator. After what we witnessed in the parking garage, we didn't think he'd be coming back in one piece."

"We had a chat. He came clean. He wasn't mixed up with those guys. Just got taken for a ride. It's fine now."

"That must have been some chat. Kata's even letting me put my hands on his computer... without him being in the office... that's like, a major deal."

Naomi knew exactly what I was looking for. It took her less than a couple of minutes to bring up the relevant security feed on the screen. I asked her to pause on some frames, rewinding and replaying some of them, zooming into the faces, looking closely at the two men from all angles.

A few minutes later, I didn't have a shred of doubt in my mind. The two men at the restaurant the previous day were Dexter and Carson. The men didn't belong anywhere near the borders of civilized society. Yet here they were, roaming the streets of San Francisco, unfettered and unchecked. They had to be stopped. Permanently.

I realized Naomi was looking at me, trying to read my expression.

"We're done here. But there's something you need to know," I said.

"Uh-oh. That doesn't sound good."

"There's a slight problem. You'll need to lie low for a couple of days."

"Uh, what's it? Is it about the weirdo?"

"Yes. There's a tracker on your car."

"Fuck! Uh, sorry. What do I do?"

"You will be safe. We'll make sure of that. The good thing is we found the tracker before he could make a move."

"I'm so glad I'm with an optimist who sees the bright side of things."

I couldn't help laughing.

"Seriously, it would've been bad had you not told us about it... and we hadn't located the tracker. That guy's a nutjob," I said.

"I know. I have a knack for attracting weirdos. This isn't the first time I've had someone stalking me. But a tracker on my car is surely a first. Oh my God! What do I do?"

"We'll figure it out. What's your living situation? Do you live on your own?"

"Yeah. I've got a small apartment."

"Where's your family? Parents?"

"Down in LA."

"Right. So, here's the deal... you'll have to lie low someplace safe until I've neutralized the threat."

"Neutralized the threat? You mean..."

"Take the guy off the streets. He's a wanted fugitive."

"Oh."

"You won't need to worry about it. He won't be coming back."

"Uh, right."

"You've got two options. You either hole up at a friend's place and sit tight there until I tell you it's fine."

"Or?"

"I'll take you to a Marshal's safe house. That's where we keep witnesses who are under our protection."

She didn't need any time to think about it. Her response was instantaneous.

"I'll take the second option, please. Uh, if it's not too much trouble."

"No trouble. But be aware it's a boring place. Nothing to do but watch TV."

"I can live with that so long as I don't have to worry about that sicko."

"Alright. But there are a few ground rules."

"Sure."

"Switch off your phone. Then leave it here or hand it to me. We can't take a chance of that guy tracking it. These men are dangerous—they aren't just street-level thugs."

"You mean it can be tracked even when it's off?"

"Yeah. Unless you take out the battery. But that's the problem with smartphones. It's not easy to just pop out the battery."

"Right. There you go. Uh, will you take out its battery?" she asked as she handed me her phone.

"We've got a device to make it untraceable. I'll show you when we go down. Now hold on to this," I replied, handing her a burner. "It's a basic burner phone. That's only to communicate with me. Don't call anyone else. Think you could do that?"

"Yeah. Sure. This thing looks like it's from the dark ages," she said, looking at the very basic cellphone in her hands.

"It is. That's the idea. You'll have to go dark. This doesn't have internet connectivity. No Insta updates. Nothing. The virtual world won't exist for you for the next forty-eight hours. Got it?"

"Yes, boss. Just keep that sicko away from me."

"I will."

"What do I do with my car?"

"Leave it here. If you need to grab anything from it, get it."

"Alright."

"Good. Get everyone together. Let's go down."

While Naomi went for the others, I signaled Slick to join me in a corner.

"Sharky's hit list just got a whole lot longer. You're officially on it now. Welcome to the club," I told him, displaying the photos on the phone I had grabbed from the hitman downstairs.

"Me? On a freaking hit list? Nah, man, this can't be happening," Slick protested.

He zoomed in on the photo, double-checking to confirm it was indeed him.

"Oh man, oh man, oh man! What am I gonna do? You gotta save my ass, Marshal. I did everything you asked," he pleaded.

"Calm down. We've got this covered for now. We'll take you to a safe house."

"Thanks, dude. I knew I could count on you."

"Listen up and listen well. This thing's not over until we take out Sharky. You better start thinking real hard about how we can get to him. I know guys like you always have a trick up their sleeve."

"Got it, boss. I'll be thinking like I've never thought before."

We stepped into the elevator and descended to the parking garage, ready for what lay ahead.

# CHAPTER 17

The parking garage had been sealed off. Cops were all over the place.

Garcia and Britt had explained the situation to the cops. It was a clearcut case of gangsters attacking a team of Marshals pursuing an investigation. We left it to the cops to figure out the exact motive. But no one cared much for that at almost 3:00 a.m. in the morning.

I asked Garcia to get a cop car to drop off Kata. Then I took Naomi to her car to grab her things. But before she could get inside, I took her around to the tire well of the rear right tire to show her the tracker.

"Oh my God! Is that still on the car? Won't it come off?"

"It will. But we'll be leaving it there for now."

"Uh-huh. I'm guessing there's a good reason for that," she said, sounding skeptical.

"Yeah. No need to tip him off that we're on to his game. Let him think you caught a ride with someone and left your car here. Tomorrow, we might just use the car as bait to lure him some place."

"Oh, I see. That's gonna be epic."

"Yeah. Grab your stuff and stay in your car. I'll have a word with my crew and swing by to pick you up in a few minutes."

I left Naomi in her car and walked over to Garcia and Britt. I quickly filled them in on all I had learnt.

"So... Mitchell was right. It's the Cadys for sure," Garcia said.

"I'm convinced. I don't know how they managed it, but they're the ones who were here yesterday."

"How could Dexter get out of supermax with no alarm being raised? Are all the prison guards in on it?" Britt asked.

"That's what I can't figure out. I can get a couple of guards or a warden being rotten, but all of them? Makes no sense at all."

"And Carson? How's he alive? His body was positively ID'd," Garcia pointed out.

"That's what we need to find out. We know Dexter put out the hit on us. But that's not their only play. We need to find out what they're up to. That's the only way to get to them."

"And when we do?" Britt asked.

"We end it. I won't make the same mistake twice. I won't be able to live with myself if those psychos ever got to Mahone's family. Are you in?"

"I'm one hundred per cent behind whatever you decide. We got into this together two years ago. We'll end it together," Britt replied with conviction.

We both looked at Garcia.

"Seriously? You need to ask me if I'm in?"

"What was I thinking?" Britt replied, shaking her head. "So, what's our play now?"

"For starters, we've got a scared girl on our hands," I said, looking toward Naomi's car.

"I'm not surprised. Have you told her about the tracker?"

"Yeah. I mentioned the option of the safe house. She jumped at the idea."

"I'm sure she did."

"We'll drop her at the safe house. How about we grab a bunk there as well and hit the hay for a few hours?"

"Yeah, man. I'm about ready to drop dead," Garcia seconded the idea.

"We won't have much time. We'll have to split up in the morning. We've got many leads to follow."

"Copy that. What are you thinking?"

"I'll head out for Dry Creek in the morning. I'm positive Dexter isn't locked up in there. But someone's going to great lengths to make it appear he is."

"If that's the case, they'll do their best to stall."

"I know. But Flynn's pulling some strings."

"What if you find he isn't there? Are you going to raise the alarm? That will set up a big manhunt," Britt asked.

"It sure will. I haven't given that a thought yet. All I do know if he's out, I'm not going to let him be taken alive. He'll do the same shit again whenever he gets the chance."

"I hear you, bro," Garcia replied.

"I'll hit the road at 0700 hours. It's a two-hour drive. Should take less in the morning. They won't let me in before 0900. But I want to be at the prison gates at the exact time so I'm back here by midday."

"If the guards are in on this... which we're assuming is the case, there might be an ambush waiting for you. One of us needs to ride shotgun," Britt said.

"I did consider that. But it could only happen on the way back. They won't have any idea where I'll be driving in from. They can't stake out the entire highway. I'll be extra careful on the way back. But you two need to be here to follow up on some leads while I'm away. We're running out of time. Whatever the Cadys are up to, we can't give them a chance to simply disappear."

"But we better make sure we're strapped with some heavy-duty firearms before we roll out in the morning. We'll grab some serious firepower at the safe house," Garcia said.

"Copy that."

"And take the truck. That thing's a beast. It can plow through pretty much anything."

"Roger that. There are a few things you two need to get done by the time I'm back."

"Go on."

"Go to this place and check up on these two guys—Daniel Cruz and Hugo Ortiz," I said, showing them the address on the business cards on my phone.

"The ones who booked the private room?" Britt asked.

"Yeah. The job titles and the office sound like a front. Dig deep and see what you can uncover. Maybe we'll get lucky."

"Got it. Anything else?"

"Find out the name of the coroner who ID'd Carson's body. That body wasn't Carson's. I had a gut feeling back then. I'm sure I shot Carson in the leg when he was in the chopper. But they told me it was a DNA match. I thought I was mistaken."

"But not anymore?"

"No. As soon as I'm back from Dry Creek, my first move is to track down the ME who fudged it. Get him to talk."

"We'll jump on it first thing tomorrow. What about Slick?"

"He's scared shitless now that he knows he's on Sharky's hit list. I told him we'll take him to the safe house. But made it clear that his only shot at staying alive is if he leads us to Sharky and the Cadys. I'm sure he'll come up with something in the morning."

"Roger that. I'll give him some more reality bites to get his brain working faster," Garcia offered.

"Yeah, do that. Now let's get moving."

I called Naomi while Garcia signaled Slick to join us. Once we got into the truck, we handed all our phones to Britt. She put them inside a small box in the trunk. The box had a thick layer of copper mesh and tape all over its inside. It was designed in the form of a Faraday cage—a mechanism to block electromagnetic fields. Once you put a phone inside the box and close the lid, it becomes untraceable.

The box was standard equipment for any vehicle on a witness protection run. Even under fear of certain death, some people cannot be relied on not to start messing about with their phones. The last thing we wanted during witness protection was high-tech criminals tracking phones and zeroing in on the location of the safe house.

I got into the back of the truck along with Naomi and Slick. Before we got going, Garcia pressed a button in the driving console. It brought down a thin, opaque screen between the front and the back and blacked out all rear windows.

I could sense Naomi was getting nervous.

"It's standard procedure when we take anyone to a safe house. So you can't figure out its location. Once the threat is over and you go back to your regular lives, we don't want you coming back for a selfie," I explained.

"There goes my cool Insta update," she replied, chuckling.

The safe house was an ordinary-looking house nestled among rows of residential homes. Safe houses are designed in a way that makes their exterior blend seamlessly with the neighborhood, giving no indication of the fortified sanctuary that lies within. It looked like any other home in the suburbs, with a front and back garden, and a garage on the side.

Garcia turned into the driveway. The door to the garage began to open as soon as he turned in. We stopped inside the garage but made no move to get out.

A few seconds later, a door leading from the garage into the house opened. The man who got out of the door hardly looked like the kind of guy anyone would imagine in charge of a safe house. He looked remarkably unremarkable in his plain, loose-fitting nightshirt and pajama pants. To anyone watching from a distance, he was just a man woken up in the middle of the night.

Nothing about safe houses is supposed to attract undue attention, from their external look to the people who open the front door. The man went to the open garage door, looked outside, and pushed a button. The garage door began to shut. That was all part of the pretense—anyone watching from outside would see the man in his nightclothes, and not some Deputy dressed in tactical gear.

As soon as the garage door shut, we exited the vehicle and entered the house. The door led to the surveillance room, located right behind the living room at the front. There was an array of surveillance monitors on one wall, displaying the feed from several camouflaged security cameras all around the house. A fully alert Deputy sitting behind a desk kept an eye on the monitors.

We were led down a narrow corridor. Beyond the door at the end of the corridor was the actual safe house—a small living room leading to three sparsely furnished bedrooms. Two bedrooms had a simple bed, a small table, and a chair. The third one was more like a dorm, with two racks of bunk beds.

Naomi and Britt got the bedrooms. The rest of us took a bunk each. But before we settled in, Garcia hooked me up with some more serious firepower than the Glocks we had been packing. I grabbed a shotgun for close-range damage. If shit hit the fan and I found myself in a firefight, I had a Heckler & Koch HK416 A5 assault rifle as a backup. The last thing he handed me was something that could open many closed doors—a Marshal's badge. A circle with the words "United States Marshal" written on it and enclosing a star.

We hit the sack a couple of minutes later. Within a minute of my head hitting the pillow, I was asleep.

## CHAPTER 18

I woke up three hours later. The sleep, even though short, was enough to recharge me.

Flynn's message had already landed on my phone. It had an attachment—an official stamped paper approving my prison meeting with Dexter. I connected my phone to a printer and took a printout. When I went out into the living room, I was surprised to find Slick sitting on a couch, deep in thought.

"I didn't take you to be an early bird," I said as I fired up the kettle for some coffee.

"Morning, Marshal. Ever since you dropped that bomb on me, sleep's been elusive. I've been doing a whole lotta thinking like you said."

"That's what I like to hear. If you want to stay healthy, you better come up with a solid plan to get to Sharky."

"I hear you loud and clear. And believe it or not, I think I've got a plan. Shit, I can't belicve I'm saying this, but I reckon I should tag along with you to Dry Creek."

"Huh? You got my attention. What's up?"

"Remember I told you how the Crips started feeling like they got hustled after the deal went down?" Slick asked.

"Yes."

"Well, ever since Sharky's crew got their hands on them heavy weapons, they've been muscling in

194

on the Crips' turf. But the Crips haven't made any move yet."

"Why do you think they haven't made a move?"

"I can't say for sure. I ain't deep in the crew like that. I do some gigs for them because I'm out here on the streets, and I owe them for keeping my ass safe in the pen. But I ain't in on their plans."

"So what are you thinking?" I asked.

"Here's what I'm thinking, Marshal. Even from behind them bars, Crips stay plugged into the streets. They might just have the inside scoop on Sharky's hideouts."

"And you think you can get them to tell you?"

"I think so. They got unfinished business with Sharky, and that might make them cooperate, especially when they know you'll take out Sharky. Makes life easier for them."

"You might be on to something there. But there's one more thing I need you to find out from them."

"What's that? I'll give it a shot."

"I need to know how Dexter got the word out about the hit. Who's the guy who delivered the information? Dexter's sitting on death row—there's no way he was out there mingling with any gangs in the yard."

"That's true. I'll see if I can get them to spill the beans."

"Good. So how will this play out? You'll meet the guy inside Dry Creek? How do you normally contact them?"

"I don't reach out to them, man. They reach out to me. They gotta get hold of a cellphone, and that only goes down at specific times of the day. I gotta slide in there as a visitor, you know? And drop the word that Sharky's after my ass too," Slick explained.

"Who will you meet?"

"Chainz. He's the Crips' shot caller at Dry Creek. That dude's dangerous. He could snap my neck without breaking a sweat if he ain't feeling what I've got to say."

"Then you better work on your charm. Get him to like what you've got to say."

"I think I can handle that. But here's the deal, Marshal. I gotta roll solo when I meet him. If I roll up with you, Chainz is gonna think I've been snitching and cutting deals. I don't need every homie in the city coming after me. You've got to trust me on this."

"Yeah, I get it. But the thing is, you can't just turn up at the prison and ask for a meeting. The way it works is you'll need to put in an application. Prison authorities review it and get back to you. But given your track record and your parole status, I won't hold my breath if I were you."

"I hear you, Marshal. That's why I was thinking, if I roll with you, they might let me slide in. But damn, ain't it funny I'm trying to figure out how to break into prison?"

"Yeah, it's a real hoot. If you're sure of this, I'll pull some strings. You promise to be a good boy?"

"You can count on it, Marshal. I'll be like a straight-up boy scout. I'm trying to leave that hustle life in the rearview. Time to flip the script, you know what I'm saying? I ain't planning on setting foot in no damn prison ever again. Just visiting for a little meet is the most I can handle."

"Alright, then. I'll give it a shot. What's this guy's name?"

"Chainz."

"I mean the Christian name, dumbass. What his folks would've named him hoping he would turn out a model citizen one day. You can't put Chainz on an official form."

"Oh. I get what you mean. It's Shaquille Nichols."

"Alright. Be ready to leave in 20 minutes."

I didn't want to take the chance of Slick's entry being refused. I decided to call Flynn to make it as official as my visit. This time, he took the call on the second ring. And this time, he had his glasses on when he looked at the phone screen and saw it was me calling. His tone was a lot more cheerful.

"How're you holding up, Cowboy? Are you on your way to Dry Creek?" he asked.

"I'll hit the road in twenty minutes. I got the paperwork you sent. I need one more thing."

I told Flynn about Slick and how he could get intel from the gang inside prison.

"That can surely get you good leads. Arranging this won't be too much of a problem. This guy will be in general population. That's normal visitation. Death row was a different deal. I'll send you the paperwork for your guy in an hour. Let me know if you need anything else."

"I will."

"Go get 'em, Cowboy. Let's close this chapter once and for all."

"Roger that."

I disconnected the call and turned around to find Naomi standing in the doorway of her room. All she was wearing was an oversized T-shirt, which went down to her knees. The words, 'Set Your Warrior Free', were emblazoned across the front. It didn't take much to guess Britt must have given it to her. Standing there with tousled hair and drowsy eyes, the dainty hundred-pound warrior looked prettier than she already was. I was in a rush but found it hard to take my eyes off her.

"What are you doing up so early?" I asked.

"Says the man who looks all ready to hit the road. Did you even go to bed? Or have you been up all night fighting crime?"

"You have me confused with someone else. I'm just a plain old cowboy most of the time."

"If you say so. But the way you look and the way you went through those gangsters yesterday, I don't think plain and old come close to describing you," Naomi said with a playful look in her eyes.

Then she suddenly felt a little self-conscious and hurriedly added: "Anyway, I wanted to say thank you before you left."

"Not a big deal. You went out of your way to help us out. It's the least I could have done."

"I've been thinking about it. Had you not offered to hang around in the parking garage... you wouldn't have checked my car... and wouldn't have found the tracker. That weirdo could have been waiting for me," she said with a shudder.

"Don't worry about it. That guy won't be bothering you ever."

"You mean you'll neutralize the threat," she said, repeating my own words, before breaking into a huge smile.

"Yeah. You could say that," I replied, mirroring her smile.

Naomi took a couple of steps and stopped in front of me. The difference in our heights became even more apparent—she was at least a foot shorter than me. It was a good thing I hadn't gotten into my cowboy boots yet. But the difference in our heights didn't get in her way as she got up on her toes, held me by the shoulders, which made me involuntarily bend down a little, and gave me a soft peck on the cheek.

"Thank you, Axel, for looking out for me," she whispered.

"Not a big deal, Naomi," I replied.

Neither of us moved as her lips lingered around my face for a few seconds, the feeling of her soft breath casting a kind of spell on me.

"Actually, it is a big deal. See you when you're back," she said, giving me another soft peck before putting her heels back on the ground.

Then she turned and walked back to her room.

I stood glued to the spot for a couple of seconds, watching the gentle sway of her hips as she walked away. I got this feeling she would turn her head to glance back before entering her room. I didn't want to be caught out staring. I got my phone out of my pocket. But before I could transfer my gaze to the screen, she turned her head and caught me staring. Our eyes locked for a second before she smiled and went inside her room.

I woke up Garcia a few minutes before we were leaving and explained the change of plan to him. Then we hit the road at 0700 hours—me driving and Slick riding shotgun.

We headed east on the I-80 for a few miles before taking the exit for the I-580. The highway snaked through empty stretches of land dotted with vineyards and orchards. We soon left the coast way behind us, heading east toward the Nevada border. The landscape shifted dramatically as we approached desert country. The road stretched out like an endless ribbon, meandering through the barren terrain, with sand and rocks as far as the eye could see.

We arrived at Dry Creek in an hour and forty-five minutes. The prison had got its name from the town. Or maybe it was the other way around. Either way, Dry Creek was a typical prison town, with its economy and demographics significantly related to the presence of a large correction facility less than ten miles from it. The prison was the central focus and employer for a large portion of the town's population.

The road to the prison made its way through the high street running through the middle of the town. We headed north for a couple of miles before turning east. From the intersection, it was a straight road toward the prison. The prison compound became visible against the far horizon almost as soon as we turned.

After driving in a straight line for five miles, we began approaching the prison's external boundary. A chain linked fence topped with razor wire was set up all around the perimeter. The actual prison compound was about half a mile further inside the external perimeter.

We approached a heavy metallic barrier blocking the road. Two unfriendly faces walked out from a booth beside the barrier. Both had automatics slung across their bodies.

"State your business here," one man asked in a voice that was borderline hostile.

"Prisoner meeting," my reply was as curt and brief as his question.

He didn't like my tone and was about to follow up with another curt remark. But I cut the conversation short by handing him the document and flashing the badge. It was as official as it gets. Surly face didn't have any option but to wave us through.

With a low hum, the heavy metal gate swung open. The massive walls surrounding the prison loomed ahead of us. I could make out the rows of barbed wire crowning the tall concrete walls. There were two guard towers at both ends of the front boundary wall, with a third one in the center. The sight triggered a nervous reaction in Slick.

"Oh man, oh man, oh man! What the fuck am I doing voluntarily heading back to the slammer? Marshal, you'll take me back on the way out, right? Don't just leave me in there."

"Shut up, Slick. Focus on what you're here for. You stop dealing dope when you get back to the city and you'll be fine. Or your ass is going to land back here. It's your choice," I replied.

"Like I said, I'm gonna be a straight-up boy scout. Leroy James is a reformed man. I'll leave Slick behind when we head out of here."

"Good for you," I said a little absentmindedly.

I was too immersed in my own thoughts. This wasn't my first visit to Dry Creek. For a Marshal, making the occasional trip to prisons for prisoner transport is a normal part of work. But my last visit to this place hadn't been a routine one. Every moment of that trip was clearly etched in my memory. That was when I had led prisoner transport for Dexter after he had been sentenced.

Dexter had been close to death when I finally opened the roof doors that day two years ago to let the cops onto the roof. It wasn't like any of the cops who came rushing out were shedding any tears for him. Dexter had also executed two of their own when he murdered Deputy Mahone.

But Dexter wasn't a pretty sight when he was carried out. Most of his upper body was broken, bruised and bloody. Blood and gunk were oozing out of his right eye. Both his arms were skewed, both forearm bones were shattered, with shards of bone sticking out through the skin. His right palm was almost split in half. The photo of the ruthless killer being wheeled out of court on a gurney was splashed across all newspapers. It hadn't escaped the attention of human rights groups and Internal Affairs.

But I had Flynn's unconditional support. Every statement made by him and every law enforcement officer at the court insisted that after his violent killings of officers on duty, Dexter needed to be quickly incapacitated with brute force. There was also the fact that Dexter was able to pull off the escape attempt because the judge wanted to make some idiotic point when he refused to have a psychopath like him shackled in court. All that took a lot of heat away.

I wasn't suspended. Not for a day. Which was a bit of a miracle.

But I wasn't done with Dexter. I wanted to personally handle prisoner transport when we made the final run to dump him in prison to rot. It was a promise I had made to Kelly Mahone. Flynn and the entire team were behind me. Given all the heat we got, it wasn't an easy ask. There was no way my name could officially be on the duty roster.

But we pulled it off. Every Deputy assigned that day called in sick. Mysterious stomach bug they caught at a dinner the previous night. Last-minute replacements were hard to find. Almost every Deputy in the San Francisco office fit for duty was miles away conducting a bust. I had to step in as a last-minute replacement.

When Dexter saw me standing beside the open rear door of the prisoner transport vehicle, he stopped dead in his tracks. He looked like an Egyptian mummy—wrapped up all over in bandages and plaster. It hadn't been even three weeks since I had broken him. Dexter looked around frantically, trying to find a sympathetic face. He found none.

I had promised Flynn I wouldn't touch Dexter. I kept the promise. I didn't say a word throughout the trip. I simply kept staring at him, playing with my gun. Dexter must have been the only prisoner in history who was relieved at being handed over to prison authorities to be put on death row.

I felt the chapter close when the gates banged shut behind me. It was time for us to move on. I had no idea that chapter would turn out to be part of a longer story—one whose final act had yet to be written.

# CHAPTER 19

"We dumped Cady's ass in ad seg last night."

I was sitting in the office of Captain Elijah Thorne—the man who headed the team of Dry Creek State Prison's Correctional Officers. The man had just informed me Dexter was in solitary confinement. I knew it meant I couldn't have a regular face-to-face meeting with him.

Technically, it was Warden Healy who headed the prison. Thorne reported to him. But the Captain was the one who got things done in the prison. The *de facto* ruler of everything going on within those walls.

Thorne was a friendly enough guy, considering his job was to keep the lowlifes residing within those walls in line. Compared to the surly faces I met at the gates, he was like a ray of light. But there was something about the ray that gave me the feeling it was crooked. Thorne was smiling a little too much, like he was aiming to be my best pal. But the smile never reached his eyes.

"What happened? Dexter assaulted someone?" I asked Thorne.

"Yeah. Mean son of a bitch assaulted a guard. Broke his hand. We let him have it good, before throwing him in the hole. A week in there and he'll get in line."

"Two years on death row hasn't toned him down?"

"Nah. Guys like him... they don't make the world a better place until it's time for them to leave. We can't wait to put the needle in him. But you know how it is in California. They haven't put anyone down for almost twenty years."

I played along with the small talk for a while. But I understood Thorne's game. He was testing me. To see how much I would push. If I didn't, he would chat with me for a while before sending me back on my way. A prisoner being in administrative segregation meant he was cut off from all external contact. No visitors.

Unless it was a visitor with political clout. I knew very well I had that clout at the time. Flynn had made sure of that. The document he had sent me had been signed by the Governor. Had I tried to throw my weight around, even the Warden couldn't have prevented me from meeting Dexter. Thorne was lower down in the food chain to be able to do much. The only way such a meeting could be stopped despite an order from the Governor would be if the entire prison went into lockdown. But it was too late for that. I was already inside for the meeting.

But the thing was, I didn't necessarily want a face-to-face meeting sitting across a table. I only wanted to confirm the guy they had in the cell wasn't Dexter. For that, I didn't need to see him up close. Just a couple of questions would tell me if the guy was him or an impostor. And if, as I suspected, he was an impostor, I wasn't about to let Thorne know I was on to him. In fact, not having a proper meeting worked for me as it would make it easier for me to act like I had fallen for their trick.

When the dust settled, what needed to be done was for Dexter to be dead. Lethal injections and political maneuvering wouldn't matter after that. And once Dexter was out of the way, I would expose the entire lot of dirty officers who were in on this.

"How about I have a chat with the guy in ad seg now? I'll have to hit the road soon," I said, cutting to the chase.

"I don't think you get the idea of administrative segregation," Thorne replied.

"I do. But this isn't a routine visit. I'm sure the document explains that."

"You sure you want to see him? I guess I'm supposed to give you some kind of access to the guy, but how this works is up to me," he replied, his tone turning a touch less friendly.

"I'm listening."

"So long as the prisoner's in ad seg, he's not allowed to get out of his cell. And you surely can't be allowed inside the cell. You'll have to speak to him through a slot in the door."

"That'll work for me. I'm not aiming to hug him. All I need to do is talk to him."

"What about?"

"Marshal stuff."

"I see. Rawlins. Get your ass in here," Thorne picked up the phone on his desk and barked into it.

A young guy, not much above twenty, walked in. Everything about him, from the way he carried himself to the way he talked, told me he was a new recruit.

"Yes, Captain," he said as he came and stood beside the desk.

"The Marshal here wants a chat with Cady in ad seg."

"Chat? You mean... get Cady up here?"

"Rawlins, how long have you been working here?" Thorne asked, without making any attempt to hide his irritation.

"Uh, three and a half months."

"How many times have we brought a prisoner up here for a chat with a visitor?"

"Uh, never. Uh, you want me to take him down to ad seg? I've never even seen that done before."

"Well, it's your lucky day today."

"Right. So, you want me to get him inside Cady's cell?"

"No. Take Brogue with you. I've told him what to do. Just open the hatch. They'll talk through that. That OK with you Marshal?"

"Yeah."

Thorne didn't realize he had slipped when he mentioned he had told Brogue what to do. He had this all planned. I played dumb—didn't let on I had noticed anything out of the ordinary.

When I followed Rawlins out of the room, another guard was out there waiting for us. A stocky man with a weathered face and enough gray in the temples to declare he was an experienced hand. His face had the same devious expression I had earlier seen on his Captain's mug. They led me through a series of fortified corridors and gates, with each checkpoint requiring authorization before proceeding further.

As soon as we entered the ad seg section, it became clear why inmates called it "the hole". It was in the basement level. There wasn't any opening for sunlight to come through. The ceiling lights were dim, making everything seem a little more shadowy than it normally would. The walls looked solid and soundproof. There were ten cells with enough distance between them so that prisoners couldn't communicate through the walls. Each cell had a heavy iron door with a hatch at around waist level.

Brogue stopped outside a cell in the far corner, opened the hatch, and looked inside.

"Rise and shine, Cady. You've got a visitor," he said, rattling a baton against the hatch.

All I could hear from inside was an indistinguishable growl. I noticed Brogue had grabbed his phone and was looking at it. His thumb tapped on the screen a few times. He then looked up at me expectantly, his phone held casually by his side. I didn't need to stress out my gray cells to realize he had turned on the recording function. Every word I said down here would be scrutinized later by his boss.

"All yours," Brogue said, turning to me.

I nodded, went down on one knee, and peered inside the dark cell. It was a small, bare room, furnished with nothing more than a bed, a sink, and a toilet. The bed was laid out against the wall on the right. A man was sitting on the far end. A well-built man. With long, unruly hair and a beard.

Wearing a patch over the right eye. In the dim light, he surely looked like Dexter.

Captain Thorne and his guys had played their cards well. They knew they couldn't refuse me a meeting. So they planned it in a way that got me the meeting, but didn't let me get close enough to the man to be able to physically verify it was him.

The man in front of me could have been anyone with a similar build and height as Dexter. He had too much hair all over his face and was sitting too far away for me to be able to observe his facial features. He was wearing a long-sleeved vest, which covered all his tattoos. His right hand was too far away and in the shadows for me to be able to observe the scar. Apart from the general build, the only thing that indicated the man could be Dexter was his eye patch. But wearing one doesn't necessarily mean you're blind in one eye.

But I had a plan. All I needed to do to make it work was get the man inside the cell to talk.

"Well, well, well. Looks like someone's been a bad boy again," I addressed the man in a sarcastic tone.

He didn't reply.

"Did you get scared when you heard I was coming? I have a feeling you deliberately had your ass thrown into solitary?"

My second remark was meant to instigate a response. It succeeded in doing so.

"You think I'm scared of you?" he asked.

His voice sounded more like a low growl, like the sound was coming from low down in his throat.

It was almost impossible to make out anything based on the voice alone.

"We both know the answer to your question. You're shit scared of me."

"Keep kidding yourself. You can't touch me in here," he replied.

My plan was beginning to work. I had gotten him to respond. Once he got into the flow, it wouldn't take me long to confirm if the man in front of me was an impostor.

"Yeah, I guess I can't. But what's with the wild man look? It's like we've switched styles. You trying to copy my style?"

"I don't get you."

"I used to have long hair and a beard when I caught you. You were clean shaven. And now look at us."

"Nothing to do with how you looked. I felt like letting it grow."

The man failed at the first hurdle. I have never had a beard or long hair in my life. Had he really been Dexter, he would have asked what the hell I was going on about.

"I must say my beard wasn't as wild as yours," I asked, just to doublecheck my theory.

"I told you it's nothing to do with you."

"Remember *plata o plomo*?" I asked, setting my second trap.

*Plata o plomo*—the choice between silver or lead was what Dexter had tried to offer me. Those were the words he had said over the phone after he killed Mahone. The words that drove me to literally tear him apart.

"What about it?" he asked guardedly.

"This beach in Mexico you were planning to retire to after breaking out of prison. Didn't really work out, did it?" I asked, making it all up as I went along.

"I'll be there one day. Wait and watch," he said, walking blindly into my trap.

His answer confirmed my suspicion. The man in front of me wasn't Dexter.

"But what's this all about? You here to make small talk with me?" the man asked.

I carried on with the conversation, gathering more proof of the deceit. I also needed to give a credible reason for my visit to the man and the guards. I didn't want them to suspect I knew the truth.

"Remember what I said when I dumped you here?" I asked him.

"What?"

"I wouldn't let Carson's girl Fiona get away. You said I'd never find her. Well, guess what?"

Fiona was just a random name that popped into my head as I spoke.

"You found Fiona?" the man asked, picking up on the name.

"Yes. She was in Cuba. Living under a false name. I hauled her ass back. And seized all her assets. She's facing trial. You've got no one left on the outside to help you get out. That's what I came to tell you," I said, my voice increasingly getting cold.

I turned to the two guards.

"Let's go. I'm done here," I said.

They were only too glad to take me back to Thorne's office.

Thorne wasn't alone when I entered the room. A man wearing a crumpled business suit was sitting opposite him, with his back to me as I entered. When I took a chair beside the man and looked at him, I was in for a surprise. He was a stocky guy of around forty, about five foot ten, with a sprinkling of gray around his temples. It was a face I had become very familiar with in the last few hours.

It was Daniel Cruz—one of the two men who had booked the private room at Tokyo Dreams for the meeting with Dexter. I had looked very carefully at the photos Mitchell had sent me as well as the video feed at the Japanese place.

If I had any doubts about Thorne's culpability, they vanished the moment I laid eyes on Cruz. Those two had somehow orchestrated the plan of getting Dexter out of prison. Cruz must have rushed to the prison after Thorne informed him about my visit. Both must have done everything in their power to ensure I wouldn't figure out the man cooling his heels in solitary confinement wasn't Dexter.

But I was also getting the feeling the conspiracy ran deeper than simply getting Dexter out of prison. His escape had been arranged for some specific purpose. Taking out a hit on me and my team seemed more of a side play.

I was surprised Thorne had managed to place Dexter in ad seg and informed Cruz about my visit, all in a matter of a few hours early in the morning. Either Thorne or Cruz was an extremely efficient person. I didn't think it was Thorne. I was sure Cruz was running the operation along with his partner, Ortiz. I wondered why that guy hadn't turned up.

I was dying to know more about Cruz. But years of practice had given me the control not to let my face and body language reveal what I felt. That came in handy as I looked stone-faced at Cruz for about half a second before giving him a nod, and then looking back at Thorne.

"Got what you wanted?" Thorne asked me as I was taking a seat.

"I guess. I just needed to tell him something."

"I thought it was Marshal business. Do you know him personally?"

"Personally? I'm a Marshal, he's a prisoner... I'm sure you know how that goes."

I noticed Cruz was hanging on to my every word. When I entered the room and before I had taken the seat next to him, I had seen him checking messages on his phone. He was still acting like he was looking at his phone, but his thumb had stopped moving on the screen.

"I know. I looked in the file and found you two have a bit of history," Thorne replied.

"You mean my history with him was mentioned in his prisoner file?"

"Uh, I don't know. In the file... online... I read it somewhere."

"I'm impressed you research your inmates so extensively."

"Well, yeah, you've got to be on top of your game. Did he look any different from when you last saw him? What was that... two years ago?"

"Yeah, two years. I couldn't get to see much of him from that small hatch. At first, I thought it could have been anyone with the same kind of build. But then I remembered I was standing in a supermax facility. Who else could it be? So, yeah, he does look the same except for the wild-haired look he's got. You've been feeding him well—he still looks as well-built as he was," I replied.

Thorne didn't know exactly what to make of my reply. It was a deliberate move on my part, to leave him, and especially Cruz, guessing.

"Was he in a talkative mood?" Thorne persisted.

"I guess. It's not like we had a lot to talk about. But he sounded different from what I remembered."

"He got clubbed on the throat when we took him down. It's a miracle he can still speak. The blow could have broken his voice box," he replied.

Thorne had a ready explanation for everything. But it sounded too pat.

"But are you satisfied with your visit?" Thorne asked, more to reassure himself.

"Yeah. I guess."

I noticed Thorne looking at Cruz, as if confirming he was happy with my answers. It was at that point that Cruz jumped into the conversation.

"Hi, I'm Michael. Sorry I couldn't help overhearing your conversation," he said extending his hand, a broad smile on his face as he lied about his name.

"That can hardly be held against you," I replied, taking his hand, "I'm on my way out anyway. You two carry on whatever it is you were discussing."

"Nothing important was being discussed. I'm an accountant, going through all the books. Routine stuff," he offered the information.

"Accountant, huh? I hope all's right with the books. No mix-ups in there."

Cruz gave me a curious look, not quite sure how to interpret my answer.

"Not a chance. This place is run on a tight leash," Thorne butted in.

"I'm sure it is. Well, I'll get moving," I said, getting up.

I had given the two men lots to think about. It was time to head back and see how it played out.

"A Marshal's work must be busy. I gather you're attached to the San Francisco office," Cruz asked as I got out of the chair.

I knew he was trying to get an idea of what I intended to do. I didn't have any doubt he already had the complete lowdown on me. A man who could pull off the feat of switching a death row prisoner could easily dig out the background of a guy who had made him drop everything and come rushing to that prison in the middle of nowhere.

"Kind of. I move around a lot," I replied, leaving him about as informed as he was before my reply.

Then I headed out. I had done what I had come to the prison for. I had the answer to the perplexing question of who Mitchell had seen at

216

the Japanese restaurant. Mitchell had been right. The man he had seen was Dexter. The man on death row had not only managed to break out of prison but had done it in a way that no one had a clue about it.

A switch. A perfect escape. Spoilt only by Dexter's lust for revenge. That was what prevented his escape from the court when he couldn't resist gloating to me about killing Mahone. This time around, his thirst for revenge would be the end of him.

# CHAPTER 20

I walked out of the prison building and headed to my pickup. There was no sign of Slick yet. When we had arrived at the prison in the morning, I had walked with Slick to the visiting area and sorted out his visit before going to meet Dexter. We had decided to meet again in the parking lot.

As I walked toward the truck, I turned on my phone, which I had switched off when I headed inside. A minute later, a message landed on it. It was an alert telling me an external device had been implanted on the pickup. It was a special security feature of the official Marshals' vehicle. Any external object like a tracker or an explosive device implanted on the vehicle would show up on the vehicle's computer, which sent the information to whatever phone number was fed into it.

The message was sent out twenty minutes ago. It told me a device had been planted on the undercarriage. The size of the external object suggested it was a small tracker and not an explosive device. It must have been planted while I was down in ad seg. It didn't need a lot of guesswork to figure Cruz must have been behind it.

I wasn't surprised, especially after having found Cruz sitting inside Thorne's office. Given the comparatively short time, they must not have had the leeway to try to open the vehicle to install a microphone inside. If they tried to tinker with the locked vehicle, I would have received a message.

I got inside the pickup, punched the code into the gun safe behind the rear seats, and grabbed a Glock. I attached a custom holster to the back of my jeans and tucked the gun into it. Then I called Garcia.

"How did it go? I take it you've just come out," Garcia said as he took my call.

"Yeah. I'm waiting for Slick to get out."

"And? What's the verdict?"

"I met a man inside. Looked like Dexter but it wasn't him. The guy was an impostor."

"What?" Garcia exclaimed in disbelief.

"You heard me. Officially, Dexter's still in prison and they've placed him in ad seg. So all I could see through the hatch on the cell door was a shadowy figure sitting at the other end of the cell."

"Man, I didn't see that one coming."

"Neither did I. They said they put him in the hole last night. Must have been after Flynn made the call. Those guys must have come to know I would land there. It was a brilliant strategy."

"But... I'm guessing there was a but coming."

"Yeah. Their strategy didn't work. Even though... I let them think it did."

I told Garcia all that happened.

"Man, these guys are good. They pulled off an almost perfect escape," Garcia remarked.

"Yeah."

"But what's the motivation of the man taking his place?"

"I don't know. My guess would be money. Lots of it," I replied.

"But he'll remain a loose end, won't he? I don't think he'd be willing to take the needle for Dexter."

"Yeah, that struck me as well. But the likelihood of a death sentence being carried out in California is close to zero these days. Still, the fact remains this guy is a loose end."

"So... this Captain Thorne... sounds like he's dirty?"

"I'm sure of that. And at least some of the guards."

"But does he suspect you're on to him?"

"Not yet. He kept digging when I met him after the meeting with the phony Dexter. I left him hanging. But what about you? Managed to dig up anything?" I asked Garcia.

"Yeah. Carson's death is beginning to look like a cover up. The coroner who ID'd the body died a couple of weeks after that. An accident that took the man and his family."

"Oh. So, there's no way to dispute the claim that Carson died?"

"I guess eventually we can prove that by exhuming the body and matching it with Carson's DNA."

"Yeah. But all that's for later. Did you find any leads on Cruz and Ortiz?"

"I'm not sure. We did check out the address. It looks like a legit government trade office. They confirmed both guys work there. But both are supposed to be on leave. The story I was given was they've gone on a vacation to Hawaii."

"Hawaii, huh?" I asked.

"I didn't buy that for a second. They're supposed to have gone last week. We know that's bullshit."

"Yeah."

"I was getting the feeling the office was a front for something else. But there's no way to verify what it is? We're kind of stuck."

"What about their phones?"

"No luck there. Both are out of service. Must have happened overnight."

"Yeah. They're getting nervous."

"You bet. But that's a dead end for now. We don't have a play left until we get a new lead," Garcia replied, sounding a little disappointed.

"Maybe not. Guess who I met inside the prison... sitting inside the Captain's office?"

"I don't know, man. I'm out of guesses."

"Daniel Cruz."

"You've got to be kidding me."

"Nope. He was pretending to be an accountant."

"No shit."

"Meeting him there was something I didn't expect. But I managed to keep my surprise in check. Just stared blankly at him."

I told Garcia all that happened in Thorne's office. And the tracker they placed on the pickup.

"Who is this guy? He surely doesn't sound like any gangster I know. And that office they worked in didn't look like an illegal operation," Garcia said.

"I don't know, pal. I've been thinking... these guys are too meticulous... too well prepared to be random criminals. They're either mercs working for some private military group... or they're CIA. Or maybe ex-CIA or something."

"You know what? That's exactly what I was thinking. I just wasn't saying it as it doesn't make sense. Why would those guys want to break Dexter out of prison? But that trade office is the kind of front these intelligence guys use."

"It's a real puzzle. It's hard getting my head around it," I agreed.

I saw Slick coming out of the visitor's gate.

"Slick's on his way out. Let's see what he's got. I'll keep you posted."

"Roger that."

As Slick approached the truck, he broke into a moonwalk, doing a nice Michael Jackson impersonation. A few seconds later, he jumped onto the passenger seat, looking excited as hell.

"Yo, Marshal. That meeting went off like fire. Chainz was out for my blood when I told him I'd hooked up with you guys. But I worked my magic on him and made it out alive. That's a big deal, man. Now listen up, I got some sweet intel that'll put a smile on your face."

"Alright, lay it on me, MJ," I said, pressing on the gas as we got on our way.

"I got the lowdown on how this Dexter dude tipped off Chainz about the hit. It was through his lawyer. Dude called Jeremy Watkins. Watkins set up a meet with Chainz a couple of weeks ago, claiming he had a killer deal to offer. He managed to get Chainz to make him his official lawyer. To get that attorney-client privilege shit, you know, so they could have a meeting with no one listening in. That's how he sprung the deal."

"Good stuff. You got any leads on this Watkins? Is he holed up in the city?"

"Yes. He's this bigshot lawyer with this fancy-ass office downtown. Chainz had his business card. I've noted down the address. I've even got his cellphone number for you."

"Nice work," I said, feeling relieved that we finally had a solid lead to work with.

"But wait, there's more. Chainz is gonna hook me up with any intel he can gather on Sharky's hideouts. These guys keep moving locations, so it ain't a hundred per cent guaranteed, but there's a good chance."

"How's he going to pull it off?"

"Sharky's got them big-ass guns outside... but in there, in the slammer, Crips rule. Sharky's guys don't have no one watching their ass. So when Chainz starts asking questions, they're gonna start squealing. He's gonna make it happen in a couple of hours, once they're all out in the yard."

"Good work. But why's he doing all this?"

"Like I said, unfinished business with Sharky's crew. Sharky took out their main man in Hunters Point last week. Him and a crew of four. Cops never caught anyone for it, but Crips know it's them. They've got a big score to settle."

I sent a voice message to Garcia. I recorded the details of the lawyer, Jeremy Watkins, and asked him to track him down. Unless we got some other actionable information from Chainz, the lawyer was our best bet to get to the Cadys.

## CHAPTER 21

It was a seven-mile run from the prison to Dry Creek. As soon as we entered the town, I turned off the main street into a side alley and stopped in an isolated spot. I got out and went flat on the ground to slither under the undercarriage. It took me less than a minute to find and retrieve the tracker. I got back inside the truck, dumped the tracker into a cavity in the central console, and got back onto the main street.

"What was that all about?" Slick asked.

"That was a tracker. We are being tracked."

"Oh, man. That's not good news. But how did you know it was there?"

"Marshal business, Slick. This is what we do."

"Uh, OK. But aren't you going to throw that thing somewhere so they can't track us no more?"

"No. It's time we had a face-to-face with these guys."

"You know who they are?"

"I have an idea."

"What if they catch up to us?"

"We'll make it easy for them. We'll wait for them here," I said, stopping in front of a diner. "I'm sure you must be dying for a bite."

"No, man, I'm good. You know what, I feel very full today. Let's hit the road, Marshal. Get back to the city. We can eat back at the safe house."

"Relax. We're going to be fine."

"But what if they come guns blazing?"

"We'll blaze back."

"With what? And, uh, Marshal, I'm not sure if you were paying attention earlier, but I'm not really a violent kind of dude."

"Good for you. But you don't need to worry. People don't come guns blazing in this town. This being a prison town, security is tighter than you'll see in any regular town. Come on, let's grab a bite," I said, exiting the vehicle.

Slick reluctantly followed me as I headed inside the diner. As soon as I opened the door, we were greeted by the aroma of freshly brewed coffee mingled with the scent of sizzling bacon. Booths with light green imitation leather were set out against both walls. I found an empty corner booth and signaled Slick to follow me.

I did a quick round of the restroom area before taking my seat. There was no one inside. The back exit was locked. I sat with my back to the wall. The seat gave me a clear view of the entrance and the main street behind it.

I figured we would have company in about fifteen minutes. Cruz and Thorne must have already heard the recording Brogue made of my conversation with the fake Dexter. Cruz would have figured out I had caught out his man. If nothing else, the phrase, *plata o plomo*, would have told him. Cruz would understand the significance of the words that was lost on the fake Dexter. And when he saw the tracker on my truck go still in Dry Creek, he would hit the road to get to us.

We ordered eggs and bacon on toast. Both of us were hungry after the early morning drive. I kept my eye on the street as we wolfed it down. Slick, for a change, used his mouth only to eat. He was sensible enough to know that now we were in the game, there was no option but to see it through.

Once we were done with breakfast, I sat back with a cup of coffee. I hadn't taken more than a few sips when I saw a van pull up next to my truck. A big guy I hadn't seen before was in the driver's seat. Cruz was riding shotgun. Both tried to peer inside the diner. But the sun had been out for a while and the street was bathed in bright sunlight. They were not able to make out much.

The driver drove the van in front of the pickup and reversed it, almost touching the truck's front rammer, trying to box the vehicle in. He stopped the van and jumped out. He was a well-built guy of about thirty, six foot two and weighing about two hundred twenty pounds, blond crew cut hair. There was a lightness in his step, indicating a good level of fitness. The words "Ex-army" were practically stamped on his forehead.

Cruz got out of the passenger door. He was comparatively smaller, about five foot ten, but stocky. He was followed by a third guy who had been sitting in the rear. The third guy was identical to the driver in build and look. All three men had stern looks on their faces. All three wore business suits.

"Don't look back. Those guys are here. Don't move unless I tell you to. Got it?" I spoke to Slick in a tone that didn't leave any room for questions.

"Yes," he replied.

I reached down to adjust the right leg of my jeans, tugging it behind the knife sheath on my boot. If shit hit the fan, I didn't want anything getting in the way of my grabbing the knife. In the confined space around the booth, a gun could easily be deflected. But not a knife with a double-edged carbon steel blade. It could wreak havoc in close quarter combat.

My assumption was the men were there to interrogate and somehow detain me so I couldn't divulge the information about Dexter's switch to anyone. I didn't think there was much likelihood of violence. But the stakes were high. It wasn't the time to work on mere assumptions. I flexed my wrists and neck to get the circulation going. I was ready for action.

Cruz opened the diner door and looked inside. It didn't take him long to spot me. I almost waved at him but checked the impulse to do that. He took a step back and said something to the two guys. Then he got back inside the van while the two men walked into the diner. Both men were carrying a sidearm in a holster under their slightly loose-fitting jackets. I took a final sip of the coffee before pushing the cup to one side.

One man came and stood next to the table while the other guy remained a few feet behind him. Both men had their right hands hovering above their holsters, ready to draw.

"Sir, I need you to accompany me to the van outside," the man standing next to the table spoke in a curt voice.

"Why would I do that?" I asked.

"Because I said so," he replied, placing his hand on his gun, which was still inside the holster.

"Not a good enough reason, pal. You'll have to show me some ID."

"Sir, I'll ask again nicely once more. Get up now and accompany us to the van."

"Oh, you're asking nicely? You know what, pal... why don't you show me your not so nice way as well. And then I'll decide what works best for me."

The man was quick on his draw.

"How does this work for you?" he asked, his gun lined on me.

"I hope you realize, pal, it's very rude to point a gun at someone's face?"

"I can be ruder. Last warning."

"Last warning? You got me. I'm not screwing around with a loaded gun in my face. But I do want to point out I asked you many times not to be rude," I said, beginning to get up.

"Turn around and put your hands against the wall," he said in a sharp voice.

"I think your boss won't like this. What do you think, Cruz?" I said, looking toward the entrance.

Both men fell for it. They couldn't resist the impulse to look toward the door. That gave me about a second to make my move. That was all I needed.

The way the man had left his entire body open to me as he turned his head, I could have done any of a dozen different things to him. From knocking him out to giving him a painful lesson he would remember—anything from breaking his balls with my knee to breaking his hand or fingers. But the man hadn't tried to physically harm me. So, I opted to simply disarm him. Taking a gun from a man with years of training on how to use it would be an embarrassing lesson in humility he wouldn't forget.

Disarming a gun is a simple technique. But it needs to happen in a second—like a reflex action. Overthink it, and you'll end up blowing it. Literally. Someone, either you or the gunman or a bystander, is likely to get shot.

I moved both my hands toward his gun hand from opposite directions. I grabbed the barrel with my left hand, while slapping his wrist hard with my right. That made his wrist move outwards, which made the barrel move inwards and toward him. The sudden wrist strike made him loose his grip on the gun, which slid into my left hand. I transferred the gun immediately to my right hand, digging the gun into his midsection. At the same time, I used my left hand to grab the gun from the back of my jeans. I pointed the second gun at the other man.

"Don't even think about it," I said to the second man, whose hand had landed on the gun in his holster, but he hadn't yet begun drawing it.

Both men froze. They had been caught completely unawares. It had taken me two seconds to turn the tables on them—a second to disarm the first guy and another second to grab my own gun and point it at the second man.

There was sudden silence all around us. The only sound that came was from Slick. He simply uttered a single word.

"Whoa!"

"Take your gun out very slowly, place it on the ground, and kick it gently in my direction," I ordered the second man while keeping my gun digging deep into the other guy's gut.

The man looked at me warily but complied.

"You've no idea who you're fucking with," the man I had disarmed spoke in a voice heavy with menace, the embarrassment of being publicly humiliated making him angrier by the second.

"Listen, pal. I've been patient with you. One more word out of you and you'll be lying face down on the floor. Don't try me," I warned him.

That shut him up.

"Turn around, spread your feet, and put your hands against the wall," I repeated the same command the man gave me a few seconds ago.

The man complied without saying a word. His clenched jaw told me he was raring to have a go at me, but the gun digging deep into his gut made him think better of it. I quickly frisked him. He was clean. I grabbed his wallet and phone and threw them on the table. I found a few flex cuffs in his jacket pocket, which I stuffed in the back pocket of my jeans.

"Both of you, hands behind your back, I'm going to cuff you now," I ordered both guys. "It's either that or I knock you out. Choose one option."

Both men obediently placed their hands behind their backs. I cuffed them both.

"Now slide into the booth. Same side of the table."

I signaled Slick to get up while the two slid into his side of the booth. I whispered to him to move to an empty booth a few tables away. He nodded and moved away.

I slid into the booth and took a seat opposite the two men. Without saying a word, I field stripped both their guns, dumping their remains—frame, slide, barrel, recoil spring and magazine—in the middle of the table.

Next, I went through the man's wallet. His license had the name Rory Brown. But the thing that caught my eye was an employee badge. It had the man's mugshot, an employee number, and a very distinctive seal—an eagle bust above a shield with a 16-point compass rose in its heart. But no name on it. I had seen such badges before. I knew they didn't have a name as part of the need to maintain secrecy. And the seal made it very clear. The guy was a CIA agent.

I looked up to see both men trying to look intimidating. Most guys tend to back off when they know they've messed with CIA. But the two men had a couple of things working against them. One, it's difficult to pull off an intimidating look when you've got your hands cuffed behind you. And two, I knew these guys and their boss had fucked up real bad by being involved in a cover up of this magnitude, and that too on American soil, where they didn't really have any jurisdiction.

"CIA, huh? I thought they would have better recruitment standards. Or is it a fake card you picked up at a pawn shop?" I asked, looking at the pair with an amused expression.

"You've no idea what you've messed with," the guy called Rory spoke through gritted teeth.

"You think this badge gives you *carte blanche* to do whatever the fuck you want to do? I've got news for you, pal. You guys are screwed," I said.

That shut him up once again. By that time, Cruz had run out of patience waiting for his men to come out with me. He had gotten out of the van again and stood at the entrance, trying to make out what the hell was taking his men so long.

"There's your boss. I'll call him over," I said, giving a wave to Cruz, signaling him to come over.

Cruz had a puzzled look on his face. From where he stood, all he could see was me sitting facing him while his men had their backs to him, like we were having a discussion. He had no option but to walk over toward our corner, the expression on his face a mix of confusion and irritation.

"Hello again. It's Michael, right?" I asked in a cheerful voice as he walked over, like greeting an old pal.

Cruz didn't have a clue what was up until he had crossed the other tables and stood next to ours. It was then that reality dawned on him. His gaze fell first on the parts of the guns spread out in the middle of the table. The next thing he saw was both his guys had their hands cuffed behind their backs.

The man was experienced enough to understand he had lost the hand. He made no attempt to go for his gun. I could make out the outline of a shoulder holster through his suit.

"I hope everything is in order with the prison's books, Michael," I asked, my voice still friendly,

232

but with an extra emphasis on the false name he had given me earlier.

Cruz had a grim expression on his face. I could feel his mind working overtime, trying to figure out a sensible move.

"I'm guessing you're holding a gun under the table," Cruz said in a matter-of-fact voice.

"I'm impressed—an accountant and a detective. Must come in real handy in the trade office where you work. Guys, why don't you squeeze in and make some room for your boss?" I said to the two cuffed guys sitting in front of me.

Both scowled heavily but obeyed my command. They had seen in my eyes I hadn't said it in a frivolous way. The two large men tried their best to squeeze against the wall. But the seats weren't wide enough for them to make room for the stocky Cruz to squeeze in as well.

"Alright, you proved your point. Why don't you and I have a chat? Just the two of us," Cruz said.

"We will. Don't you worry about that. You'll get my full attention soon. You've got a lot of explaining to do. Pull up a chair and join us. We'll set some ground rules before we talk," I replied.

"Alright," he sighed, pulled a chair, and sat down. "What next?"

"How was Hawaii? I heard you're on vacation," I asked.

"How about we cut out the bullshit?" Cruz replied, trying hard to control his irritation.

"Really? You want to do that? Lay your cards on the table? Let's start with your real job, Michael. Or is that Daniel?"

"OK, you got me. I think you already know I work for a trade office. I'm a trade analyst."

"I thought you wanted to cut out the bullshit. I'm not asking about the job you use as a cover," I said, tossing Rory's wallet on the table, with his CIA badge open.

Cruz was silent for a few seconds. He simply glared at his two subordinates with murder in his eyes.

"It could be fake, you know," he made a half-hearted attempt to still play me.

"Sure, it could be. In fact, I asked GI Joe here if he got it at a pawn shop," I said, looking at Rory.

"Alright," Cruz sighed once again. "You got me. How about the two of us have a chat now? My men can wait in the van."

"You want to chat... you come out clean. I'm guessing you know everything about me."

"Yeah, Marshal for five years. Headed their SWAT team. On temporary assignment since yesterday. Joined the Marshals as an army vet with ten years' service record. Retired Major Axel Blaze. Special Forces. 75th Rangers. Delta Force. Distinguished Service Cross, Silver Star, Bronze Star. I had told these two to be very careful and keep their distance while talking to you," he replied.

The two cuffed guys kept their eyes glued to the table while Cruz talked.

"Right. Your turn now. Tell me exactly who you are. Then we'll talk."

"Alright. You already figured out a lot. I really am a trade analyst now. With a special focus on arms trafficking. But I did spend a decade in the field before this. Mostly Eastern Europe, the Middle East and Africa. And eight years in the Service before that. Marines. Ask me anything else and I'll answer."

"What does Ortiz do?"

"You know about him?"

"You two seem to come as a package deal. All the intel I got from my sources told me you two are always together."

"Well, yeah, he's my partner," Cruz replied with a wry smile. "Same job profile as mine. Similar background."

"Where's he?"

"I'll tell you about him. How about we hit the reset button... make this thing a little more civil?"

"You mean cut your musclemen loose?" I asked, unable to resist taking another dig at the two cuffed men.

"That would be a good start. They'll go wait in the van while we chat."

"You two promise you won't jump me if I cut you loose?"

"They won't," Cruz replied on their behalf.

"Alright. Bend forward," I said, holstering my gun, pulling out a boot knife, and cutting through their flex cuffs.

Cruz handed them the van keys.

"Shall we clear the table? If that's fine with you?" Cruz asked, looking in turn at me and the parts of the two disassembled guns lying in the middle of the table.

I nodded.

The men picked up the parts and headed out without looking back. Cruz turned off his phone and placed it on the table between us. I ordered more coffee.

It was time to talk.

# CHAPTER 22

"This whole thing... it's not something recent. I don't even know where to begin."

Cruz was fiddling with a fork, trying to organize his thoughts.

"How about you tell me why the CIA's messing about with prison breaks?" I asked.

"It's a long story. This was such a clean operation. Perfectly planned. How did you even get to know about it?"

"I know you've been a field agent. You're good at this stuff—getting people to talk to you. But that's not the way it's going to work today. You guys fucked up bad. Put my men in danger. It's up to you to convince me it was for a good reason."

"I know we fucked up. But I don't understand how your guys were impacted by what we've done."

"You really have no idea? Dexter played you, in that case."

"I seriously don't have an idea. But I know we fucked up. Alright, I'll answer all your questions. And then you tell me your story. Do you know the history of the Cady brothers? How they became the biggest arms dealers on the planet?" Cruz asked.

"I've got some idea. But why don't you take me through it."

"Alright. The way they made it big... well, they simply lucked out. Happened to be in the right place at the right time. This was the end of the eighties. Their family had moved to Eastern Europe for a few years. And then the Soviet Union collapsed. All these new countries were being formed, most of them with a huge arsenal, including nuclear weapons, and not much of a government controlling them. Everything was up for grabs. All you needed was to be a wheeler-dealer. And these guys were good at it. It was all over the papers at the time. You must have read about it."

"Yeah."

"And that they were captured in a joint operation by the ATF and DEA."

"Yes."

"What isn't known about it was it was our guys who coordinated everything at the back end while the deal was being made."

"I did wonder why there wasn't any mention ever of the CIA's involvement."

"We got burnt early on. Stayed in the background after that."

"Got burnt how?"

"We used the Cadys' network to supply weapons to an insurgent group in Latin America. I can't give you specifics, but we were left with egg in the face. Even more so when we discovered later the Cadys had managed to get their hands on nuclear rods from one of their contacts."

"Nuclear rods? You mean weapons grade?" I asked, genuinely surprised.

"Yeah, man. U-235. 95% enriched. Their contact was an ex-KGB operative. He had access to decommissioned Soviet stockpiles."

"No shit."

"That was the whole reason we launched the multi-agency international operation. The Cadys were searching for a buyer. That weapons grade shit is worth a lot of money... but only if you get the right buyer. And finding buyers with that kind of money, while keeping it hush-hush so you don't get a bull's eye painted on your back... well, it isn't an easy task. When we heard whispers of nuclear material on the market, we set up the sting. Involved DEA and ATF. And you know how we nabbed them in Dubai?"

"Yeah."

"What didn't come out was the operation wasn't the success it was claimed to be. Everyone was in too much of a rush. The operation had been on for a year. Everyone wanted results. There was too much pressure. The agents moved in too soon. We nabbed the Cadys, along with a big arsenal—guns, explosives, short-range missiles..."

"But not the rods?" I asked.

"Right. We never found them. And once the Cadys got caught, they lawyered up. And wouldn't consider any deals."

"Because they thought they could use the rods to arrange an escape?"

"Yes. We realized that later when we brainstormed about it."

A wild thought suddenly struck me. The Cadys' escape attempt from the court had been a highly professional affair. It could only have been pulled off by someone with access to huge resources. I wondered if it could be someone in the CIA trying to save his ass—helping them escape in exchange for the location of the nuclear rods.

"Was it one of you guys who orchestrated their escape from the court?" I asked, trying hard not to let emotion enter my voice as the long-buried anger at Mahone's killing began to rise once again.

"What? No, man, you're way off target. I know people think we do a lot of shitty stuff... but not that, man. Not on American soil," Cruz replied, sounding a little indignant.

I felt convinced he wasn't putting on an act.

"Who was it then?" I asked.

"I don't know. I can only guess. Something on that scale... it must have been some well-funded insurgent group, some foreign regime, someone desperate to get their hands on the rods. My guess would be either a Middle East terrorist cell, maybe ISIS, or it could be the Iranians. They've been trying forever to enrich uranium to weapons-grade level. It would give them a jump start to get their hands on these rods. I've tried asking Dexter directly. But he didn't tell me."

"OK. I believe you. But again, why did you guys get involved in breaking him out?"

"Yeah. I'm getting to it. We thought the matter was buried once Dexter was sent to death row and Carson died."

"You guys really believed Carson died?" I asked, sounding unconvinced.

"You mean you knew he was alive?"

"I had my suspicions. I'll tell you in a minute."

"Well, there was a DNA match. There wasn't any reason for us not to believe it."

"Alright. Go on."

"Six months ago, we again began hearing rumors of someone looking to sell nuclear rods."

"Let me guess... that was Carson rising from the ashes with a new look."

"How do you know all this, man? I can't figure out your deal. Not more than a handful of people within the CIA know Carson's alive," Cruz said in a surprised voice.

"It was my eagle-eyed Deputy... he spotted both brothers. I always knew in my gut that body two years ago wasn't Carson's."

"What made your doubt it?"

"I had shot Carson in the leg while he was escaping in the chopper. The burnt body that was supposed to be his didn't have any bullet hole. But like you said, the DNA evidence came out. And I figured I might have been mistaken. Things were crazy on the roof that day. So, I decided to ignore my gut feel. But once I got the call from my guy saying he thought he had seen the Cadys, I got on the next flight to San Francisco. Carson is an easy guy to spot if you know him well. His plastic surgery didn't make him as invisible as he thinks it did."

"You've got a point there. That man's deluded. He has been all over town for a week. When we met for the first time, he had this cocky attitude about him... like he was getting a big kick out of being out in the open in front of us. He calls himself Ronin these days."

"Yeah, I know."

"Why am I not surprised?"

241

"Did you guys catch on to him from the start?" I asked, bringing the conversation back on topic.

"Not really. We had never interacted personally with the Cadys before this. Which was a good thing, or he might have caught on to us from the start. We had prepped well, which included a backgrounder on the Cadys' operations as a case study. But when we set up the first meeting, we had no clue who we'd be running into. And, unlike you, we didn't have any doubts about Carson's death. But all the meetings were being recorded. When one member of our back up team saw the recording, he did think the guy resembled Carson. And then, in the next meeting, the dude brought up the topic of Dexter. That was the clincher."

"So, how did it play out?"

"When we set up the sting this time, we went solo... didn't involve any other agency."

"How did you initially touch base? Did Carson handle everything? Was their lawyer involved at any time?"

I already knew the lawyer wouldn't be involved in this kind of a deal. I asked the question to confirm if Cruz had any idea about the lawyer and the fact he was dirty as hell, making shady deals for Dexter.

"It was Carson. No lawyer. You don't have lawyers in these kinds of deals," Cruz replied.

"Just making sure. So, what happened?"

"Ortiz and I posed as the buyers, working for a rebel group in Latin America."

"Venezuelan?" I asked, remembering Mitchell had told me their vehicles had Venezuelan diplomatic plates.

"Yes. Seriously, man, how much do you know?"

"Not much. Just some intelligent guesswork."

"Well, that's a little too intelligent for my comfort."

"You guys shouldn't have been moving around in Hummers with Venezuelan diplomatic plates."

"You know about that too? Fantastic. And here I was thinking we were the seasoned pros at this. We deliberately did that so those guys would buy our cover. We knew they'd surely check the plates."

"But why Venezuelan?"

"It had to be some Latin American country. Ortiz and I don't really look like we could be representing an African or Middle Eastern group."

"Yeah. Right."

"And we had a couple of good contacts at the Venezuelan embassy."

"It was a good cover. But Dexter let you down. I'll tell you about it in a minute. Go on," I said.

"Right. It took some time before Carson took the bait. But once we began talking, he brought Dexter's name into the conversation. He said only Dexter knew the exact coordinates of where the rods are hidden. It was then that he revealed the rods were inside the country. We didn't have any option but to play along. We told him we had the money and the connections to bribe the hell out of the entire prison system."

"So... is Thorne dirty or not?"

"Well, he is. He did it for the money. But we had to work to get him onboard. He agreed to it only on the condition that we'd do a switch and not a prison break."

"But he doesn't know what your operation is all about?"

"No."

"Who does he think you guys are?" I asked.

"He doesn't think about it. That was part of the deal. We do this switch for a week or less, and he gets paid. No questions asked."

"Who else is in on it? The warden?"

"No, just Thorne and three prison officers. The warden, deputy warden, no one has a clue."

"Very impressive. You guys did pull off the perfect switch."

"Until you came along. But I still don't get how you found out. You told me your Deputy saw them somewhere. Was he able to make a positive ID just by a passing glance?"

"He might not have under normal circumstances. But Dexter screwed it up for you. Your planning and execution were close to perfect. But he's an egomaniacal psycho. That's what got him caught out. Do you know how I was able to catch him at the courthouse two years ago?"

"Not really. I just know the bare facts. Dexter killed three officers. One of them was a Marshal from your team. But you stopped his escape. With brute force."

"Do I detect a hint of judgment?"

"No, man. No judgment at all. I'm just stating the facts I know," Cruz replied defensively.

"Dexter would have escaped. But he couldn't resist the urge to boast to me about killing my guy."

I told Cruz about Dexter's threat of "*plata o plomo*". And how he revealed his location by calling me on the radio. And then what I did to him once I had caught up.

"Man, I've seen his scars. You're one guy I don't want getting mad at me. But hang on... so, is that how you caught out my guy in prison—*plata o plomo*? That was a smart move," Cruz said.

"Trapping him wasn't too difficult. I knew you guys must have prepped him. But unless the man was actually there and part of what went down that day, there's only so much he could have done to prevent his cover from being blown."

"I know."

"What's going on with the nuclear rods? Are you sure they exist? And on US soil?"

"The rods do exist. The ex-KGB operative I told you about... he was real. We received confirmation from multiple sources he had managed to smuggle the rods out of Eastern Europe. As for whether they are on US soil, I only have Carson's word for it. But there's a high probability he isn't bluffing. And we can't take a chance on it."

"So, do you guys have a fix on them?"

"Not yet. They've been stalling. But it's supposed to happen tonight."

"And that's why you came running all the way here so I wouldn't fuck it all up by blowing the whistle on Dexter?"

"Yes," Cruz replied, looking me straight in the eye.

"And how do you know the Cadys won't just take off and sell the rods to some other buyer?"

"We know there's a risk. We've taken precautions. They agreed to pre-conditions before we got Dexter out. They are only allowed to move in the vehicle we've provided for them. That Hummer your man saw—the one with the diplomatic plates. We've got live tracking on that and their phones. Two of our men drive them around."

"How long has Dexter been out?"

"Two days."

"Has he been compliant?"

"Yes."

"No. You're wrong."

"Why? I've held up my end. Told you the entire story. It's time for you to tell me what you're doing out here in Dry Creek."

"Fair enough. Guys like Dexter never play by the rules. Even before you broke him out, he had already set up a hit on me and my team—all of us who were part of the security detail during his prisoner transport. They have already made two attempts. We rebuffed both. Caught the men. And got them talking. That's how I knew."

"When did all this happen?"

"Last night. And the hit is not just out on us. He's even going after the family of my Deputy he killed at the court—the one for whom I almost physically tore him apart."

"Fuck!" Cruz said and went silent for a few seconds.

I could see his mind was on overdrive. He had just found out Dexter might not be as easy to control as he was hoping. And if this mission didn't turn out the way he had planned, it wouldn't be just his career going down the drain. He would be responsible for losing the nuclear rods as well.

"I hope you believe I didn't have a clue about this," Cruz finally said.

"I believe that. But I also believe you inadvertently helped him set up the hit."

"What? What do you mean inadvertently?"

"You must have paid Carson an upfront amount to seal the deal. I won't ask you to confirm it, won't even ask how much you paid, but I know that's the only way these guys got their hands on the resources they needed to float the hit. I don't think Carson has been swimming in cash all this while he's been away."

This time Cruz didn't respond. I took his silence as confirmation of my claim.

"So, you see, pal, it looks like we are at cross-purposes. Because no matter what, I'm going to hunt down Dexter," I said, holding his stare.

"Even if it means we lose the chance of getting our hands on the nuclear rods... and they land in the wrong hands? On American soil?"

"You don't need to sell me the patriotic pitch, Cruz. You know I'm a soldier. Always will be. I'm not about to do anything that puts the rods in the hands of any nutjobs. Securing them takes priority. But if you think you're going to give the Cadys a free pass after that, I'll tell you in straight terms—that's not gonna happen. I'll hunt them down."

"I've got no problem with that. Make no mistake—we didn't break Dexter out to give him a free pass. That fake Dexter you just met... you think he'd be willing to spend the rest of his life on death row?"

"I was wondering about that. Who is the guy? And what's your plan for him?"

"He's just an actor playing a role. A role that pays well. But that's about all the commitment he has to this thing. He'll carry on with the charade for four days. That's it. After that, we get him out and cut him loose. We can't keep him in there forever."

"And what happens then? You can't have an empty cell forever," I pointed out.

"The plan is to dump Dexter's ass back in prison."

"And pretend like none of this ever happened?"

"Yes."

"Well, there's one little hitch."

"You?"

"Yes."

"But why? You gave him what was coming to him. And it was well deserved—I'll be the first person to accept that. But why not let him rot on death row?"

"There's this small issue of the hit out on us. He had that done while he was on death row inside prison. And when he put my Deputy's family on the list, he crossed a line he can't cross back."

Cruz remained silent, not really knowing how to respond.

"Also, this neat little plan you've devised isn't going to work out. It's already beginning to fall apart. It's not just me who knows Dexter's out. His stupidity made sure of that. He's recruited a local gang and is supplying military-grade guns to them. We got Dexter's name from one of the hitmen. You won't be able to keep a lid on this for long. And it's only going to get worse. That deal you're hoping will go down tonight... that's not gonna happen. I can see from your face you're beginning to realize that as well," I said.

"I know, man. There are too many things that can go wrong. All we can do is try to make sure they don't. Me and Ortiz, we've got our careers on the line."

"That might be the least of your worries if the brothers manage to escape. Not just escape, but get their hands on the rods and sell them to someone else. I'm sure they would have an alternative buyer lined up. Whoever arranged the escape attempt two years ago, you think they'll just hang around and let them sell the rods to you? The Cadys are dangerous, but they wouldn't want to fuck around with the kind of people who could arrange multiple explosions in the heart of San Francisco and then whisk Carson away in a chopper. That could be the only reason for them to be stalling, because your cover is good. I don't have any doubts about that."

Cruz was beginning to look more worried by the second.

"You said the exchange was going to happen tonight. Did they give you a time and location?" I asked.

"The time... yes. 10:00 p.m. But not the location."

"You sure they're not playing you? When was the last time you had a definite location on the Cadys?" I asked him.

"They're being constantly monitored. Their phones, the Hummer, our guys..."

"Yeah. But when was the last you talked to them?"

"Last night. It's not like we're friends."

"But how about your men? When was the last time you heard from them?"

"This morning. I had a word with them before we left San Francisco. I left Ortiz at the base office to monitor things while I rushed here."

"How often do you touch base with them?"

"They leave a message on the hour. Every hour."

"When was the last contact?"

"I don't know, man. It's 10:00 a.m. now. I guess they must be making contact right about now. I'll have to check. You're beginning to make me nervous," Cruz replied, turning on his phone.

"Make the call. I sure hope I'm wrong. But these guys... they are twisted."

"Give me a minute. I'll go make the call," Cruz said as he hurriedly walked over to another booth to call his partner.

# CHAPTER 23

When I turned on my phone, I found it had two missed calls—one from Garcia and the other from an unknown number. I called Garcia.

"You gotta watch your phone, bro. We've been getting worried," Garcia said, as he took the call on the first ring.

"Sorry, pal. You won't believe the bombshell conversation I just had."

"Hang on, Britt's with me. I'm putting it on speaker."

I brought them up to speed with everything Cruz had told me.

"CIA broke out Dexter?" Britt asked, her shock evident in her voice.

"Man, I didn't see that coming," Garcia added.

"I know. Even though I got the idea when I saw him inside the prison, but it was still a shock when he said it to my face," I replied.

"Are you sure about the rods? That makes this a whole new ballgame."

"Yeah. I'm still trying to get my head around it. Did you find out anything about the lawyer?"

"That was the reason I called."

"Slick said he's this bigshot lawyer with a fancy-ass office downtown."

"Fancy-ass my ass. He's got this space at the back end of this building that looks good from the front. But the office entrance is through the back alley. Back alleys are the same everywhere. Britt and I parked ourselves there soon after we got your message. No sign of the guy yet. And the office is locked. I've asked my guy to track his phone to get a location. I'm waiting for him to get back."

"Good. He's our best lead for now. Let's first find out if the CIA guys still have the Cadys. Wait for my call. It's time I hit the road. I'll be with you guys in a couple of hours."

"Roger that. But wait, there's one more thing... you know the Deputy back at the safe house— Matthews? He just called me to say your girlfriend's been driving him nuts."

I could hear Britt chuckling.

"What? What girlfriend?" I asked.

"Your Japanese babe, bro. Back at the safe house."

"Hardly my girlfriend, pal."

"I don't know, man. You've got this way of working your charm on the low. Anyways, she told Matthews it's extremely important she talks to you. He called me as he couldn't get through to you."

"Oh, right. I've got a missed call from an unknown number. That must have been him. I'll call him."

Before I could call the safe house, I saw Cruz get off his call and walk back to my table. He looked worried.

"Worrying news?" I asked him.

"I'm not sure. I can't get a hold of anyone. And Ortiz's line is busy. I've left a message to call back immediately."

"There's no point hanging around this place. Are you guys headed back to San Francisco?"

"Yes," Cruz confirmed.

"Let's hit the road. Whatever either of us does next, it will have to be back there."

"Makes sense. But, uh, where do we stand now? Do we have some sort of understanding?"

"First get a handle on whether you still have the Cadys. And let me know. We'll take it from there. I'm not blowing the lid on Dexter until you've got your hands on the rods. That's all I can promise for now."

"Thanks. That's all I need."

We exchanged numbers as we got up. I signaled Slick to join me. We walked out to the pickup.

"Hang on, Cruz. I've got something for you," I called out to him as I opened the driver's door.

I reached in, grabbed the tracking device I had uninstalled from the undercarriage, and handed it to Cruz.

"I believe this is yours."

He looked like he was about to pretend he didn't have a clue what I was talking about. But then he decided against it.

"No more bullshit. It's a promise," he said sheepishly.

We were soon on our way to San Francisco. As soon as we hit the highway, I called the safe house. Matthews soon put Naomi on the line.

"Hey, Axel," Naomi answered in an excited voice.

"Hey. Everything alright?"

"Yeah. All cool. The thing is, I remembered something I think might help you grab the weirdo."

"Good. What's it?"

"You guys can do all the high-tech spy stuff, right? Track phones... shit like that."

"I guess."

"I'm not sure if I told you, but that day, he made an origami dragon from a napkin and gave it to me. I thought it was really cute. But that was before he began hitting on me. Anyway, when I got home that night, it was in my pocket. Next morning, I was fiddling with it when I found something written on it with a pen. Some characters in Japanese and a number. I can speak Japanese because my parents speak it, but I can't read it. So I don't know what the words meant. But the number... I think it could be a phone number."

"It sure could be. Where's it? Do you have it with you?"

"No, that's the thing. It must be lying in a corner in my living room. That's where I threw it."

"No problem. We'll take you there to retrieve it. This could be very important. Good you told me."

"Shall I go over to my place and grab it? I'm sure it will be alright to get out in the daytime."

"No. Don't even think about it."

"Uh. OK," she replied, sounding unconvinced.

I felt I needed to give her some reality bites so she wouldn't get too lax and do something stupid— like wanting to leave the safe house. It wasn't like she was a prisoner there.

"Naomi, listen to me. I didn't want to scare you yesterday, but I think that guy has been tracking you since that night when you thought some guys in an SUV were watching you. That means he knows where you live. You get what I'm saying?"

"Yeah," she replied, her voice suddenly very subdued.

"Don't worry about it. It's just a matter of a day or so. We'll catch these guys soon. But until then..."

"Yeah. Sure. I get it. I'll sit tight."

"Good. Hang in there. I'll have a word with Britt. She'll pick you up from the safe house and take you to your place for a quick visit."

"Uh, OK. Uh, you sure we'll be fine? Just us two girls?"

"Just two girls? Let me tell you about Britt. She isn't just any girl. When it comes to combat missions, she's a one-woman wrecking machine. I would pick her any day to watch my back. I wouldn't just send you out with any rookie Deputy. You hear what I'm saying?"

"Loud and clear. That's one hell of a reference. No worries."

"Good. Wait for her. I'll catch you later."

I called Garcia again. When he came on the line, I asked him to put me on speaker before telling him and Britt what I had just learnt from Naomi.

"Sounds like a promising lead. I'll go to the safe house now and take Naomi to her place," Britt said.

"Roger that. Garcia, I'm on my way. Should be with you by 1200 hours."

"Copy that."

Even before I had gotten off the call, I had begun getting the ring from another incoming call. This time, it was Cruz.

"What's up?" I asked.

"I hate to admit it, but you were right about the Cadys," Cruz said, sounding dejected as hell.

"What happened?"

"When Ortiz didn't get the call from our guys, he tried calling them back, but no luck. Then he went to this house we have arranged for them to stay in. All he found was our two guys, hands and ankles cuffed. No sign of the Cadys."

"Believe me, pal, it doesn't give me a kick to say, 'I told you so'. But your two guys are lucky to be alive. What did they say? Dexter must have left them alive for a reason."

"Yeah, they left a message. Dexter said the deal's still on. But they'll do it on their own terms. They won't move around at our beck and call."

"They said the deal's still on?"

"Yeah. They'll call us and let us know the time and location. But if they find us trying to track them, the deal's off. What do you make of it?"

"They've got you by the balls," I said the first thing that came to mind.

"Thanks for stating the obvious. But seriously, what do you make of all this?"

"Seriously? Alright. Your cover is still intact. They don't suspect you to be anything but what you told them. Or your guys would have been dead. That's one piece of good news."

"Uh-huh. And the bad news?"

"I'm not done with the good news yet. They don't want to mess with you until they've got their hands on the money and can vanish. And it's not like they don't have a lot of men and weaponry at their disposal. It means they're scared you've got the resources to track them down. That's why they have made the threat of the deal being off if you try to track them."

"Hmm... makes sense. But that doesn't help us."

"It will. Trust me on that."

"Alright. And the bad news? Beyond the obvious."

"You mean beyond your nuts being in their hands?" I asked, unable to resist taking another dig at him.

"Yes, if you could be so kind as to further expound your theory?"

"OK. The bad news is I don't think they plan to hand you the rods. They've got another buyer lined up, or else they wouldn't have dared to piss you guys off. All they see you as now are standby buyers in case the other guys fall short for some reason. And more importantly, they want to make sure you don't screw up things for them until they're done and ready to take off."

"So, basically, we're screwed."

"Looks that way. But this thing isn't completely FUBAR yet. You're not all out of options."

"I don't know, man. I've got brain freeze right now. Ortiz is in the same boat. We're in panic mode. The best option in this case would be to launch a full-on multi-agency manhunt, but..." Cruz stopped mid-sentence.

"But you can't. Because one man's supposed to be in prison and the other dead. Right?"

"Yeah, man. But what did you mean we're not out of options? Can you think of something?"

"I think I've got a couple of ideas."

"I'm listening."

"You know there aren't any free lunches?"

"I know, man. I get it. What do you want?" Cruz asked.

"There are two conditions. Both non-negotiable."

"I'm listening."

"First, everyone in my team has a target on his back. We've got active contracts out on us. This will be a joint operation, but my team will take the lead. Your guys will provide back up and intelligence."

"And the second condition? I think I already have an idea."

"I think you do. Dexter isn't coming out of this thing alive."

"Right," Cruz said, letting out a long sigh. "I promised you earlier you'll get no more bullshit from me. Well, I meant it. I could say it's all fine and let's go ahead with it, but you know it's not just up to me."

"I know that. If you had said yes immediately, I wouldn't have believed you."

"I'll have to take this to Ortiz and my boss. We all know we're fucked if the Cadys get away with the rods. I've no doubt they'll agree to it. But give me some idea of what you have in mind. I need to have some kind of a plan to take to them."

"Alright. What I have in mind... and I know it'll work... is rather than us chasing them, we'll make them come after us. We'll lure them in. Give them baits so irresistible they can't help coming after them."

"I'm listening."

"I told you how your entire operation got blown because of Dexter. The man has a psychotic streak for vengeance. That's what fucked up his escape attempt from the court, simply because he wanted to talk to me and gloat about killing my man. He has such a burning hatred for me he even put his freedom from death row in jeopardy by putting out hits on me and my men. The rods, the money, all that's important, but he won't rest until he sees me and everyone I care for dead. I'm your irresistible bait for Dexter. I've got a similar bait in mind for Carson—someone he can't resist coming after. Dangle the baits in front of both brothers. They'll come out of whichever hole they're hiding in."

"But how will they see the bait? I mean, they'll come after you only when they know for sure you're going to be some place at a specific time."

"That's where you guys come in. You'll dangle the bait in front of Dexter when he calls. He'll surely call, just to keep you hoping he'll stick to his word. Tell him there's this Marshal who's been snooping around. Talk to him like he's your best pal and casually slip my name into the conversation. Tell him you've handled it at the prison. I went away but called you again demanding a meeting at a specific time and place

259

in San Francisco. I can bet anything he'll be there to take me out."

Cruz was silent for a few seconds.

"You know what, I can see this working, man," he said, his voice getting all excited. "Who's the bait for Carson?"

"That I can't tell you until we've got a deal. I'm not worried about myself. But we will need a bulletproof plan for the other person. I can't put that person in harm's way. That's why my team will call the shots."

"I get it. Let me make some calls again. I don't have a doubt I'll get them in line."

"Good. Get back to me soon."

"I will. One more thing..."

"Yeah?"

"I didn't know Dexter would set up a hit on you guys. I wouldn't have let that happen had I known. You get that, right?"

"I do. No worries."

We were more than halfway back when Slick got a call from his man, Chainz. Some of the information he received was confirmation of what I already knew. Sharky's gang was in disarray after the seizure of their guns and warehouse in Hunters Point the previous night. We had substantially reduced their numbers, but they still had enough guns and men to pose a serious threat.

But the information that caught my attention was the gang had some kind of a setup in Japantown, which they were using as a kind of temporary base. That surprised me—Japantown is considered a safe area of the city. But it also raised the possibility it had something to do with Carson.

The last thing Slick mentioned was something big was about to go down way up in the High Desert in the Sierra Nevada mountain range in Northern California. The place Chainz mentioned was somewhere north-west of Reno near the Nevada border. But he had no clue about what was going down.

I wouldn't have thought much of it except it seemed to have a connection with Carson. That area was where his fake corpse was found along with a crashed helicopter. My thoughts were interrupted by another call. This time it was Mitchell.

"Hey, Mitchell. All fine with you and Em?"

"Yeah. There were two Deputies parked outside her place. I realized there wasn't much need for me to be there. Caught a few hours sleep and flew back. I've just landed. Where are you?"

I gave him a quick update on all that had happened. Then asked him to make his way directly to Watkins's office building.

Half an hour later, we followed the I-80 across the Bay Bridge into San Francisco. Officially called the San Francisco-Oakland Bay Bridge, it's the more hard-working but less sexy of the city's bridges. Unlike the Golden Gate Bridge, which is the beautiful gateway to the Pacific Ocean, the Bay Bridge is more functional, cutting across the Bay. At 8.4 miles, it's almost five times as long as its prettier sibling.

Once we crossed the bridge, we took the exit toward Civic Center to reach downtown. Garcia was waiting for me to show up in the back alley outside the lawyer's office. I was about two minutes away when I got a call from him.

"I'll be there in two minutes," I said as I took the call.

"Good. Something's about to go down here. The lawyer arrived ten minutes ago with two bodyguards. Looked nervous as hell. He left one bodyguard as a lookout at the entrance. Now there's this black van that's been casing the place. The men inside don't look like model citizens."

"How many men?"

"No idea. It's blacked out at the back. I just saw two men in the passenger cabin. But hang on... Fuck! They just took down the bodyguard. They've got suppressed guns. Four men have just come out of the van... walking fast toward the entrance. They've dragged the man's body inside."

"I'm almost there. Sixty seconds," I said as I stepped on the gas and swerved through lanes, cutting across cars, leaving a trail of irritated drivers honking like mad.

"Can't wait, bro. I'm heading in. We can't let the lawyer get taken out."

"Copy that. I'll follow you. Watch your six."

"Roger that. The door to the back entrance is open. Black van parked next to it. Office is on the second floor. Take a left from the landing. I'll take out the driver and head upstairs. Over and out."

# CHAPTER 24

I turned into the back alley thirty seconds later.
I slowed down, turned off the ignition, and cruised
to a stop near the entrance, a little distance from
the van. There wasn't enough time to grab heavier
firepower from the gun safe at the back. I asked
Slick to get in the back seat, stay low, and watch
the street. I knew he wouldn't try to run. He was on
Sharky's hitlist—the only way for him to survive
was to stick with us.

I grabbed a suppressor from the glove
compartment and ran toward the van, screwing it
onto my Glock. The van driver was slumped
sideways in his seat. I needn't even have bothered
to look—when Garcia said he'd take care of the
driver, it was as good as done. I stepped inside the
back entrance, gun held straight out in front of me.
A man was lying dead just inside the door, shot
multiple times.

I rapidly went up the stairs, staying as quiet as
possible. Once I arrived at the landing, I peered
into the corridor. The entrance to Watkins's office
was about twenty feet away. Beyond that, I saw a
man lying motionless on the floor. There was a
small puddle of blood beside his chest.

I tiptoed toward the office's open door. I
stopped for a second beside the doorway before
peering inside. I saw Garcia talking softly to a
woman who looked like she was on the verge of a

nervous breakdown. A man was lying on the floor just inside the door. This one looked knocked out, not dead.

"Stay here and hide. You're safe now. We'll try to save Watkins," Garcia told the woman, signaling me to move out with him.

"Uh, what if he wakes up?" she asked in a nervous voice.

"Trust me. He won't," Garcia replied over his shoulder as we rushed out.

"Watkins ran upstairs?" I asked.

"Yup. The bodyguard down at the entrance warned him about the men before they got him. Watkins ran for the stairs to the floor above. His bodyguard ran with him, but he was late and got shot. They left the woman hanging around, but she had the presence of mind to duck under a desk. The gunmen left one guy here and three of them have gone after the lawyer."

"You clipped the guy they left?"

"Yeah."

"How many floors above this?" I asked as we ran toward the stairs at the end of the corridor.

"Only one can be accessed from this floor. The floors above that are blocked from the rear. You can only get to them from the front."

"Good. That makes it simpler," I said, as we rushed up the steps.

We reached the stairwell on the third floor. The layout there was slightly different. There wasn't any corridor going out from the stairwell. There was just a door. It was one of those self-locking doors that could only be accessed by a keycard. But someone had placed a small wedge, so it wasn't shut properly.

We opened the door cautiously and moved in with guns at the ready. But what we saw beyond the door caught us by surprise. We were standing at one end of a bustling, open-plan office filled with rows of cubicles laid out within a large rectangular hall—a maze-like expanse of partitioned workspaces. The place was alive with activity. Most of the cubicles looked occupied. The air hummed with the sound of ringing phones, clacking keyboards, and the low murmur of conversations.

"What the fuck!" Garcia exclaimed. "There must be a hundred people in there."

"Good place to hide in plain sight. Before trying to find him, let's take out the gunmen. I don't think they're here to take prisoners. They must have fanned out. I think I already see one of them over there. I'm going after him. You take this side. Let's try not to create a panic and a stampede."

"Roger that. I've spotted a second one. Going after him," Garcia replied.

The cubicles were laid out in four rows in a grid-like pattern, with three narrow walking lanes between them for accessing the cubicles. Each cubicle had a five-foot high partition around it. There were two wider passageways at both ends of the rows of cubicles. Garcia walked down the passage near the door to go after his guy.

I kept low as I walked rapidly to the passage at the other end to take down the man who was moving slowly along, peering into each cubicle as he went forward. I kept scanning the rest of the area as I walked—I didn't want to fixate on the target and get caught out by the third guy.

I grabbed a bunch of folders lying on a table to hide the suppressed gun in my hand. As I closed in on my target, I saw him lock eyes with a man moving in the middle walking lane. Both men shook their heads slightly. Bingo. I had just found the third target.

I decided I had no option but to kill the man in front of me. Taking him down with non-lethal force would alert the third man. If that happened, it was certain he would begin firing and create a panic.

The man was about ten feet in front of me. When I saw him move to a space next to an empty cubicle, I took two quick steps and shot him twice just above his neck, the bullets severing his brainstem. As the man crumpled soundlessly and fell, I caught him, dragged him into the empty cubicle, and dumped him on a chair.

I got out and cut across the cubicles to move into the middle lane, my eyes fixed on the third man. I momentarily looked in Garcia's direction. I couldn't locate him. But I got sight of him a couple of seconds later when he stood up after taking out his guy. I signaled to him about the third man. Garcia nodded and began moving toward him.

But our stealth operation came to a sudden end when a woman screamed. It came from a cubicle a few yards ahead of our target. I saw a man scrambling out of the cubicle, trying to shield himself using a lightweight woman he was almost carrying in his hands. He dumped her in the middle of the lane and then ran in a zigzag manner in the direction of Garcia.

The third gunman sprinted after the fleeing man, taking wild shots at him. People scrambled into whatever cubicle they could dive into as the sound of terrified screams filled the air. A few of them dived to the floor to get out of the way of the bullets. That slowed the gunman's progress. And by that time, I was almost upon him.

I could have tackled him and taken him down. But he would have let out a few more wild shots. The cardboard-like cubicle partitions wouldn't save the people hiding behind them. I had no option but to shoot the man. A double tap to the base of the skull ended his reign of terror.

Garcia had grabbed Watkins by that time. I knew there would be a mad rush to the exit any second. People could get hurt. I got on top of a table in a cubicle and began to address everyone.

"There's no need to panic. We are US Marshals. The gunmen are all down. There's no imminent danger to anyone," I said in a commanding voice, holding up the Marshals' badge.

My announcement was met with a clamor of voices asking a hundred questions. I held out my hand to get some silence.

"This is a crime scene now. I need all of you to make your way to the front of the office and exit the building. Cops will be here any minute."

The sound of authority in my voice gave most of them some assurance things were under control.

Most of them dutifully began making their way to the front.

I made a quick call to 911 as I walked over to Garcia. We had three to four minutes before the cops arrived. We needed to get some quick answers from Watkins before that.

When I joined Garcia, he had kind of convinced Watkins we were the good guys. But the man still looked terrified as hell, staring wide-eyed at the dead assassin lying a few feet away.

"I need you to focus, Watkins. You would've been lying there dead had we not taken out those three killers. What you do in the next two minutes will decide whether you remain alive until the end of the day. Tell me you get that?" I said, holding him by the shoulders and forcing him to look into my eyes.

"Uh, yes. Uh, who are you guys?"

"We are the men you helped Dexter put out a hit on."

"Hit? What..."

"Don't even try. You have less than two minutes now, before we take you down to your office and leave you there. You don't want to take a gamble on your life with those men down there."

"No. Please. Can you really help me? Who are you? I mean, really, who are you guys?"

"Before I tell you... do you remember the hit now? One minute forty-five seconds left. Tick tock, tick tock."

"Yes. But it wasn't personal. I was just doing what my client told me to do."

"Save the bullshit. We're US Marshals. We can take you to a safe house. We're your only shot at staying alive," I said, showing him the badge.

I knew he would jump at the chance of saving his skin.

"Once the cops get here, your chance is gone. They'll interview you and let you go. All the best with staying alive after that, with Sharky on the prowl," Garcia added.

"No. Please. I'll do anything."

"Give us the dope you have on Dexter and Carson. You know damn well you're a loose end for them. Your only hope of staying alive is if we catch them before they vanish. If they do, you're on your own. One minute thirty seconds left before we walk down."

"Yes, I get it. After all I've done for them, all I am is a loose end," Watkins said, his voice almost breaking up.

"Not the time for self-pity, Watkins. We're giving you a shot at staying alive. Grab it while you can," Garcia cut in.

"Yes, I get it. I'm trying to think. Well... I got Dexter's false identity made—driving license, social security, passport... the works. His new name is Dean Paxton. He looks different on the passport. And Carson already has an ID in the name of Ronin Andrews. All the details are in my laptop down at the office."

"Dexter looks different how?"

"He's no longer the wild jungle man he looked like until yesterday. He's all clean shaved now."

"When did this happen?"

"Overnight. He looked like a shaggy man when I saw him yesterday."

"But still missing an eye?"

"He's got a glass eye. Looks almost like the real thing in the photo."

I exchanged a knowing look with Garcia. That was great intel. Dexter could have easily given the slip to anyone who had only seen him recently. We still knew what he would look like even in his new avatar, because that would resemble the look he had before he went to prison.

"That's a good start. What else? When are they getting out? How?"

"I don't know exactly when. Maybe tonight… latest tomorrow… All I know is soon. But I do know how. They have a Cessna waiting in a private hangar north of Palo Alto. Both of them are good pilots."

"Where are they holed up?" I asked, keeping up the intensity of questions, not wanting to give him time to cook up a story.

"I don't know exactly where they are now. They were at a place these Venezuelans got for them. But they never told me where it was."

"Where have they stashed the nuclear rods?"

"You know about the rods?"

"What do you think, genius? He just grabbed a random idea from thin air?" Garcia shot at him.

"They never told me. But I can make a guess."

"Go on. Clock's ticking. Forty-five seconds."

"Back in the day when the Cadys were considered respectable, they made an investment— a large tract of desert land near the Nevada border.

The plan was to set up a casino and resort. But the bottom fell out of the plans when they suddenly became fugitives and fled the country. That land was in the name of a shell company, which remained under the radar even when all their assets were seized two years ago. I wasn't their lawyer then—I wasn't the kind of high-flying, high-priced suits they went in for those days. But when Carson rose from the dead a couple of weeks ago, he contacted me."

"Why you?"

"They needed dirty work done. I had bailed some of Sharky's crew earlier. He recommended me."

"Alright. What's the land got to do with the rods?"

"That's where they hid a stash of arms before they fled. I came to know about it as that's where Sharky's crew went to get a large haul of automatics. All military grade. Once I knew about it, I kept digging further. I kind of knew this day would come... when I become a loose end. Anyway, I think they smuggled the rods in at the same time as the other weapons. I think that's where they'd still be, unless they moved them last night."

The information seemed solid. It made perfect sense. Verifying it wouldn't take long. And it fitted in well with what Chainz had told Slick about something big about to go down in the High Desert in the Sierra Nevada mountain range.

"This place... is it north-west of Reno?"

"Yes. Surely that wasn't a guess?" Watkins asked, genuinely surprised.

"It wasn't. Your two minutes are up. It's time to go down."

"But, please... I told you everything. Believe me, I can help you get them," Watkins pleaded desperately as we got him moving toward the landing.

"Prove it. Grab your laptop and come with us. We'll have to get out of this place before the cops arrive. Get moving now."

His feet suddenly got wings as he rushed down the stairs with us. He gave a gasp when he saw his bodyguard's body lying in the corridor. Then he averted his face and carried on to his office.

"We're getting out of here in thirty seconds. Grab whatever you need. You aren't coming back here," I ordered Watkins while Garcia had a quick word with the secretary.

I signaled Garcia to join me in a corner.

"We've got a real chance at the nukes as well as grabbing the Cadys," Garcia said.

"Yeah. But if they find out Watkins survived, they might run before we get a chance to grab them."

"I know. You think we have time to pull a deception? Float the news he's dead? There will be cops swarming this place any minute."

"We can take a shot at it. Let's get the lawyer, secretary and this guy out of here," I said, pointing to the knocked-out man, the only one in the kill team still alive.

"You do that. I'll stick around and explain things to the cops. But I'll leave out the part about

Watkins. Say I haven't got a clue about what happened to him."

"Roger that. Let's get moving."

I grabbed the knocked-out man, hauled him on to my shoulder, and hurried downstairs, with the others following me. We were inside the pickup before the first cop car turned into the back alley. Garcia had stayed back near the entrance. He waved the cops over, holding up his badge in the other hand.

# CHAPTER 25

I pulled out of the alley just as a second cop car was making its way in. I drove a couple of blocks before pulling into a parking garage. That seemed to be a safe place to lie low until I had sorted out a few things.

Before I could talk to Watkins, I got a call from Mitchell. He was calling from the alley behind the lawyer's office, which was buzzing with cops. I gave him the location for the parking garage.

Sharky's hitman, who I had dumped in the back of the pickup, was still out. Garcia had clipped him real hard. I handed Slick a set of flexicuffs and asked him to cuff the guy and keep an eye on him.

Before I turned my attention to Watkins, my gaze fell on his secretary, who was sitting quietly in the back seat. She sat clutching her bag tightly, her hands still trembling from the shock she had experienced. Her eyes darted around nervously, scanning the surroundings.

"Hi! I'm Axel. What's your name?" I asked her.

She stared at me with a slightly surprised expression initially, like she didn't expect anyone to address her directly.

"L... Linda," she whispered, stuttering.

"Linda, you're safe now. There's nothing to worry about. We'll soon take you to a safe house until all this blows over. Alright?" I said calmly.

She nodded vigorously, unable to come up with a response initially.

"Thanks," she finally said in a trembling voice.

In the meantime, Watkins had been busy with his laptop, getting all the relevant information together. He had images of Dexter's and Carson's passports, under the aliases Dean Paxton and Ronin Andrews, open on the screen. With his glass eye and clean-shaved look, Dexter looked more or less the same as how he looked before his escape attempt.

I took out my phone and clicked a photo of the screen. The next thing Watkins showed me was the location of the private airstrip and the details of the Cessna waiting for them.

Finally, he gave me the coordinates of the location up in the High Desert near Reno. It was a large tract of land of over three hundred acres with a ghost town in the middle of it—the remains of a mining outpost. Even if the rods were present at the spot, they wouldn't just be lying in the open. They would be in an underground bunker. Locating them wouldn't be an easy task.

Mitchell had driven in and parked next to me by that time.

"Man, what have you guys been up to? The place looked like a warzone. Cops were going nuts back in that alley," Mitchell said, giving me a bro hug.

Mitchell had been a worried guy when he left for LA last night. He had reason to be—had he not been a keen-eyed investigator, he and his five-months pregnant wife could have become the target of hitmen. My blood boiled at the very thought, but I was glad to see him come back a relaxed man. Flynn must have put some of the most capable Deputies on her protection detail.

"Just the usual stuff, pal. There's something about your city and hitmen roaming its streets. Someone has to take them out," I replied.

"Looks like I missed most of the action."

"Don't hold your breath on that. We've still got a shitload of trouble to deal with."

I brought him up to date with what I had learnt from Watkins.

"Man, that's solid intel. So, how are we playing it?"

"The first thing is to take all these guys to the safe house. I need to give some third degree to the killer we've got cuffed in there. Can't do it here in front of the others. The woman in the backseat is already on the verge of a nervous breakdown. Let's switch vehicles. Whose car are you driving?" I asked, looking at the sedan he had driven in.

"It's a rental."

"Here, grab the keys to the truck. Drop off these people and give me a call. I'm texting you the registration number of a Cessna the Cadys plan to use. And the coordinates of an airstrip. Find out all you can."

"Roger that."

I opened the trunk of the car, walked over to the back of the pickup, grabbed the cuffed guy who was just about beginning to stir, dragged him over to the car, dumped him in the trunk, and locked him in. The parking garage wasn't the kind of desolate place I needed to put the fear of death in the man.

I knew exactly where to take him. I headed away from downtown and drove toward some abandoned docks on the eastern edge of the city. It was a ten-minute drive. On the way, I called Cruz.

"Man, this has been one hell of a day. Tell me you've got some good news," Cruz said in a weary voice as he took my call.

"I might have something to cheer you up."

"C'mon, man, make my day. What's the news?"

"I think I know where they've hidden the rods."

"Seriously? You're not toying with me, are you?" he asked guardedly.

"I don't have the time, Cruz. But you need to do something immediately to prevent the Cadys from getting to know we're on to them."

"Sure. Shoot."

"I'm guessing you've got solid connections in local PD? Not regular cops but high up in the chain?"

"Uh, I guess. What's it about?"

"I need you to float a rumor."

I told Cruz about the shootout in the building and how we needed to make everyone believe Watkins was killed.

"Watkins is the guy who knows most of their secrets. If they get to know he survived, they might change their plans and vanish," I said.

"Leave that to me. I'll make it happen."

"You'll need to get on this immediately. Cops are already all over the place. I don't think Watkins's name will come in the initial report as he's not on the scene. But you need to set the story straight."

"I'll do it. What about the rods?"

"I'll text you the coordinates after the call. But they are for a big area—a three hundred-acre spread around a ghost town near Reno."

"Reno?"

"Yeah. You'll have to send a large tac team up there. The exact spot where they've hidden the rods might not be easy to locate. But so long as your men have the place surrounded, the Cadys won't be able to move the rods from there. My guess is they'll send men to pick them up once they get their payment. Maybe the men are already there, waiting for the exact location. Use drones or satellites to scan the place for any activity. But be discreet. Hold back and play the waiting game."

"Yeah, sure. I get it," Cruz said, sounding excited as hell.

"And if you do bump into Dexter, you might not recognize him immediately. He's got a haircut and is clean shaved now. With a glass eye."

"No shit. How did you get all this?"

"Ear to the street, Cruz. You've been in the field. You know how it works."

"I guess I've been behind a desk too long. But Blaze..."

"Yeah?"

"Anytime you're looking for a job, we have an opening for you."

"Good to know that. Let me know when you hear from Dexter."

"You said when, not if. Are you sure he'll call?"

"Yes. Not before the evening, when he's close to getting his payment, but he will," I replied with conviction before ending the call.

I stopped the car at a desolate spot next to the bay. I texted the coordinates to Cruz. Then I got out, drew my gun, popped open the trunk, and took a step back. I had frisked the man before shutting him in and knew he wasn't armed. But the cuffed man had managed to grab a wrench, which he tried to swing at me. I shot him in the right shoulder. The man cried out in pain. I grabbed him by the collar, pulled him half-way out, and dumped him on the ground.

"You know who I am?" I bent over him, glowering menacingly.

I knew everyone in the gang knew our faces very well. They were all being paid top dollar for our heads. I saw a flash of fear cross the man's eyes before he nodded.

"I won't have the slightest problem putting a bullet in your skull and dumping you into the bay. If you have any doubt about that, let me know and I'll give you further demonstration."

"No, man, no doubt," he gasped, pain and fear wracking his features.

"Here's what you're going to do—you'll call Sharky, tell him you got the lawyer, but the cops came and there was a shootout. Everyone else is dead. You managed to escape but got shot and will lie low somewhere. You do that, I'll let you live. If you stall, I'll kill you now. I don't have time to waste on you. Got it?"

The man understood it wasn't an empty threat. He didn't need further convincing.

"Yes. I'll do it," he said, agreeing immediately.

"Get inside the car," I ordered, opening the passenger door.

It was too windy outside and I didn't want Sharky to try and figure out the location. The best thing was to keep the conversation short and simple.

"Unlock it," I ordered, holding out his phone.

The man dutifully touched his thumb to the Touch ID sensor. I found Sharky's number and made the call. The man did exactly as told. Sharky seemed convinced Watkins was killed. He didn't really seem to care much about his guy. Just asked him to lie low and got off the call. It was apparent this wasn't a gang with any ties of loyalty.

"Where's Sharky holed up?" I asked the man.

"There's this place in Japantown. A restaurant this guy owns. But it's being redone. It's got plastic sheets all around, so no one can see what's going on inside. But I don't know if he'll be there now. That's where we holed up last night."

"What's the name of this joint?"

"No name. But it's the only one there with those blue plastic sheets on scaffoldings all around the building. It's close to that weird Japanese tower."

"The Pagoda?"

"Yeah, that's what they call it."

"Who owns this restaurant?"

"This weird guy—Ronin."

"Was he holed up with you guys?"

"No, man, these guys are loaded. Must have been in some high-end hotel."

"Which guys? Ronin and who else?"

"There's this other guy. He looked like a wild man—crazy hair and all. But he was all clean-shaved this morning."

That's all I needed from the man. I got out of the car, walked over to the passenger side, and asked him to get out. While he was focusing on the task of getting out of the passenger seat with minimal pain to his shot shoulder, I clubbed him with my gun and knocked him out. I dragged him to one side and propped him in a sitting position against a wall.

I used his phone to call 911 and told them he was shot and bleeding. I wasn't entirely convinced a hired gun like him deserved any sympathy, but I had promised I would leave him alive if he talked.

I threw the phone in the bay, got in the car, and made my way to Japantown to check out Carson's place. I cut across the Financial District and got on to Pine Street. Japantown was a couple of miles further on. I had just gotten onto Nob Hill when I got a call from Britt. I realized I had forgotten about her and Naomi in the rush of things.

"Hey, Britt. How did it go?"

"Pretty smooth. We went to Naomi's place, got the dragon, and had the Japanese written on it translated as well."

"So, what did it say?"

"Not anything mysterious or witty. All it said was 'Want to live the dream life? Give me a call', followed by the guy's name—Ronin."

"That's it?"

"Yup. The man isn't exactly a poet."

"Does the number work?"

"I didn't want to risk alerting him by calling the number. I've passed it to Mitchell. He's got his guy on it. We should get a location soon."

"Good work. Are you back at the safe house?"

"No. I brought Naomi for a coffee and a bite. She seemed too jittery. I think you scared her by telling her Carson knew where she lived."

"Yeah, I did. She wanted to head out on her own. I gave her some reality bites," I told Britt.

"Yeah, that's what I thought. She lives a couple of blocks from here. So, we came over to J-Town."

"J-Town? That's where I'm headed. But you better watch your back, Britt. That's where Sharky's guys were holed up last night."

"You gotta be shitting me. This is supposed to be one of the safest neighborhoods in the city."

"I guess that's why it would be the last place anyone would expect them to be. I just found out Carson owns a place there. I'm less than five minutes away. Where exactly are you?"

"Café called Akira's. West of the Pagoda."

"How long have you been there?"

"Twenty minutes. The guy at the counter reads Japanese. He was the one who translated the message."

"Other than the café, have you moved around the area much?" I asked.

"No. We parked the car on Buchanan and walked over. We've been in here ever since."

"I think we're good, in that case. You got baseball caps by any chance?"

"I should have a couple in the car. You want me to grab them?"

"No. That's a block away. Stay inside. You'll be less visible. Hang tight and stay low. I'm on my way. See you in five."

"Roger that."

# CHAPTER 26

Japantown is spread over five blocks to the south of Pine Street. But its epicenter is around the Peace Plaza north of Geary Boulevard. The tallest structure in the Plaza is the hundred-feet tall five-storied Peace Pagoda—a gift from the Japanese city of Osaka to San Francisco way back in the 1960s.

I parked my car and walked briskly toward the Pagoda. I bought three Giants baseball caps from a shop before making my way to the café. The bills pulled low would at least make us less easy to recognize if we happened to bump into any of Sharky's crew.

I did a quick scan of the entire pedestrian area in the Plaza. Carson's restaurant was easy to spot. The guy had been right. The blue shrink-wrapped scaffolding all around the two-story building was clearly visible from a distance. The good thing was it was diagonally opposite Akira's café to the west of the Pagoda, with an open walking space of at least a hundred yards between them. The chances of Sharky's goons walking across the Plaza to have coffee at that place were slim.

Before approaching the café, which was located next to a three-storied mall, I took out the binoculars from my crossbody bag and examined the restaurant for any movement. The place looked dead—no one around on the outside. There was no way to make out the layout inside.

While I was doing the recon, I got a call from Garcia.

"All sorted?" I asked him.

"Yeah, man. It wasn't fun. Too many hysterical people in that office. I felt bad for the cops. But it's all handled. No one there has a clue what happened to Watkins."

"Good. I've sorted that out. They'll spin a story saying he got caught in the shootout."

"That'll keep Dexter relaxed," Garcia replied.

"I've sent Mitchell to the safe house to drop them off. We've also got Carson's number. Mitchell's guy is working on it."

"No shit. That's big, bro."

"Yeah, I've got one more number we need to track. Sharky's. I'll text it to you. Get Mitchell's guy cracking on it as well. I'm in Japantown. About to meet Britt. I'll keep you posted."

"Copy that."

I ended the call and headed toward the café. But rather than walking across the open Plaza, I took a circuitous route. Once I was outside the café, I observed its interiors from the window before heading in. Britt and Naomi were seated at a corner table.

"Hey, girls. How are you holding up?" I said as I walked in and took a chair at their table.

"Ready to kick some ass. Huh, Naomi?" Britt replied.

"Yo, girl," Naomi replied, giving Britt a high five.

"Britt has just taught me some cool moves," she added, looking at me with bright eyes.

"Ready to kick your stalker's ass, then?"

"Sure. Bring it on."

"Easy, tiger," I said, smiling.

"I heard you guys turned the lawyer's office into a battle zone," Britt remarked.

I gave them a quick update of everything I had found out.

"Looks like we've just got a few hours to grab them before they vanish," Britt said.

"Yeah. We won't let that happen. This has to end today," I replied.

"All those killers were holed up in that building?" Britt asked incredulously as she walked to the front window and peered at the restaurant.

"Yeah. I found that hard to believe. But Carson owns the place."

"He's more of a nutcase than we thought, if he thinks he'll simply keep flitting in and out of the country with no one ever catching on."

"He very well could have, if Mitchell hadn't recognized him... if Dexter hadn't sent men after Mitchell... Dexter's mad need for revenge got them caught out," I replied.

I noticed Naomi's face had lost some color.

"You alright?"

"Yeah. Just thinking... he would have come after me last night, if I hadn't bumped into you," she replied nervously.

"Don't go there. It will end soon."

"How? They still might escape in that plane."

"We're not out of options yet."

"Yeah. But there's one option with a better chance of bringing him out in the open."

"What?" I asked even though I already understood what she had in mind.

"He asked me to give him a call. I'll do it. Arrange a meeting."

"Too risky, Naomi. These guys are dangerous. We can't expose you. At least not until we've run out of options."

"But why wait until the last minute? We may no longer have a shot once he skips the city. I told you this has happened to me before. It was horrible. I don't want to face it again. I don't want to live in fear... having to look over my shoulder all the time."

I looked at Britt, not sure what to say.

"And shouldn't this be my choice? I want to do it. I know you guys can keep me safe," Naomi added, trying to sound brave.

Neither of us replied. We had seen this before. Witnesses offering to do something risky in a rush of adrenaline and then losing their nerve at the last moment.

"You guys can handle it, right? Or aren't you confident you can handle them?" Naomi persisted.

"Nice try," I replied, unable to resist a smile.

"Good. So, that's settled. Now tell me how to handle this."

"Hang on. Nothing's settled."

"Naomi's right, Blaze. She's our best shot at grabbing them," Britt gave me the confirmation I needed.

"Alright. If you're sure..."

"One hundred per cent. I want to get this over with. Just tell me what to do. I may look lightweight, but I can be tough when needed," Naomi said with as much determination as she could muster.

"Good. Let's get on with it. Britt, any word from Mitchell about the phone?"

"I'll call him now."

While Britt made the call, I began prepping Naomi.

"The first thing to decide—rendezvous time and place."

"Rendezvous? Oh, right. I get it. It's just that I've never heard anyone use the word," she said, laughing a little nervously.

"Yeah, I get that often. Anyway, tell him you'll be at one of the benches around the Pagoda at 1600 hours."

"1600 hours? That's like 4:00 p.m. Right?"

"Yes. That's one hour twenty minutes from now. Next, let's get your story straight. You need to have a clear explanation for why you're calling two days after he gave you the number. He's going to be suspicious. Especially because your car hasn't moved since yesterday. You'll need an explanation for why you left it there?"

"Uh, right. For why I left it there, I guess I can just say I was too shaken up after the shootout that happened in the parking garage. So, I got a friend to drop me. You think that works?"

"Yeah. Sounds logical. He would know about the shootout. The thing is, he won't ask you about the car. He can't let on he's been tracking it. You'll have to slip it into the conversation. And also where you were last night. Give him a logical explanation for that."

"So… I stayed at the friend's place? I was so nervous after the shootout, I left my keys and stuff back at the restaurant. Does that work?"

"Yeah. I'd believe that. But then I'd wonder if it's a girlfriend or a guy?"

"Oh. Does it matter?"

"You know it does. If a guy's stalking you, I'm sure he wouldn't want to hear of a boyfriend. Or you could give him the boyfriend's detail and then we grab him trying to take out that guy," I replied.

"That sounds like a better plan. How about I tell him you're my boyfriend?" Naomi said with a naughty smile.

"I don't think that's going to work. He's too scared of me. He might drop the idea altogether," I said, trying to keep the conversation professional.

I could sense Britt was kind of listening to our conversation while she talked with Mitchell on the phone.

"Alright. I guess it's a girlfriend. Cool?" Naomi asked.

"Yeah."

Before I could say anything else, Britt got off her call.

"Carson's number is live. He's in San Mateo. About halfway between here and the airstrip in Palo Alto," Britt informed us.

"San Mateo? Well, the good thing is he isn't too far off. I've begun prepping Naomi," I replied.

"Yeah, I kind of gathered that," Britt replied with a mysterious smile.

"We still have to figure out why I'm calling after two days. How about... I didn't even know there was a message inside the dragon until today. I took it home the day before, spent last night at a friend's, and when I got back home today, I picked it up again and discovered the message while fiddling with it. Then I came to J-Town to figure out what it meant. And when I got the message, I decided to call."

"I think that works. But keep it a bit casual. Just tell him you're here for a couple of hours before you head into work," Britt suggested.

"Yeah, sure. So, is that it? We've got everything covered?" Naomi asked.

"One last thing... how did you get inside your home?" I asked.

"Um, I went back to the restaurant to collect my keys?"

"But why's your car still there?"

"Oh!"

"You didn't go back. You collected the key from a neighbor who you couldn't wake up in the middle of the night."

"Yes, that makes sense. Uh, are we all covered now?" Naomi asked, taking a deep breath.

"Yes. If this works, we need an hour to set things up to make this foolproof. Don't agree to meet him earlier than 4:00 p.m."

"Right."

I had been carrying a stash of burner phones in my bag. I took out one and handed it to Naomi.

"Use this. I don't think he has your number but, if he asks, tell him it's a second phone you sometimes use. You forgot your phone behind at work along with the other stuff. OK?"

Naomi nodded her head, suddenly beginning to look less sure of herself.

"You've got this. Let's grab that prick," Britt said, in a voice meant to reassure Naomi.

Naomi nodded somberly before breaking into a giggle. Britt looked confused for a few seconds but laughed when she caught on.

Naomi took a deep breath before calling the number. It kept ringing. Carson didn't take the call.

"What do I do?" she asked unsurely.

"Give it a couple of minutes," I said.

Naomi nodded but kept staring at the phone, clutching it tightly in her hand, nervously biting her lip, too fixated on the idea of trapping Carson to be able to focus on anything else.

"Did Mitchell mention anything else? About the plane these guys plan to use, or Sharky's phone?" I asked Britt, more to break the tension than anything else.

"He said he's on it. He'll call back as soon as he has an update."

Before I could say anything else, the phone rang. Naomi looked at me nervously. I nodded. Britt squeezed her hand reassuringly.

"You can do this, Naomi. It's time to put an end to this madness," Naomi said to herself, taking a deep breath.

Her demeanor changed as a determined look came on her face. Then she took the call.

"Hello," she said in a voice that was playful and alluring.

The nervous-looking girl I was reassuring a few seconds ago was suddenly replaced by a charming, almost seductive woman as she took Carson on a journey he hadn't imagined he would be making. Naomi's tone was velvet, smooth and sensual, wrapping around his senses like a seductive spell. As she chatted in a carefree manner, like to a friend she knew intimately, I could feel a seductive web being spun on the man—her playful banter had a hint of mischief, her laughter had a melody that tickled the imagination, her tantalizing giggles had a quality that left Carson longing for more.

By the time Naomi got off the call, I didn't have any doubt in my mind—Carson would be there at the appointed hour, come hell or high water. In the call lasting not much over five minutes, Naomi had got the man wrapped around her finger.

# CHAPTER 27

"What do you think? Will he be there?" Naomi asked, still flushed after her spellbinding act.

"Oh, he'll be there all right. Right, Blaze?" Britt replied, looking at me.

"Yeah," was all I could manage.

But I soon snapped out of the spell Naomi had cast. We had an hour and five minutes to come up with a foolproof plan. I walked to the café windows, looking at the layout of the Plaza once again. I had no doubt Carson would be accompanied by Sharky's men. And they would come packing heavy firepower. I realized we would need backup. Just the two of us wouldn't be able to form the secure perimeter I wanted in place to ensure Naomi's safety. We would need Garcia in sniper position. I called him.

"I was about to call you. We got a trace on Sharky's number. He's with Carson. Both numbers are in San Mateo," Garcia told me as he took the call.

"Carson will soon begin moving toward Japantown. Maybe even Sharky."

I told him about Naomi's phone call.

"You sure he'll bite?" Garcia asked.

"You should have heard the way she talked to him. That guy will be here, even if he has to walk all the way. But we need you here, pal. In sniper position. Better hit the road."

"Copy that. What's the range?"

"Two hundred yards. Even less. It's possible we may not need a shot at all. But best be ready. They'll be armed with automatics."

"No problem. I'll grab an M24 from the armory. Rendezvous in twenty-five minutes."

"Roger that. Is Mitchell around?"

"Yeah."

"Tell him I'm waiting for an update."

"Roger that."

Mitchell called me a few seconds after I got off the call with Garcia.

"Any updates, Mitchell?"

"Yes. I've got everything. The plane you mentioned—it's parked in a hangar at that private airstrip. Five miles north of Palo Alto. Fueled and ready to go."

"You'll need to head there, pal. Disable the plane any which way. And then watch the place like a hawk."

"I hear you. I'll head out there. It's about a half an hour drive from here."

"You need to be well-armed. If Dexter manages to somehow arrive there, you need to be ready to take him down. We'll head out as soon as we've grabbed Carson."

"Roger that," he replied, ending the call.

The only thing left to do before those guys arrived was a recon of Carson's restaurant. I needed to assess the number of men in there and the firepower they had stashed. I didn't want to be caught flat-footed against an army carrying heavy-duty hardware.

I walked back to the table. Naomi had ordered coffee and small delicate-looking Japanese cakes for us. The café guy had just laid out the order and had headed back behind the counter.

"Ladies, would either of you have a compact mirror?" I asked.

Naomi immediately took one out of her bag. It was pink. But it didn't matter as I wasn't planning to use it anywhere public.

"I'm dying to hear about what you plan to do with it," Britt asked.

"Don't you want me to look nice when I take out the bad guys," I replied.

"Seriously?"

"I'm going on a recon mission. Carson's place has this scaffolding all around it. I'll check it out. See how many guys and weapons they have in there."

"Right," Britt replied, finally satisfied I wasn't losing my mind.

"Have you been here before?" I asked Naomi.

"Yeah. Many times."

"How enterprising is the guy behind the counter? Is he willing to make a quick buck?"

"What do you have in mind?"

"I want him to go with takeaway coffees to Carson's place across the plaza. Tell them he's doing a promotion for his joint. No one refuses free coffee. All he needs to do is hand them coffees for each man in there and head back. And tell us how many men there are in there. It will also make any men on the second floor come down for the coffees. Makes it easy for me to look around. Think he'll do it?"

"I'm sure he will. He's a college kid. They don't mind extra cash. Want me to talk to him?"

"I'll come with you. But you better do the talking."

"OK."

He was a typical college kid. Ready for a little adventure that got him some extra pocket money. Fifty bucks did the trick.

I put on the Giants baseball cap, pulled the bill low, and walked out of the café. I took a circuitous route toward the restaurant, before taking up position near the side of the two-story building. It had scaffolding all around it, which was kind of shrink wrapped in a blue plastic covering. I made a small tear in the plastic to peer inside. The side wall of the building didn't have any windows. All the windows on both floors were on the front and back of the building.

I took a quick look around, before slashing the bottom of the plastic wrapping. Then I slid inside and stood up in the space between the scaffolding and the building wall, shielded from the eyes of any passersby. A minute later, a text landed on my phone. The café guy had handed out three coffees.

That was my cue. I began climbing up the metal structure of the scaffolding, using its interwoven bars as a makeshift ladder. I stopped as soon as I was level with the second floor, took out the compact mirror, and examined the back end of the floor. It had three large open holes where the windows were missing as it was still under renovation.

I ascended further to have a quick peek at the roof. There wasn't much to see there. It was just a flat, empty roof. I went down again to the second-floor level, moved sideways, and stopped beside the gaping window hole. I used the mirror to examine the room. It was empty. I entered the room. All it had inside were some makeshift beds.

I walked very carefully toward the door, acutely aware the sound of footsteps could alert the men downstairs. I opened the door slowly and realized the room was more like a back office to a big seating area outside. It was empty as well. The room next to the one I walked out from was locked. I couldn't possibly break the lock without alerting the men downstairs.

I tiptoed back to the window, got out and went sideways on the scaffolding to enter the other room through the window. This room had what I was looking for. Two big wooden cases. I knew before I opened the first one there would be guns inside them. I found M-16 automatic rifles and mini-Uzis stacked neatly in the boxes.

I had seen all I needed to see. A plan of action had begun to form in my mind. I went out the window again and moved to the side of the building once again before descending. Once I was on the ground, I moved to the back windows of the first floor and used the mirror to look inside. The first floor was simply one big hall. I spotted three men with disposable coffee cups near the entrance at the other end of the hall. I retreated to the side again, used the mirror to check for any passersby, before stepping out.

When I re-entered the café, Britt was getting Naomi set up with a radio.

"What did you find? I'm sure you've come back with a complete action plan," Britt asked.

"I think so," I replied, grabbing a napkin and drawing a layout of the Plaza on it. "Garcia will be here in five minutes. I'll get him in sniper position on the roof of the mall. It's the tallest building around. With a clear view of the entire Plaza, including the Pagoda as well as the restaurant. When those guys arrive, they'll go into the restaurant first. That's their base of operations. They've got a big stash of guns in there. M-16s, Uzis…"

"Sounds like they're all set for war."

"Yeah. That's the reason Sharky's crew has been sticking with the Cadys. They were small-time crooks before they got their hands on these weapons. But that's the reason they pissed off other gangs. It worked well for us. We wouldn't have been here without the intel the Crips gave to Slick."

"That's right. But the guns won't matter. We're doing a stealth approach, right?" Britt confirmed.

"Yes. We aren't waging all-out war."

"Right. What next once those guys arrive at the building?"

"I'll position myself on the roof of the restaurant."

"Uh-huh. Why?"

"When this all goes down out in the open near the Pagoda, we don't want their men coming at us from back there. The way we're doing it is once Garcia signals us the men have left the building and are taking up position around the Pagoda, I'll enter the building and take out any men they leave in there. And then I'll go out and start taking out the other guys stealthily. Garcia will be our eyes. He'll pinpoint the exact location. You and Naomi won't enter the scene until I give you the go-ahead. I'll do that only when most peripheral threats have been neutralized."

"It's possible Naomi might not have to make an appearance at all."

"Yeah, it's possible. But I don't think Carson will approach the place on his own. He'll surely have some men close to him. And these guys will have automatics. We'll have to be careful. We can't have them start a full-on gun battle in the middle of a public place. Naomi might need to make an appearance simply to draw him away from the gunmen. We'll have to play it by ear," I replied.

"Copy that."

"Naomi, Britt will be close to you at all times. I won't be visible but will be close enough. You'll make yourself visible only when I give the go-ahead. After that, we'll see how it plays out. Before Carson comes out, he'll certainly call you. Tell him you're in the mall and will make your way out. Ask him to wait near the Pagoda. Any questions?"

"Uh, no. Copy that. I'll rendezvous at 1600 hours," she replied, mimicking me, trying to use humor to hide her nervousness.

Garcia walked into the café just at that moment, a big duffel bag slung across his shoulders. Inside his big bag were two smaller bags. He handed one each to Britt and me. Inside each bag was a Heckler & Koch HK 416 A5 assault rifle with a suppressor and magazines. The rifle was the sub-compact version with an eleven-inch barrel and an effective firing range of 330 yards.

Britt set us all up with radios. She placed a micro earpiece inside Naomi's left ear. Once her hair fell in place over her ears, the piece was invisible. A tiny mic attached inside the front of Naomi's dress was pretty much invisible as well. We made her use the mic and earpiece a few times to get used to them.

It was finally time to split up. We gave fist bumps to Britt and Naomi before heading out.

Garcia and I walked into the mall and went up to the third floor. We flashed our Marshals badges to the security guy to get him to open the door to the roof. Garcia took out the M24 rifle from the duffel bag, assembled it, and set himself up near the edge. I scanned the layout below us and was satisfied. Garcia would have a clear view of everything.

"Watch your six, pal. I'll take up position on that other roof," I said.

"Copy that. Head on a swivel, bro."

Garcia latched the roof door from outside once I left. That was standard protocol for such an operation. He couldn't afford to have some idiot walking on to the roof and spoiling his focus.

I used the same route I had taken earlier to approach the restaurant from the side. Less than a minute later, I was positioned on the roof. In the middle of the roof was a kind of a trapdoor for accessing the roof from inside the building. It was locked from inside.

I opened the bag and checked the rifle. It was assembled and ready to use. All it needed was a magazine. And a suppressor, if required. I wasn't planning on using it. At least not while grabbing Carson. It would come in handy later, when we went after Dexter. I put the rifle back in the bag, took out my Glock, and screwed the suppressor on.

And then I relaxed and began the wait for Garcia's signal.

# CHAPTER 28

"Four men approaching the restaurant," Garcia's voice came through my earpiece ten minutes later.

"Copy that. Do you have a confirmed visual on Carson?" I asked.

"There's one guy in the middle. Surrounded by the other three. Guy in the middle has same height, physical structure, and posture as Carson. I'm sure it's him but can't make a positive ID. He's wearing a hat."

"It's close enough."

"Wait. He took his hat off before entering the building. It's Carson."

"Copy that," I replied.

We waited, senses on high alert.

"Incoming call to Naomi's phone. She's taking it now," Britt's voice came through the earpiece.

"Copy that," we both replied and waited.

"It's on. Carson will meet her at rendezvous point in five minutes," Britt confirmed.

A noise behind me suddenly alerted me to an unanticipated problem. It sounded like someone was trying to unlock and open the trapdoor from inside the building. I didn't waste a second. I slung the bag across my body, grabbed the scaffolding, and descended below the roof's edge. A few seconds later, I heard voices above me. The ledge of the roof jutted out a little, partially blocking the view from the top. But if someone did peer out over the ledge, he would spot me on the scaffolding.

I spotted a foot hold in the brick wall. I placed my toe on it, let go of the scaffolding, and pushed my body toward the wall. Then I hung on, supporting my body weight on one toe while gripping the corner of the wall with my right hand.

Garcia had been watching all this from his higher vantage point. He couldn't see me through the plastic around the scaffolding but must have gathered what I had done.

"Maintain position, Blaze. I'll let you know as soon as the roof's clear."

"Roger that. I'm clinging to the wall," I whispered back.

I remained in that position for about two minutes. My tense muscles felt each one of those one hundred and twenty seconds.

"You're good to move back to the scaffolding. But roof's not clear. There are two men posted on the front edge, eyes glued to the Plaza. You'll have to take them out."

"Roger that," I said as I pushed myself away from the wall and got back to the comfort of the scaffolding again.

I waited for Garcia's next message. I would take out the men as soon as Carson left the building.

"Carson has exited the building with three men. All three have open duffel bags slung across their bodies," Garcia informed us.

"Copy that. They'll have M-16s and Uzis inside the bags. Our objective is not to let them use the guns. Zero collateral damage."

"Roger that."

It was time for me to move. I climbed up until my eyes were level with the edge of the roof. I saw two men standing together about fifteen yards away, one of them scanning the Plaza with binoculars. The other man had an M-16 ready in his hands, with a hundred-round drum magazine attached to it.

I couldn't believe these guys. The way the man held the gun, he didn't look like he was much of a sniper or even a pro at handling the gun. At the first hint of trouble, the man would simply empty the magazine, spraying one hundred 5.56×45mm NATO cartridges into everyone across the Plaza. I needed to take him out fast. There was no way I could take down the men with non-lethal force without warning the remaining man inside the building. The time for a light-touch resolution to violent situations was over.

I took out the Glock with the suppressor already attached to it. I took careful aim and shot the gunman at the base of his head. It was a kill shot—it ruptured the spinal cord. The man began collapsing without a sound. The other man sensed something was happening and lowered his binoculars to turn around. I shot him twice. A double tap just above his ear. The man was dead before he began falling.

But I didn't bother waiting for him to hit the ground. I moved down and sideways, before entering the second-floor room from the window.

"Carson's group moving toward the Pagoda. One man with him. The other two have spread out," Garcia's voice came through the earpiece.

"Roger that," I replied.

I was already familiar with the layout. I moved fast toward the stairs leading down to the first floor, without bothering to muffle my footsteps. The man below knew two guys were on the roof and one of them could well be coming down. The man was standing near the entrance, watching Carson's team moving out, a rifle slung across his back. There was too much noise coming from outside for the man to have heard me.

I shot him point blank at the back of his head, caught him before he fell, and dragged him inside.

"Three targets inside the building neutralized. I need positions of the others."

"Copy that. When you get out the entrance, there's a row of trees at your three o'clock. About thirty yards from the door. One man is positioned there. He's the closest to you. But he could spot you if you step out of the building," Garcia informed me.

I shut and bolted the door from inside, headed to the back of the building, stepped out the window, and exited the building from the same place I had used earlier—through the plastic wrapping around the scaffolding. I had exited a little behind the row of trees, out of the line of sight of the man. I kept my gun back inside the bag.

There were a few people walking around the Plaza. I didn't want to cause a scare.

I walked rapidly toward the trees. As I got closer, I spotted the man. He had his duffel bag in front of his body, his hand inside it, clutching an automatic. I stealthily approached him and stopped behind the cover of a tree close to him, shielding myself from his line of vision.

I took out my boot knife—a 5.4-inch double-edged carbon steel blade. Then I took a quick step, slipped my right arm around the man's neck, pulled his head to the side, and plunged the knife into his neck. The blade sliced through the carotid artery and jugular vein. The man went limp.

"Target down. Guide me to the next one," I spoke into the earphone as I dragged the dead man back and propped him up on a bench slightly hidden behind the trees.

"Your twelve o'clock. Fifty yards. Beside the florist."

I began sprinting to my right, trying to utilize the cover of the trees as I approached the man using a circular route. The direct route would require me to walk through the open space of the Plaza. I came to a stop a few yards behind the man.

Taking the man out posed a problem. Even though he was standing partially hidden by the shopfront of the florist, there wasn't any space around the shop for me to hide him for a few minutes. A man with blood gushing out would get noticed. It could cause a panic. Carson was still forty yards away from me, with the gunman standing next to him.

I would have to take out the man without spilling blood. I didn't spend any more time thinking. I took a few quick steps to stop immediately behind him. In a swift move, I wrapped my left hand around the back of his head and grabbed him around his right ear, grabbed his chin with my right hand, twisted his head to the left and anti-clockwise, before giving it a powerful clockwise jerk. The entire move didn't take more than a second. The man's neck snapped. He went limp and began sagging to the ground.

"Target down. Only two active targets remain," I informed the others as I put the dead man's arm around my shoulders, kind of dragged him toward a bench, and propped him in a sitting position.

I assessed the situation. Carson was located near the Pagoda, about forty yards from me. He was pacing around, his eyes fixed on the mall entrance, waiting for Naomi to come out. But there was a problem. A group of tourists had moved near him and were milling about, taking photos. I knew Garcia would no longer have a clear shot.

"What's the play?" Britt's voice came through my earpiece.

"Garcia, any chance you can get the last gunman?" I asked.

"That's a negative. I don't have a clear shot."

"Naomi, are you ready?"

"Yes," she replied in a firm voice.

"Britt will move out first. She'll mingle with the crowd around Carson. I'm only seconds away from him. You won't be alone."

"OK. Sounds good."

"You need to draw him away from the crowd. Any direction that gives Garcia a clear line of sight from the top of the mall. Can you do that?"

"Yes. I can."

"Alright. Britt, time for you to move out. Naomi, wait for my signal."

"Roger that. I'm heading out," Britt replied.

Britt walked out of the coffee shop. She had the Giants baseball cap on, bill pulled low. She walked casually, taking small bites out of a cake in her hand. Nothing about her suggested she was there for any reason other than having a stroll around. I gave her fifteen seconds to get close to the Pagoda. It was time for Naomi to make a move.

"Naomi, move whenever you're ready."

"OK," she replied.

A few seconds later, I saw Naomi walk out from the direction of the mall. She looked hesitant at first, and a little nervous. But she soon got a hold of herself. I witnessed the same transformation I had seen earlier, when the nervous woman waiting for the phone call was suddenly replaced by a charming, almost seductive woman. With each step, her posture straightened, her shoulders squared, and her gait became more purposeful.

When Carson's eyes fell on Naomi, he took a couple of steps toward her. But the gunman stopped him. Carson gave Naomi an awkward hug when she came close. Naomi looked a little stiff but didn't move away. We couldn't catch the initial part of the conversation as Carson tried to have it in Japanese. But Naomi was smart. She replied in English, paraphrasing some of his comments, like she wanted to make sure she got what he was saying.

Carson soon gave up and switched to English. He tried seducing her with dreams of the wealth he had come into.

"What are you hanging around this city for? A stupid waitress job? Take a leap of faith. Come with me tonight. I'll show you the life."

That was possibly the worst pickup line I had ever heard in my life. Carson was a lot of things, but a smooth-talking ladies' man surely wasn't one of them. But Naomi took it in her stride, keeping him talking until Garcia had a clear shot.

"Come with you? And do what?"

"See the world. Europe, South America, Japan. Any place. Lavish parties, lounging by the pool, sipping champagne..."

"That sounds cool," Naomi replied, making a sincere attempt to sound enthusiastic, but not quite succeeding.

"It's a once in a lifetime chance. Grab it. I've got a private jet waiting."

"Private jet? Really? Where?"

"Palo Alto."

"That's cool. But why is this guy with the gun following us? He's making me nervous."

"Don't worry about him. That's the only downside of being rich. People are jealous."

Naomi's plan worked. Carson placed his hand around her waist and guided her away from the Pagoda. He had no idea he was moving directly toward me. The gunman began moving away as well.

But the sound of a woman's scream suddenly stopped all three in their tracks. There was a commotion at the other end of the Plaza. I could guess what it was—some woman had stumbled upon the body of the guy I had left on the bench. It wouldn't take Carson and the gunman long to guess what was up.

"I've got a clear shot on the gunman," Garcia's voice came through the earpiece.

"Take it," I said.

A second later, the gunman went down, as the 7.62×51mm NATO cartridge traveling at more than twice the speed of sound ripped through his midsection at an angle, causing maximum damage and tearing through his heart. No one heard the shot—not just because Garcia had a suppressor on the rifle, but also because of the commotion at the other end of the Plaza.

But the clatter of the guns falling out of the open duffel bag as the man fell alerted Carson. He immediately realized it was a trap. His reaction was fast. He grabbed Naomi, picked up the M-16 from the ground, and began retreating, using Naomi as a shield while trying to wield the gun properly.

But wielding a rifle over three feet in length and weighing over nine pounds isn't an easy task. You have to be reasonably strong and a real pro for that. And Carson surely wasn't one. I had been moving toward him all this time, my gun pointed at his head and ready to shoot at the first sign of a real threat to Naomi. Britt was closing in from behind Carson. He was so engrossed in his multitasking that he never saw me until I was almost upon him.

The moment Carson saw me, a look of sheer terror gripped his face. He had managed to get his finger on the trigger by then, and he pulled it. The gun wasn't pointed anywhere specific, but the bullets coming out of it and ricocheting were no less deadly. I was close enough to take a shot without any danger of hitting Naomi. I shot him in the shoulder. Just a flesh wound—I wanted him able enough to talk. But it was painful, nevertheless. Carson screamed as the rifle fell from his hand.

# CHAPTER 29

I wrapped my arm around Naomi's trembling body and pulled her away while kicking Carson at the back of his ankles, sweeping his feet out from under him. Carson fell to the ground, landing heavily on his back. Britt had moved in by then. She roughly turned him over and cuffed him.

"Are you alright?" I asked Naomi.

"Yeah," she nodded, slightly shaken but in control.

"You did great. But it's time you headed to the safe house for a few hours while we put an end to all this. Alright?"

"Uh, alright. You think I'm still in danger?"

"I'm just trying to be extra careful. Britt will take you to the safe house."

"Sure. Uh, will I see you again?" she asked, not letting go of my hand as she looked in my eyes.

"Yes," I replied without breaking eye contact.

Naomi nodded and let go.

Garcia had come down and joined us by then.

"That went like clockwork, huh?" he said.

"Sure did. The old SOG team still alive and cracking," I replied.

"You two sure you can handle things without me?" Britt asked, looking slightly reluctant at having to babysit Naomi.

But we had discussed this earlier. We all agreed that if we caught Carson alive, the one thing that would get him talking would be his terror of me for what I had done to Dexter at the courthouse.

"You know it's just a matter of wrapping things up. Most of the work's already been done," I replied.

"Yeah, I know. Watch your six," she said, leading Naomi away.

Carson was still lying face down, Garcia's foot on his back making sure he couldn't move. I signaled Garcia to remove his foot. I frisked Carson, found a phone, and slipped it into my pocket. Then I grabbed him by the back of his collar and hauled him up.

"Remember me?" I asked him, my face inches from his, my eyes boring holes into his.

Carson was too petrified to reply. I gave him some reality bites before hauling him away.

"You see that crowd over there—that's one of your guys with his throat slit. Over there by the florist, is a second guy with his neck broken. The two men on the roof of your restaurant are dead. So is everyone else with you. You're the only one still breathing. Got it?"

He nodded his head, still unable to speak.

"Who's got the keys to the vehicle you used to drive here?"

"Uh, him," he said, pointing to the dead man lying a few feet away.

Garcia frisked him and grabbed the keys.

"Cadillac," Garcia said, dangling the key ring.

"Where's it parked? What color?"

Carson didn't reply.

"Don't make me ask you again," I spoke, digging my fingers into his shoulder next to his bullet wound.

"It's black. Parked on Post Street, next to the antiques shop," he gasped.

"Let's go," I ordered, hauling him roughly by the elbow.

"Where are you taking me?"

"Shut up and keep walking. You'll soon have the chance to talk all you want."

"No. Arrest me. I'm not going anywhere. Help! Officer," he shouted to a couple of cops rushing on to the scene.

But there was too much commotion for them to have heard Carson. I dug my gun hard into his ribcage. That shut him up. We hauled him to Garcia's pickup truck. I threw him into the back before turning to Garcia.

"What's our play now? Do we have a location on Dexter?" Garcia asked.

"Not confirmed. But I think he's in San Mateo. That's where Carson came from. And we tracked Sharky's phone there as well."

"But where in San Mateo?"

"We've got a close enough approximation. It's next to the bay. That's why I asked you to grab the key to his car. I'm sure this place is not their regular haunt. Check out the GPS in the car. We just might get lucky. Let's take the car with us when we go there. We might need it to gain access to the place. I'll put the fear of death in him while you get the car."

"Copy that. I'll get the car and wait for your signal before we drive out," Garcia replied before walking away.

I opened the front door and pressed a button in the driving console, the same one Garcia had used last night when we took Naomi and Slick to the safe house. The button brought down a thin, opaque screen between the front and the back, disabled the internal opening function of all the rear doors, and blacked out all rear windows.

As the screen went down, I thought about my line of questioning for Carson. I mainly wanted confirmation from him on two things. The first was the exact coordinates for the nuclear rods, for which all I had was Watkins's guesswork. The second was Dexter's location. I had already figured out everything else. I knew I would have to question him in a way that wouldn't give him the chance of slipping in a lie.

I closed the front door and got into the back. Carson was slouched in a corner, trying to stay as far away from me as possible. I grabbed him, pushed him down, cut off his cuffs with my boot knife, and hauled him back up again.

"Now we'll talk," I said ominously. "Before we begin, I want you to understand I know almost everything you have been up to. When I ask questions, you'll give me straight answers. Do you know what will happen to you if you lie even once?"

He just looked at me silently, fear painted large all over his face.

"It's only fair I explain everything to you before I begin the interrogation," I said.

I reached over, grabbed his right hand, pulled it roughly toward me, and grabbed two of his fingers in each hand.

"You must have seen Dexter's scars, but you weren't around to witness what I did to him. This was how I grabbed his fingers before tearing them apart with a jerk, almost splitting his hand into two," I said, giving a slight jerk.

Carson let out a scream even though I hadn't done anything yet that would have given him any pain. It was all psychological.

"No. Please. I'm not tough like Dexter."

"That's why I thought it was fair to warn you first. I never gave him that warning," I replied in an icy tone.

Carson tried to withdraw his hand from my grip, but I held firm, keeping the tension on his fingers.

"You want to get out in one piece, you'll answer all my questions truthfully."

"Yes, I will."

"Why are all of you holed up in San Mateo?"

He looked surprised. He couldn't figure out how I knew about the place.

"I told you I know all about what you've been up to. The Venezuelans, Dexter's prison break, the nuclear rods, that ghost town of yours, that airstrip in Palo Alto..."

Despite his fear, his mouth dropped when he heard me mentioning all his secrets.

"How do you know..."

"Never mind how. I want you to confirm all the facts one by one. You lie once and you'll experience pain like you've never known before," I said, giving another little jerk to his fingers to remind him what lay in store for him if he lied.

"No. Please. Ask me anything," he said, beads of sweat forming over his eyebrows.

"Tell me about San Mateo. Why were you hanging around there?"

"It was random. We just needed any place midway between San Francisco and Palo Alto. Sharky picked the place."

"What's the address?"

"16, Beach Road."

"How many men does Sharky have there?"

"Uh, six... maybe seven. You have taken down most of his crew since yesterday."

"Why did you double-cross the Venezuelans?"

"The Iranians gave us the same deal. And we owed them... for that courthouse escape. We didn't have a choice. They would have come after us."

That was information Cruz would have given his right arm for. He had a list of suspects in his mind, with the Iranians being among them, but there was no way for him to be sure.

"But you think the Venezuelans won't come after you?"

"We planned to vanish before they came to know," Carson replied.

That's what I expected. I also realized Cruz and Ortiz had played their cards well. Never once did the Cadys suspect they were anything other than who they claimed to be.

"That's why Dexter stayed back and sent you alone?"

"No. It's simply because the less he's seen out in the open, the better."

"And you thought you are unrecognizable after your plastic surgery."

"I thought I was," he said lamely.

"Why haven't the Iranians picked up the rods yet?"

I was taking a wild shot with the question. Cruz had told me there were men assembled at the site in the ghost town, but there wasn't any activity going on. All I could do to prevent Carson from bluffing was act like I knew everything. But I needed his answer to confirm my suspicions.

"They haven't made the money transfer yet."

"Who are the men at the site?"

"It's the Iranians. Ready to get the rods once we give them the coordinates."

"When will that happen?"

"At 10:00 p.m. Look, you could easily make a big cut in the deal. Ten million dollars. No, twenty million dollars. Just say the word," Carson said, his eyes starting to shine again as his cunning brain began to work.

"You guys really don't have a soul, do you? You fuck around with nuclear rods... hundreds of thousands of people could die, but you couldn't give a fuck. All you want is your money. Well, I've got news for you, pal, you're not going to see a dime of it. And you try that with me once more... you'll never use your hand again. Got it?"

"Yes," Carson replied, the light dying out in his eyes.

"Back to the questions. What are the coordinates?"

"Uh, I don't know."

I could sense he had begun to get the feeling I wouldn't go through with my threat.

"Wrong answer. I warned you not to lie. You've been truthful until now, so I'll give you one pass. Don't screw up again. What are the coordinates?"

"I really don't..."

His words got cut off midway as he screamed. I had just broken his ring finger. It was bent backwards at a ninety-degree angle, in a position it wasn't designed to be in.

"What are the coordinates?"

"I can't," he gasped.

I broke his middle finger. It joined the other finger in the same skewed position.

"What are the coordinates?" I asked again.

"In my phone," he cried out, sobbing in pain.

I took out his phone from my pocket and handed it to him.

"Use your left hand. You've got thirty seconds before I break a third finger."

He had the coordinates up on the screen in twenty seconds. I took a screenshot, set the phone on permanent unlock mode, and put it back in my pocket. I had all the information I needed. But I needed Carson to drive the car when we arrived at Dexter's place in San Mateo. I would need to sort out his fingers.

I still had his right hand with the broken fingers in my grip. I didn't want to forewarn him about what I was going to do. Fixing his fingers would mean extra pain for a few seconds before it subsided. I placed my fingers behind his broken ones, which were trembling from their raw nerve ends at my very touch. I placed my thumb on his palm for leverage. Then with a sudden jerk, I pushed both fingers back into their joints. Carson screamed again.

"Why did you do that? I've given you everything," he sobbed.

"I just fixed your fingers temporarily. The pain will go down now."

I pulled out my knife, sliced a strip off his shirt sleeve, and tied it around the fingers to make them immobile.

"You should be fine now."

I opened the door with the key, got out, and locked him in again.

It was time to take out Dexter.

# CHAPTER 30

"Did you get what you wanted?" Garcia asked me when I got out.

He stood leaning back into the black Cadillac parked behind the pickup, waiting for me to finish the interrogation. I texted the exact coordinates of the nuclear rods to Cruz before replying.

"Yeah. We're good to go. Got anything from the GPS?"

"16, Beach Road."

"That's the one. I don't completely trust every word he told me, but the intel I have is there are nine men in the house, including Dexter and Sharky. It's going to be intense."

"Copy that. Let's end this once and for all. How are we playing it?"

"I'll lead in the Cadillac. Once we're there, let's check the layout and decide. We might need to get Carson to drive to gain entry into the place," I replied.

"Copy that. Also, Mitchell called. He has located the plane and staked out the place. Trying to figure out how to disable it. Either way, he won't let that thing take off."

"That's good enough. I don't think it's going to come to that. Dexter isn't leaving that house for a few more hours. But he might get suspicious when he hasn't heard from Carson. We can't let him vanish."

"Roger that. Let's go."

We headed south on Highway 101 toward San Mateo. It was about a twenty-five minute drive. When we arrived close to our destination, we stopped at a lookout point on top of a low hill. The plan was to study the layout of the house.

But we had forgotten about the Bay Area's fog. It was that early evening time again when the wisps of fog that must have begun to emerge from the San Francisco Bay an hour ago had started to thicken. The fog had crept forward and had begun engulfing everything in its path, including all the houses along the beach. Visibility was getting low by the minute.

We could still make out the rough layout of the houses, which were big, and set some distance apart from each other. Each house had a boundary wall on all sides, with sturdy gates blocking entry to the houses within them. It was a logical deduction there would be security cameras in place. But we doubted that Sharky's crew, who had just rented the place for a few days, would be skilled enough to manipulate the cameras and monitor the feed.

In either case, we could try using the fog to breach the perimeter unnoticed. But it would be foolish to completely bank on the fog and risk the chance of getting caught under heavy fire from inside the house. We decided to split up and launch simultaneous attacks from the front and rear. I would get Carson to drive the Cadillac while I stayed hidden in the backseat. I would create enough mayhem at the front to give Garcia the chance to slip in from the rear and launch an attack.

Garcia left first. He took the dirt track at the back of the houses, left the truck a little distance from the target house, walked back, and took up position. As soon as he left the truck, I began driving toward Beach Road. About a couple of hundred yards before the house, I stopped and got Carson in the driving seat while I got into the back.

"Listen to me carefully. You'll drive to the gate and ask them to let you in. Act normal. You do anything to make them suspicious, you'll be the first one to catch a bullet. Understood?"

"Yes. If we get out of this, you promise not to kill me?"

"Yes. I won't kill you."

It wasn't a false promise. Carson was as ruthless and devoid of a soul as his brother, but he wasn't the bloodthirsty beast his brother was. I was determined to put an end to Dexter. But once that happened, I doubted Carson could ever be a threat to anyone while serving out multiple life sentences in prison.

Carson drove slowly toward the house. He stopped outside the gate and began honking and flashing the headlights.

"We're at the front gate now. Are you in position?" I asked Garcia over the radio.

"In position," he replied.

"Copy that. I'll give you a heads-up once we're in."

It took a minute for two men to walk over to the gate from inside the house to open it. That was further proof that this was an untrained bunch of thugs who wouldn't know the first thing about maintaining a secure perimeter.

"Remember, act normal. No false moves. You don't want to be the first casualty," I reminded Carson, digging the gun into his back as the men approached.

"Yeah, I remember," he whispered back.

As soon as the men saw the Cadillac through the hatch, they stepped back and opened the gate wide. That was their last mistake. Both men were armed with automatics slung with straps across their bodies. But they had grown lax as soon as they saw the Cadillac. As Carson drove in, I shot both men with my suppressed gun. Both men dropped dead without a sound.

Carson rolled the car to a stop in the driveway. He had done his part. From this point onwards, he would only be a hindrance to my plans. I had promised not to kill him. I struck him hard on the side of his head with the gun. He wasn't wearing the seatbelt when he headed in. He simply flopped to the side onto the passenger seat.

I was about to exit the car and approach the house when I saw a security camera installed on the front wall of the house move. I realized we had lost some of our advantage. Whoever was operating the camera knew something was wrong. The best option under the circumstances was to create enough confusion at the front to give Garcia a clear entry from the back.

The front wall of the house was made up of floor to ceiling windows meant to provide an unobstructed view of the bay. I decided to make an entry they wouldn't anticipate.

"Give me a sitrep, bro," Garcia's voice came through my earpiece.

"Wait ten seconds. Then make a breach."

"Roger that."

I pushed Carson onto the passenger seat, strapped a seatbelt around him, slipped into driving position, and put on my seatbelt. I started the car, reversed a little, and then stepped on the gas, sending the car hurtling across the manicured lawn, up five steps, and into the huge living room through the glass front. I took out one more man in the process. He had been peering through the glass doors and realized too late that he was in the path of a 4,500-pound missile headed his way.

The car smashed through the glass, went through the living room, smashing all furniture in its path. I applied the brakes and rapidly turned the wheels as the car hurtled toward the back wall of the huge living room. The car swerved and turned, hitting the wall sideways. It had lost a lot of momentum by then and the impact wasn't jarring enough to incapacitate me.

But the moment the car stopped, I came under heavy fire from the front and back. The car shielded me from the fire, but I was trapped. I grabbed my duffel bag from the back seat and took out the assault rifle. I caught a break when a lack of return fire from me gave both gunmen the impression I had been knocked out in the impact. Both men stepped out from behind their cover and made themselves visible. I slipped in a magazine and took out the target advancing from the front. A burst through the windshield stopped him dead.

I opened the door, dived on the floor, and began firing at the target in the back. I shot out both his ankles. The man screamed and fell to the floor. I fired a short burst dead center at his chest.

A burst of automatic fire from the back of the house told me Garcia had made a breach.

"Five targets down in the front. No sign of Dexter or Sharky," I spoke into the mic while switching magazines.

"Copy that. Two down at the back. I don't have a visual on anyone else."

"Copy that. I'll move toward you. Let's clear this floor before moving up."

The house had the large, open living room area in the front and three bedrooms behind it on the first floor. There were two sets of stairs at both ends of the huge living room leading to the second floor. That floor had three more bedrooms.

It took us less than a minute to clear all the rooms on the first floor. As we moved from room to room, we could make out the soft sound of footsteps above us.

We walked out to the living room and fanned out, taking one staircase each. We matched steps as we moved up, keeping our rifles in high ready position, until we reached the landing on the second floor. The door of the room in front of me was shut. I signaled Garcia to cover me from the other end as I stood to one side of the door and tried the handle. It was unlocked.

I was about to push it open but something made me stop. The place was too quiet. There were two dangerous men waiting for us in one of the three bedrooms on that floor. While we were clearing the first floor, the men had been moving around on stealthy feet. They could easily have booby-trapped the door.

I was proved correct when I moved the door a couple of inches. I saw a string stretched along the bottom of the door. I peeked through the crack and found it was tied to the pin of an M67 fragmentation grenade. Had I rushed through the door, it would have exploded with me inside the room. I signaled Garcia to retreat a couple of steps.

"Booby-trap inside the door. M67 grenade," I whispered into the mic.

"Well spotted," Garcia's whisper came through the earpiece.

"I'll disable it and retrieve the grenade. Hold position."

"Copy that."

I pulled my boot knife. The razor-sharp blade sliced through the string. I checked the door for any secondary traps but found nothing. I pushed the door open, took a quick look around the room, and found it empty. I tiptoed toward the corner, retrieved the grenade, and stepped out again.

I signaled to Garcia to check the corner room at his end while I covered him. That room had been rigged the same way. Garcia retrieved the grenade from the room and tiptoed back.

"I'll explode the grenade inside the bedroom. That will make them come rushing out," I whispered into the mic.

"Copy that," Garcia replied.

I removed the safety clip from the grenade, held its spoon in place with my thumb, stepped forward, and rolled it inside the door before shutting it. I dived back toward the staircase and went flat on the steps, below the level of the second floor.

A couple of seconds later, a thundering explosion followed. And then, complete silence. I crept up the steps, stayed low, and waited. The door of the middle room opened. The barrel of an M-16 came into view before a man followed it. It was Sharky. We fired at him simultaneously, taking him down in the crossfire. He was dead before he hit the floor.

"Don't even think of shooting at me. I've got the house rigged with C-4," Dexter's deep voice came from inside the bedroom. "I'm coming out now so you can see for yourself."

Dexter stepped out with a remote control in his hand.

"We can all leave this place alive to fight another day. Or I'll press this button and the whole place goes up."

Without saying a word, I shot Dexter in the head. The HK416 rifle empties its magazine at 850 rounds per minute. I pressed the trigger for a little over a second. That was all the time it needed for my 20-round magazine to empty its lethal dose into him. Dexter wouldn't go after anyone again. Ever.

The trigger mechanism in his hand fell harmlessly on the floor. Dexter shouldn't have told me the place would blow up once he pressed the trigger. Until the pressing of the trigger set off the detonator, C-4 was as safe as putty. His tendency to boast had got him once again.

"I don't think this guy's putting out any more hits, bro," Garcia commented.

"You know what, pal? I think you might be right."

We made our way out and stood on the steps outside the living room. The fog had lifted for a while. The view of the San Francisco Bay was magnificent.

# EPILOGUE

There is a reason San Francisco is called Fog City. The wisps of fog swirling gently and rising from the tranquil waters of the Bay on most late summer afternoons claim as much right over the city as any of its denizens. So much so that the fog has an official name—Karl.

I cut through Karl's gray veil enveloping the mostly empty streets as I drove through downtown and entered the underground parking garage. I parked the pickup, pressed the button for the elevator, and waited.

I glanced at my watch. The time was 0230 hours. Late night or early morning—depending on how tired or energetic you felt. It had been a long day. I had hit the road for Dry Creek at seven in the morning. We had done what we had come to the city for. The outcome had always been a foregone conclusion. Evil forces like Dexter could never be reasoned with. That kind of wickedness doesn't stop until you physically put an end to it. What we did wasn't about rules and laws; it was about right and wrong. And protecting innocent lives.

Cruz and Ortiz had managed to secure the rods. As for the impostor in the cell within Dry Creek, he was let loose before he began to raise hell. Cruz managed to spin a story about a prison break and Dexter getting killed in a final encounter. We decided to keep quiet on the matter. What those guys had done was about protecting lives. But as for Captain Thorne and the three guards on the take, we couldn't close our eyes. That was about greed, pure and simple. They became the fall guys. They were forced to resign, effective immediately.

Garcia was back in Miami. He planned to spend a few days sipping Mojitos on South Beach, until another gator poacher forced him into the swamps again. Britt and Mitchell had flown to LA—it was time for them to get back to their regular lives.

As for me, there was one more stop to be made. I got inside the elevator and pressed the button for the eighth floor.

When the elevator doors opened, the familiar fluorescent display welcomed me yet again. But the place looked empty. Not a soul in sight. All tables and chairs pushed to one side. I was about to call out when I saw a gorgeous woman walking out from one of the private rooms.

"Welcome to Tokyo Dreams. I'm afraid we don't have a table tonight. All we have are private rooms at the back. And I'm afraid it's going to be self-service. All the staff have left for the night," Naomi said as she came to a stop inches from me.

The difference in our heights was a little less apparent this time. She had high heels on. It wouldn't really have mattered. When she held me by the shoulders, I was automatically drawn closer to her. Her perfume further pulled me in.

The fog swirling through the streets had taken hold of my senses. It would be a while before I would see daylight again.

## – THE END –

### BLAZE RETURNS
### (Book One)

Deputy US Marshal Carter has gone missing in Little Butte, Nevada. The Dawsons own the town. A Mexican cartel is moving in. A gang war is coming to town. Blaze returns for one last assignment to find Carter before all hell breaks loose.

### LETHAL FORCE
### (Book Two)

When Blaze takes out a Mexican cartel's operations in Nevada, the cartel sends hitmen after him and everyone he cares about. Bad move. What the cartel doesn't realize is, it has messed with a Lethal Force.

### HARD TARGET
### (Book Three)

When Blaze stops at an isolated gas station, he stumbles upon an execution about to go down. Blaze's intervention gets a pack of mercenaries after him. What they don't realize: when it comes to deadly sport, Blaze is a master of the game.

### MEAN STREETS
### (Book Four)

Midnight in New York City. A car stops at an intersection. A girl in the back gives Blaze a distress hand signal. The chase that begins in Manhattan takes Blaze on a treacherous chase through the city that never sleeps.

### NO ESCAPE
### (Book Six)

Chaos erupts in Bison Creek, Wyoming. Two slain officers. Blood-soaked ex-Marine Logan on the scene. A sinister link between a cult and a pharma company. But one man will move heaven and earth to dig out the truth—Blaze.

### FEAR CITY
### (Book Seven)

Blaze heads to Boston after a shadowy group of investors—rich, powerful, and ready to bulldoze anything in their way. Blaze is up against these ruthless players who would sooner bury the truth than face it. They play dirty.
But so does Blaze.

### DEAD CALM
### (Book Eight)

The book goes into Blaze's past as a US Army Ranger. Blaze promises to rescue a dying friend's kids from the Taliban. The hunt takes him from Afghanistan to a trafficking network run by the Bulgarian mafia.

### NO MERCY
### (Book Nine)

CIA agents in the Middle East are turning up dead. Blaze must save trapped agents and stop a rogue analyst from blowing their covers. With the Italian mafia and terror outfits in the picture, Blaze has only one rule: No Mercy.

## WARPATH
### (Book Ten – April '25)

Blaze and his Delta team head to Mexico to dismantle a powerful drug cartel. They take it apart piece by piece. But when the cartel brings the fight to US soil and targets Americans, Blaze makes it personal and goes on the warpath.

## CROSSFIRE
### (Book Eleven – July '25)

Yemen's going up in flames. Americans are caught in the inferno. Blaze and his team are sent to extract an Al-Qaeda informant, who is the key to saving lives. They face betrayals and deadly odds. Blaze won't just hold the line—he'll obliterate the enemy.

## ABOUT REVIEWS AND NEWSLETTERS

Thank you for reading my book. I hope you enjoyed it. If you could take a moment to leave a review on Amazon, even just a sentence or two, it would mean the world to me. Should you wish to share any thoughts or feedback, I can be reached at billrunnerauthor@gmail.com.

I invite you to join my mailing list on my website: https://bill-runner.com. You will receive updates on new releases, special offers, and the occasional free audiobook voucher.

Made in United States
North Haven, CT
15 February 2025

65868068R00202